Sign up for our newsletter to hear
about new and upcoming releases.

www.ylva-publishing.com

Other Books by Shaya Crabtree

You're Fired

Tight Knit

Shaya Crabtree

Chapter 1

It was perfect. Sort of.

Lara double, then triple checked her angles. Her webcam rested precariously atop the coffee table on a stack of knitting books that were due back at the library a week ago. The camera lens framed her couch, and Lara centered herself in the shot, sitting on the ravine between the cushions like the middle child in the backseat of a car.

The arms of the loveseat were decorated with scraps of unfinished work she couldn't bring herself to complete. Sleeves of sweaters overlapped with six-inch scarves, and the colors melted into a rainbow that looked aesthetically pleasing but not too organized. If Lara couldn't be proud of her work, she could at least be proud of her set design. On screen it looked like she had so much creativity she was forced to spread her energy across several projects, and she spent time nudging each piece into frame to make herself look busy.

The neck of a sweater fell to the ground, and Lara extricated it from the claws of her cat. "Rocket, not right now."

She tossed a fresh ball of yarn to the other side of the living room for him to play with out of frame, then checked her watch. Still five minutes to go.

To be safe, Lara checked her email one more time. She scrolled through the dozens of messages Roger Feldman had sent, searching for the most recent. Yes, the time was correct. Less than three minutes now.

Lara had never met Roger Feldman, but she knew of him. Everyone did. *The Trend Bender* was the premier online gossip mag of the distasteful and easily amused drama queens of the world. A good review of Festive Feline Fashion could put Lara in the next tax bracket. A bad review, well, Lara didn't want to think about it. She hadn't wanted to risk the interview at first because she hadn't needed it. She was getting press from plenty of other publications. Her business was doing fine. Until her life had gone to shit, her motivation had disappeared, and her orders became more backed up than a California highway. Now Lara needed this. It was the fresh start she so desperately craved.

The Skype ringtone chimed, and Lara scrambled into position: seated with one leg draped over the other, settled into the couch. It was the most natural position she could design, and when she hit accept on the call, she hoped Roger thought she looked as comfortable as Lara did when she looked at her reflection in the little call window.

Moments later, Roger's face popped up. He was calling with his phone resting below him on his desk, giving Lara a great view of his chin.

"Hi, Lara." He waved. "Can you see me?"

"Yep! I can see you." He was blurry, but it didn't matter what he looked like anyway. Lara wasn't the one writing about him.

"Great. We've got about—" He checked his watch. "Twenty minutes. Let's get started, shall we?"

"Sounds good."

"So tell me about your business."

Lara was caught off guard. This was the infamous Roger Feldman? Readers clung to the words of a man who opened his interviews with questions that a high school yearbook editor would ask? She had spent all morning preparing for this?

"Really?" Lara asked. "That's your question? I've already talked about this in every single interview I've given. Don't you think people know about my business by now?"

Roger swiveled slightly in his chair, clearly taken aback. "I figured you'd be willing to tell the story again," he explained. "It's a good one. Young woman builds a successful business out of her favorite hobby and makes enough money to quit her job. I've read all of your news coverage: *The Star*, *Chronicle Weekly*. I've done my homework, Ms. Spellmeyer. I'm not asking you the basics because I'm ignorant. I'm asking because most business owners I talk to are eager to discuss their work. You're not?"

"I am," Lara said, a bit too quickly. "I mean, I like my work. I love my work." She was stumbling now. Were her words meant to persuade Roger or herself? "I just prefer to talk about more specific details. I hate repeating myself. Everyone knows the general story by now."

"Everyone, huh?" Roger looked smug, and Lara hoped that was just her blurry connection.

"That's not what I meant. Of course not everyone has heard of my business, but I assume most of the readers on your site have. Your numerous emails mentioned how an interview with me has been much requested." If he could play the leverage game, so could she.

"That's true. You're a hot topic," he conceded. "At the moment, anyway." Lara didn't care for the way he tacked on that addition. "Still," he continued. "People love a good origin story. How does one build a cat sweater empire out of nothing?"

Lara wasn't falling for his tricky wording again. She wasn't a boastful person, and she wasn't going to start being one now. Instead, she'd be so humble that Roger couldn't make her out to be egotistical unless he cut nearly all of the interview.

"I wouldn't call it an empire. I run a website people order cat sweaters through. It's fun. I'm not a millionaire."

"That's it?" Roger asked, mockingly. "'It's fun' is all you have to say?"

"Like I said, I've talked about this before. It was a fun hobby for me that accidentally turned into a business. I didn't expect this. The details are pretty boring."

"The general details, you mean."

She just managed to avoid heaving a sigh. "Yes."

"Well, let's go into some specifics, then, like you asked."

Good. Finally some real questions.

"A woman messaged me a few weeks ago, saying that a sweater you sent her caused her cat to have a severe allergic reaction. Would you like to comment on that?"

Fuck. This was not what she'd prepared for. Had that woman really contacted Roger?

"I wouldn't call it severe," Lara said.

"Are you a vet?"

"What?"

"Are you a veterinarian?" Roger asked.

Lara didn't appreciate the patronizing. "No, but—"

"So you have no medical authority to categorize the situation?" Roger's face was so blank, so impersonal. His mouth was hidden behind the hand holding his chin, and his eyes were hidden behind the glare his office lights cast over the lens of his glasses. He didn't care about the well-being of that cat. He cared about the drama of the situation.

"That specific cat had a long list of medical issues that I wasn't made aware of," Lara said firmly. "If the owner had told me that the cat was allergic to wool, I would have made the sweater out of a different material. The issue has been corrected, and I use hypoallergenic yarn now just to be safe. That cat is fine, by the way. All the sweater did was make him sneeze. I don't think anyone could call that severe."

"Corrected how?" Roger asked.

"I offered to give the owner a refund and send her a new sweater."

"Was the cat allergic to the second sweater?"

"I never sent it," Lara said. "The owner turned down my offer. All she wanted was her money back."

"So she didn't trust your work?"

"Maybe," Lara said, thinking out loud. "I don't know. It wasn't my work that was the problem. The order form on my website specifically asks which materials the customer wants their sweater made out of. If she knew the cat was allergic to wool, she shouldn't have chosen wool."

"So you're blaming the victim for the incident?"

Lara blinked. This was hardly victim blaming. "If a lactose intolerant woman orders a glass of milk, is it really the restaurant's fault if she gets sick?"

Roger shifted slightly. "I have to say, Ms. Spellmeyer, this seems like a touchy subject for you."

It was, clearly, but Lara tried not to let it show too much. She adjusted her hair, making sure she didn't look too frazzled. "I'm sorry. It wasn't the best situation, as you can imagine, and I thought the issue had been buried. I didn't expect you to bring it up."

"What do you do when you're approached with these kinds of questions online?"

"Pardon?"

"You have over one hundred thousand Instagram followers. Surely an Internet celebrity such as yourself must get tough questions like that on a daily basis."

"I don't consider myself an Internet celebrity. People follow me for the cat pics, not for me. I don't post personal stuff. You don't get a lot of hate comments when all you do is post pictures of cats."

"I see," Roger said. He was quiet for a moment. His chin bobbed as he rocked in his chair. "Well, I think that's all for today."

"Oh." Lara glanced at the clock. "Aren't we supposed to have ten more minutes?"

"Well, you know." Roger adjusted his glasses along the slope of his nose. "The extra time is a precaution. Sometimes you get everything you need sooner than you expect."

He was blowing her off. This guy had pestered her for an interview for more than two months and now that he'd finally gotten it, he was cutting it short after ten minutes of nothing. She knew he was definitely writing the article. He'd told her the date it would come out. So what was he going to base it on? The questions about the allergic cat?

Wait, when had Feldman started pestering her for an interview? She did some quick time calculations in her head.

Oh shit.

Chapter 2

Two days had passed since the *Trend Bender* article was published, and Lara couldn't bring herself to leave the house. Everyone had read it by now, and it wasn't just the people in town that Lara had to worry about. For once, the digital world was worse than the real one. Lying in bed all day wouldn't stop the hateful string of comments from appearing on her social media, but that hadn't stopped Lara from trying. She was tired. The embarrassment and regret barely let her sleep. It was nine in the morning, but she had gotten maybe three hours at best. She'd spent the night tossing and turning, and when she hadn't been doing that, she'd been checking her phone. First, she'd deleted dozens of comments about the article on her Facebook page, then the Twitter messages requesting follow-up interviews from people who had no intention of letting Lara tell her side of the story and every intention of dragging her back under the bus for another daily news cycle.

She buried her head under her pillow, but still her phone buzzed. And buzzed. And buzzed. Frustrated, she re-emerged from her tomb of suffocation to see the same two words written on her screen over and over again. *Cat Killer*. *Cat Killer*. *Cat Killer*. Someone had commented that on every one of Lara's Instagram posts from the last month. Dealing with people who had read the article was one thing, but confronting people who had only heard about the article through a warped game of telephone that turned cat allergies into premeditated murder was something Lara wasn't equipped to handle. Then there were trolls who didn't even know who Lara was; they'd just heard about the scandal on Reddit and shown up to gleefully watch her career burn. It was the final straw.

Defeated, she turned off her notifications and went back to sleep, hoping that things would somehow be different by the time she woke up.

They weren't. Her phone woke her up a second time, and what Lara thought was the alarm she'd already snoozed ten times turned out to be a phone call. She accepted without thinking.

"Lara?"

Even though she hadn't heard it in four years, Lara knew that voice instantly. Once upon a time, she had woken up every morning to that scratchy voice saying her name from the pillow beside her.

"Yeah?"

"It's Paige Daley."

"I can hear that," Lara said. "What do you want, Paige?"

"This morning one of my interns read a story about your business that was published in *The Trend Bender*. *The Daily Page* is going to recount it. I was wondering if you wanted to make any additional comments for the newspaper to run." Paige's voice sounded rehearsed, like an automated recording.

"Is this a nightmare?"

"Pardon?"

"I'm still asleep, right? Please don't tell me that my ex-girlfriend actually just called me for the first time in four years to tell me that her newspaper is going to publish a horrible article about me in a town that already hates me and my entire family."

"It's nothing against you," Paige said. "The article made national news, and we'd be remiss if we didn't cover such a big story about one of Perry's own."

"It's a gossip column, Paige. I thought you took that job because you were passionate about real local news."

"I did, Lara. You know that better than anyone. I know we haven't talked in a while, but I'm still me." Paige could try to appeal to their history all she wanted, but Lara had decided a long time ago that she and Paige didn't know each other as well as they'd thought. "Besides," she continued. "This *is* real local news."

The sad part was that Paige wasn't wrong. With a population of only a couple thousand people, Perry was tiny. Lara making a national fool of herself probably was going to be the most interesting thing to happen for at least the next month. It didn't help that she was a Spellmeyer. Perry loved to hate on the Spellmeyers. A girl has one alcoholic grandfather and suddenly the whole town treats the entire family like Roger Feldman looking for his next career to ruin.

"You've got to be kidding me." It was too early for this. Lara hadn't even had coffee. Somewhere in another room, Rocket was meowing for breakfast. Usually the cat's whining would get on her nerves, but nothing could annoy Lara more than Paige Daley.

"Do you care to comment?" Paige asked when Lara was silent for too long.

"My comment is, 'Go fuck yourself.'"

"Mature."

There were Paige's true colors. Lara was wondering how long she could keep up the professional facade. Apparently, the answer was forty-five seconds.

"And it was mature of you to call someone whose heart you broke to ask them to help you get ahead in your job and open themselves up to even more public ridicule?"

Paige was silent for the briefest of moments. Lara almost thought she had gotten through to her, but—

"Yes," she said, too much confidence booming in her voice. It sounded overdone, which was surprising. Lara had never known Paige to be lacking in confidence. She was explaining the situation to herself, not to Lara. "I'm putting aside my personal differences for the sake of professionalism."

Lara rolled her eyes and channeled all her energy into making sure Paige somehow saw it through the telephone. "And that is exactly why we broke up. You care more about professionalism than people's feelings. How could you ask me this? How could you run a gossip column like that? In what universe is this the hard-hitting news you always claimed to be so passionate about?"

"Lara—"

"Roger Feldman is a scumbag who leeches onto every little mistake someone makes and blows it out of proportion to get hits on his website. I had one bad day and gave one bad interview, and now people are acting like it's the end of the world."

"Is that your comment?"

"The part about Roger Feldman being evil or the part about you ruining our relationship and abandoning your ethical principles?"

"That's not what happened, and that's not what's happening now either, but I'll take that as a yes."

Of course. Paige was probably getting off on this. She always had to win. She had to show Lara that her business was the more successful one. She had to prove that choosing journalism over their relationship was the better life decision.

The silence stretched out. Lara didn't know what to say. Paige was clearly going to do whatever she'd set out to do, and rationalizing wasn't going to get Lara anywhere. Should she hang up? Should she cuss Paige out some more? She didn't have the fight in her. So she spoke to Paige like a human being, hoping that her ex was still one somewhere in her heart.

"So you're really going to run this article, huh?" The words hit Lara as she said them. As fulfilling as yelling at Paige had felt, it wasn't going to improve her public image. With all that Lara had said in the last five minutes, Paige could easily write an article far worse than Roger Feldman's.

Paige was quiet for a moment, as if she was actually considering Lara's plea. When she spoke, she sounded off the record, but Lara actually couldn't tell if Paige was being sympathetic to her plight or rubbing it in her face for the fun of it. "It's my job, Lara. If I don't run this, I look out of touch with Perry. Or like I'm playing favorites trying to protect you. I'm not."

Would that be so bad? This situation was far worse for Lara than it ever would be for Paige. "God forbid you put my feelings first for once, huh?"

There was a grunt on the other end of the line. Then: "I'm sorry, Lara. I'm really not doing this to mess with you."

"I'm sure."

"It's not like I follow your life," Paige snapped. "I didn't know about this story until my intern brought it to my attention. I'm covering it because it's my job. It's a local interest piece, and I thought I'd be nice and give you a chance to defend yourself. If you don't have anything else to add, I'll leave you alone. It was nice talking to you again."

Paige was going to hang up? No. She didn't get to decide when this conversation ended. She didn't deserve the luxury of backing out at her own convenience when she was the one who had made the mistake of calling Lara in the first place. If she wanted this story so badly, Lara was going to make her suffer for it.

"Was it nice, Paige? Was it—"

The click on the other end of the line cut her off. Just like that, Lara was right back where she'd started.

Actually, no. She was worse off.

Mozart Cafe had the perfect name. It was outdated but classic. The coffee shop had always been *the* hangout spot in Perry. Even before Lara was old enough to appreciate coffee, even after the corporate monsters of Starbucks and Dunkin' Donuts had wormed their way into the hearts of Perry's residents, Mozart Cafe was still the place to meet for a Saturday morning brew with friends. She had almost missed it these last couple of years she'd been living in Oklahoma City—as much as she could miss something from Perry.

When Lara walked in, April was already seated at a small corner table just big enough for the two of them. Lara waved at her, stood in line with a fairly sizable crowd of other zombies looking for their morning caffeine boost, and ordered a cup of joe before joining April in the seat opposite her.

She was just starting to feel settled when she noticed the name written on her cup. Instantly, the good mood she was nearing was wiped away. "Really?" She scrubbed at the marking with her thumbs, but the marker refused to come off. "I told them my name was *Lara*."

"What'd they write?"

Frustrated, Lara spun the cup around for April to read. The fact that she couldn't do anything about it bugged her more than what was written.

"Spellmeyer?" April asked. "Well, it is your name."

"But it's not the name I told them to write. I hate my name. I hate that everyone knows my name. I hate being nothing but another Spellmeyer to this town. I've been gone for four years, but only a couple weeks of being back, and it's like I never left."

"You having a bad day?" April asked.

"Try bad week."

"Tell me about it."

"You're a super mom with a penchant for community engagement. How do you have a bad week?" Lara grumbled, feeling sorry for herself.

"Are you kidding? I'm a single mom of two kids *and* I work in my son's high school. Trust me, I have my share of bad weeks."

"Okay, fair enough. I might have been exaggerating out of self-pity." Lara had definitely heard about April's bad weeks before. April liked to talk her head off to someone who would actually listen to her, unlike her ex-husband. It was the reason, Lara was convinced, that April liked her so much. Lara liked April because she was the only person in town who didn't judge Lara by the rumors she'd heard or by the stories about the Spellmeyer family.

They'd met in the yarn aisle of the craft store, each reaching for the last ball in a specific shade of blue. After laughing over the coincidence and swapping stories of what project they needed the yarn for, April had let Lara have both the yarn and her phone number so they could get together and talk about knitting sometime. Lara had known right then and there that if she needed something, April would always be there for her, and Lara had vowed to be there for April, too. Even when Lara had moved away, they'd still regularly kept in touch. Saturday morning coffee dates with April were one of the few good parts of being home. If April wasn't straight, Lara would probably be in love with her.

"A few days ago, I had this interview, and I totally bombed it," Lara said, relishing the chance to vent. "All of my customers have been complaining since the article came out, and I don't know how to fix it. I've never lost this many orders before. I was already stressed out because I had too much on my plate, but now I'm stressed out because I'm scared I don't have enough. This could ruin my business. All because of one bad interview. My life is a total joke."

"Don't say that, Lara. You're being too harsh on yourself. I'm sure the situation isn't as bad as you think it is."

Lara wished she could believe in April's optimism. "That's not even the end of it. It was so bad that a couple days later, Paige called me. As if national humiliation wasn't enough, my ex-girlfriend decided that my hometown needed to hear about the situation in depth."

"What did she write?"

"I don't know. She said the article would be in today's paper, but I can't bring myself to read it. I don't want the entire town of Perry reading this story. They already hate me enough. You're the only person here that likes me."

"That's not true."

"Name one other friend I have," Lara said.

"The dozens of friends we're both going to make when Tight Knit starts."

Right—their idea for a weekly knitting circle that anyone in the community could join. Lara had grown up going to her grandmother's knitting club, and the nostalgia of simpler times made her desperate to bring the tradition back. April was hosting the first meeting, and Lara had promised to do whatever she could to help.

"You know what you need?" April asked.

A miracle? A fresh start? A sense of accomplishment and fulfillment?

"A girlfriend."

April wasn't wrong, but Lara had so many other concerns closer to the top of her worry list that needing a girlfriend didn't have time to be on her radar. Usually.

"Yeah, right." Lara rolled her eyes. "The last woman I dated was Paige Daley. I think it's safe to say that my taste in women is horrible, and I can't be trusted to properly manage my own romantic life ever again."

"Then let me manage it."

Lara raised an eyebrow. Her confusion fueled April's smile, as mischievous as Lara had ever seen it. April leaned forward on the edge of her seat.

"I have a friend."

"Oh no. No, no, no."

"You'll love her."

"Let me guess," Lara said. "She's the only other lesbian you know."

"Yes! You two would be perfect for each other."

Lara was pretty sure she knew every lesbian in Perry, which was to say she knew herself and the one other out couple who had been together for about fifteen years. As touched as she was by April's gesture, Lara didn't know how she felt about being set up with an older woman or ruining a perfectly happy marriage. "I don't know, April. I've got too much on my plate to worry about dating right now."

"Nonsense. Love waits for no right time. I'll introduce you two at Tight Knit."

Lara had a feeling that her definition of love was very different from April's. It wouldn't hurt to meet the woman, though. The whole point of starting Tight Knit with April was to get to know more people. This woman probably already knew who Lara was, though. Lara couldn't imagine what type of person would be okay with being set up on a blind date with a Spellmeyer.

"You sure this woman doesn't hate me? She's probably sitting at home drinking her morning coffee and reading whatever slander Paige wrote about me right now."

"This article can't be that bad."

"You don't know Paige."

April took that as a challenge. "Here. Let me go get the paper."

"No, April!" Before Lara could stop her, April was out of her seat and at the front of the store, browsing through the news rack. She found what she was looking for and came back to the table. Lara thought about spilling her coffee on the paper so that no one in the store could read it ever again, but the rack held what felt like an endless supply of copies; she couldn't spill coffee on them all. Besides, April held tightly onto the pages, flipping through until she found Lara's segment featured somewhere in the middle.

"'Local Business Receives National Attention—And Critique,'" she began.

"No! Don't read it out loud!" Lara's voice dropped to a hushed whisper. "There's people here!"

April didn't listen. "'Lara Spellmeyer is well-known throughout Perry for her successful online business.' Looking good so far."

"Great. Stop reading now while I'm ahead."

"'But recently her firm Festive Feline Fashion has fallen under fire.' Holy alliteration. I don't know if I can read this out loud."

"Awesome. Please stop."

"I'll just skip down. Get to the good parts."

Lara buried her face in her hands. If she couldn't see anyone in Mozart, then they couldn't see her either.

"Feldman assures his audience that he remains an unbiased reporter whose primary goal is to provide a platform where all sides of any story can be told. However, Feldman admits that he can relate to Mrs. Rushmore's negative account of Lara's business. He too claimed to feel viciously attacked by Ms. Spellmeyer's cold-hearted attitude."

"Viciously attacked?" Lara resisted the urge to slam her head into the table. The public embarrassment was already great enough without her making a scene. "They make me sound like some kind of guard dog. I don't even like dogs. I run a business for cats."

"Wait, hold on. It gets better. 'Spellmeyer, however, contests Feldman's integrity, insisting that her words were bent out of context and that the situation was blown out of proportion. She says that her seemingly poor attitude was merely the result of a particularly bad day. She also contends that all issues with her products mentioned in *The Trend Bender* had been resolved long before the article's publication. While Spellmeyer also had some choice words for Feldman that cannot be legally transcribed in print, her upset is a clear indication that her passion is still very much alive, voiding Feldman's claims that she no longer cares about her business.' See, that's not so bad."

"Paige wrote that I cussed him out so obscenely that she couldn't repeat what I said. In what world is that 'not so bad'?"

"She also used the quotes that you gave her to defend yourself."

"You weren't there, April. I didn't say that stuff to defend myself. I said it to hurt Paige. I blew up at her. The article doesn't *sound* bad, but I was there, and the whole conversation was awful. I can't remember the last time I lost control like that."

"Yeah, well, love makes us do things we're not proud of."

Lara's name had received plenty of slander in the past week, but this was by far the worst. "I do not love her."

"Someone's being defensive," April teased. "No wonder you didn't want me to set you up on a date."

"I'm not being defensive!"

April gave Lara a pointed look.

"Fine, I am defending myself, but can you blame me? I do not love Paige Daley. I can't believe I ever did. Thinking about it makes me nauseous. Who was I?"

"All I'm saying is that if you truly didn't care about her, you wouldn't be so torn up about this article. An article that is not that bad, I repeat."

"I do care. I care greatly," Lara said. "But that care is fueled by hatred, betrayal, a need for justice and revenge. I feel a lot of things towards Paige Daley, but none of those things are love."

"Whatever you say." April snapped the newspaper pages in front of her face like a dad avoiding a conversation. "Here, let me read some more."

"Please put the paper away," Lara pleaded. "I can't bear it anymore."

"Fine. Just let me check one more thing."

"Is it the obituaries?" Lara asked. "I might be in there: Lara Spellmeyer: murdered by Roger Feldman and Paige Daley, who were acquitted of the crime they obviously committed by a heavily biased jury of Lara's peers. She accomplished nothing and is survived by everyone. No one will miss her."

"Hush." April set the paper on the table and sifted through it, her frown drooping lower and lower as she neared the back page. "Of course. It's not in here again."

"What isn't in there?"

"Do you remember how I said I was going to put out an ad for Tight Knit so that plenty of people came to the first meeting?"

"Yeah." Lara was too petty to read *The Daily Page*, but no one else in town held the same grudge against Paige Daley that Lara did. Everyone would have seen the ad by now. It was one of April's many great ideas.

"The ad was supposed to run a few days ago, but it never did. I've been checking the paper every day, and it's still not in here."

Classic Paige. Screwing over Lara was one thing, but screwing over the nicest woman in Perry was another. "Did you call them?"

"Only about a hundred times. I need to talk to Paige, apparently, but I can't get ahold of her."

"Sounds like Paige."

"I'll have to take a day off and go down there sometime next week." April sighed and rubbed her temples. "Maybe you can call her again and butter her up enough to give me a civil conversation."

Lara felt bad for April—she could sympathize with her fruitless plight—and the words were out of her mouth before she could stop them. "I could help you. Maybe."

April perked up. "Really? You'll call her?"

Lara shook her head. "No, I'll…" Lara's eyes closed in a feeble attempt to shield herself from her own stupidity. "I could go down there for you."

"Lara, that would be wonderful! Are you sure you're not too busy?"

After that *Trend Bender* article? "Definitely not."

"Oh, thank you so much." Not even April's smile could make Lara feel great about what she'd just agreed to do, but it did help a little. "You could use this to your advantage, too," April added. "Doesn't she owe you a favor after what she did to you? Make her feel guilty. Get her to apologize and run the ad as penance."

"It's not penance. It's a business transaction. You paid her. She should run the ad no matter what." But it would be nice to get something in return for all the things that Lara had done for Paige over the years. Still, would one last opportunity to be vindictive make up for having to see Paige's face again?

It would have to be. Lara couldn't let April down.

"I'm so excited!" April gave a small squeal. "This knitting circle will be great for the town."

It would be. Everything April did was great for this town. If everyone were like her, Perry wouldn't be such an awful place to live, and Lara never would have moved away. April was the only person who had always been on her side. And if the press was so hell-bent on making her life worse, then Lara had better keep her only friend around to help her get through it.

Chapter 3

People like Roger Feldman and Paige Daley were the reason Lara's phone screen was cracked.

Okay, that wasn't true. Rocket had punted her iPhone off the kitchen table last week, like her grandmother chucking pucks down a shuffleboard table on her annual cruise. Staring at her screen's GPS, Lara tapped the fractured glass like a challenge. If she pressed just a little harder, the screen would burst and fade to black. No more bad reviews, no more anger, and no more excuses for putting off buying a new phone. She could tell April that she hadn't been able to find Paige's office.

She couldn't do that, though. Lara had been dreading this meeting all weekend, but if she put it off, the ad would never be published before Tight Knit started. She had to do this.

Lara's eyes shifted from the fractured glass of her phone screen to the smooth pane of glass on the storefront in front of her. The frosted gold letters of the sign glittered in the sunlight. *Home of Perry, Oklahoma's Only Newspaper: The Daily Page.*

God, she really hated that name.

When Lara stepped into the office, she let herself see the building for the first time. For a small-town newspaper, *The Daily Page* was an impressive operation that seemed out of place in the historic downtown district otherwise populated by rustic buildings and ancient local landmarks. The open glass architecture of the building was reminiscent of some of the nicest places in Oklahoma City, and the main floor had a sleek, minimalist layout. The ringing of phones accompanied the din of lively conversation, and the way the floor was swamped with employees—running from station to station, chatting with others, and carrying stacks of papers and folders—gave the place an urgent feel, as if this quiet little town had real news to report on, as if everyone here was convinced they had come across the next big scoop that was going to launch their name into journalistic stardom.

Lara located the receptionist, an older woman almost out of place among the young staff, and approached the desk, her head bowed lest someone recognize her. "I have an appointment with Paige Daley."

"I'll let her know. You can wait over there." Lara's eyes followed the receptionist's guiding hand to the waiting area.

"Um." Lara bit her lip, ashamed of what she was about to say. "Do you have a copy of Saturday's paper?"

"Probably. You're Lara Spellmeyer, right?"

Fuck. Was there a picture of her in the article? God, this was a mistake. Lara wanted to say the woman had confused her for someone else and walk away to forget this ever happened, but the woman worked here. She obviously recognized Lara. There was no point in denying it.

"Yes, I am."

"How's your grandmother doing?"

Oh. Right. She recognized Lara because everyone in Perry recognized Lara. "Better. Not great, but better."

"I'm praying for her. Tell her we miss her at Bridge." She ducked beneath her desk and rummaged around. Moments later, she reappeared with the newspaper in hand. "Here, you go. Saturday's paper."

"Thanks."

Lara took it quickly. At least her embarrassment wasn't on the front page. Still, she tucked the paper beneath her own folder and carried it discreetly to the waiting area. No one else was there, and Lara claimed the best seat in the house, the one in the corner farthest away from the receptionist, a.k.a. the only person in the world who knew that Lara Spellmeyer was about to read an issue of *The Daily Page*. Lara took a deep breath, made sure no one was watching her, and dove in.

There was no picture, only a headline that wasn't even the largest print on the spread. The article was given poor real estate, tucked away in the corner of a page next to an ad for fertilizer, which said a lot about where Paige thought Lara belonged. Lara knew she should be happy that Paige hadn't made the article such a big deal, but she wasn't. It still existed, and it still made her look bad. The fact that Paige didn't consider the story major news almost made it worse. It was a routine story, unsurprising for anyone. Just one more piece of evidence that confirmed what Paige and Perry already knew: Lara Spellmeyer was a screwup.

Even the article was uninteresting. Most of it April had already read. Everything else was didactic, the small, boring details that no one cared about. There was one piece that caught Lara's eye, though: the byline. Where Lara expected to see Paige's name, she saw someone else's instead. Lorraine Bauer.

Who the hell was Lorraine Bauer?

"Lara Spellmeyer?"

Lara didn't mean to greet the assistant with a scowl, but she could feel her lips slouch into a frown regardless. She grabbed the manila folder in the chair beside her and stood from her seat.

"Sorry for the wait. Ms. Daley is ready to see you."

Lara nodded and thanked the young woman, trying to be as polite as possible despite her sour mood. She was an innocent bystander. Lara's anger was best reserved for people like Roger Feldman. Or Paige Daley.

Lara took a deep breath, centered herself, and let the assistant guide her into Paige's office.

Paige hadn't aged a day. She'd aged years. She looked so different, rigid behind her work desk in a blazer, not as she had once looked slouched behind her school desk in jeans. Lara almost didn't recognize her.

Paige didn't have as much trouble placing Lara. The pen twirling between her fingers screeched to a halt as her green eyes flashed with recognition.

"What are you doing here, Lara?"

"You wrote an article defaming my business no less than two days ago. Are you really that surprised to see me show up?"

"I heard you were in town, but I didn't expect to bump into you here. Figures you'd come to yell at me about the article again." Paige sank into her seat and rolled her eyes, preparing for another verbal beating.

"I didn't. I'm here on other business."

Lara tossed the manila folder onto Paige's desk. It was merely a flake on the snowfall of papers already blanketing the surface. Each page was a different color, a different size, and twisted into different angles. The desktop was a mess, almost as disorganized as the cabinets and shelves behind Paige. Drawers were open. Awards were displayed crookedly. It reminded Lara of Paige's old dorm room, and she felt herself sinking into her seat like it was the bean bag chair at the foot of Paige's old bed. As soon as Lara caught herself drowning, she sat up, straightened her spine, and held onto the arms of the chair like a raft. She was here on business, not to take a stroll down memory lane.

"And what would that be?" Paige's voice was tired, gruff. Lara expected to see the signature pack of cigarettes peeking its head out of Paige's blazer pocket, but it wasn't there.

"I'm here for a friend. April Helm. She put in an ad for last week and it never ran."

Paige's eyebrows twitched as she clicked the tip of her pen closed and picked up the folder. She sifted through it meaninglessly, eyes not moving enough to read the text.

"That's the ad," Lara said.

"So what is it that you're asking me?"

"I'm asking you to do your job."

Paige flipped the folder from cover to cover again, no more attentive this time than she had been the first. "What is it that you want me to do exactly?"

"Run the ad tomorrow."

"Why would I do that?"

"Because my friend paid for it, and you're obligated to."

"Right. *Friend*." Paige sounded unconvinced. It wasn't like Lara could blame her. Paige knew exactly how many friends Lara didn't have.

"Look," Paige said, her voice softening. Lara knew that opener well. It was Paige's "I don't want to be the bad guy" façade that she only put on right before playing the bad guy, a way of shifting blame off herself. She never could own up to being an asshole. She always had to pretend that her own assholery somehow hurt her too. "I can't help you if it's not your ad. If the order is under her name, she's the one who's going to have to contact me."

"She's been trying. For a week. She's talked to every person here but you, and they've all told her that you're the person she needs to get in touch with. Except, apparently, you don't answer your calls."

"I'm busy."

"Busy answering other complaints? Busy calling me when I don't want to talk to you?"

Paige bit her tongue. Literally. Lara watched the teeth clamp down like a cheetah suffocating its prey.

"I'm not helping you," Paige said.

"Because I'm me?"

"Because you're not the client."

"The client sent me."

"Are you family?" Paige asked. "Lovers?"

"No."

"Then, no, I won't let you manage her accounts."

Lara scoffed. "Good thing you stick to arbitrary rules of conduct. If only you stuck to your deadlines too." It felt good to be crass, but Lara was bluffing. If insulting Paige didn't get her anywhere, then it was nothing but selfishly cathartic. She'd promised April she could do this. She'd promised herself she could do this. "Look, you owe me this."

Paige raised an eyebrow. "Owe you? I've already told you: I don't owe you anything."

"After running that article on me, yes, you do."

"That wasn't personal, Lara, and it has nothing to do with this ad."

"Yeah, right," Lara taunted. "It was so not personal that you weren't even brave enough to put your own name on the article. You threw some intern under the bus."

"Lorraine's name is on the piece because she's the one who found the story, and she wrote most of the local content. I gave her credit where credit was due, and she was happy to take the lead."

"Then why were you the one to call me?"

Paige rocked back in her chair ever so slightly. "I figured you'd rather hear from me than a stranger."

"I would have preferred the intern."

Paige took a deep breath. Her nostrils puffed out like a dragon disturbed from its slumber, but her chest fell and her face relaxed before the fire could burst forth from her mouth. The papers in her hand wavered. Her mouth opened as if to speak, but as quickly as she faltered, her jaw clenched shut again. Paige slapped the file flat against the mess of the desk and slid it back to Lara. A few of her own papers scattered with it. Paige didn't seem to care.

"I think you should leave."

Lara's heart stopped. She'd blown it. "So this was all a waste of time?"

"Looks like it."

Of course this was a waste of time, just like thinking she could do something nice for April in the first place, just like thinking Paige would actually help her after what had happened between them. Lara shut her eyes and tried not to have a brain aneurysm on the spot. She settled for accepting the migraine pounding at her temples as punishment for her defeat.

Lara picked up the folder and put her brain power toward thinking up an excuse for April rather than thinking up another way to convince Paige to do something that she clearly wasn't willing to do. "Fine. I'll see myself out. Not like you'd even exert yourself to show me the door."

As Lara got up, she heard the scratch of the other chair sliding across the wooden floor. Paige opened the door before Lara could get it for herself. It was simultaneously the most gentlewomanly and the rudest Paige had ever been.

Well, maybe not *the* rudest, but she sure didn't seem sad to see Lara go.

"Sorry we couldn't come to an agreement." She was all business again. Too calm, too formal. Paige never did let herself feel. She had never operated like a normal human being with emotions. She hadn't been able to give Lara the love she'd felt four years ago, and she couldn't give Lara whatever she was feeling now.

Lara scoffed at the formality. An agreement. She hadn't wanted a business contract. She'd wanted Paige to not let her down just one time. She was stupid for ever thinking there was a chance of that happening.

Paige went back to her desk, and Lara lingered just outside her open doorway, fuming and disappointed. Being back in the main part of the building only made her feel worse. Everything was so organized and productive. It was the exact opposite of how Lara felt.

Lara was so out of it that she didn't realize just how much her loitering was offsetting the scheduled balance. A young woman with a flowing scarf and springing curls of red hair barreled down the hall with green eyes locked on her phone. By the time Lara noticed that she was in the way, it was too late. The redhead collided with her, shaking them both up and causing the girl to drop her mobile. The shrill inhale of a gasp and the shattering crack of broken glass pierced Lara's ears before she had time to stabilize herself from the impact. The redhead crouched to retrieve her phone as Lara struggled to regain her balance.

"Sorry!" The girl's voice was youthful and high pitched. Lara could tell the apology was some combination of actual guilt and grief over her broken phone.

Lara was in the middle of opening her mouth to say that accidents happen and she was sorry about the phone, but when the girl rose to her feet, her eyes bulged out at the sight of Lara. It scared Lara enough to silence her.

"Oh my god, you're Lara Spellmeyer! You're actually here!"

The girl reached for Lara's hand and practically yanked her arm out of her socket with her handshake. "I'm Lorraine Bauer, the one who covered you in *The Daily Page.* I'm a huge fan!"

"If you're a fan, why would you want to publish anything about that *Trend Bender* article?"

"You made national news! That's awesome!"

Had she read the article? "I made bad national news."

Lorraine shrugged. "All press is good press."

"Tell that to my sales," Lara said. "I had almost ten people call and cancel orders this week. Two of them were from Perry."

Lorraine pouted, but she didn't look as guilty as Lara was trying to make her feel. "I'm sure things will turn around soon. You have over one-hundred thousand followers! BuzzFeed wrote an article about you! People love you!"

They used to. They wouldn't for much longer if people like Roger and Lorraine had anything to say about it.

Lara heard footsteps and braced herself for another impact. She was prepared for a collision, but she was not prepared to see Paige emerge next to her.

"You have a following of that many people?" Paige asked. "I didn't realize it had become that successful." Her voice was laced with disbelief, but also astonishment.

Lara shrugged, feigning humility. "They're mostly there for the cat pics. Customers send me pictures of their cats wearing the sweaters, and I post them. I don't think anyone is actually there because of *me*."

"You didn't tell me that," Paige said. Her voice was soft. It had lost all of the bark she'd used in her office. She spoke to Lara like Lorraine wasn't even there. Their conversation became more personal than it had been the entire time they were shut alone in a room together.

"I haven't seen you in four years," Lara said. "Why would I tell you anything?"

Paige tried to stutter out a response but came up short. Lorraine broke the tension, blissfully unaware of anything but her own excitement.

"How could you not know?" As annoying as the girl was, Lara enjoyed watching Paige wince, clearly just as annoyed by Lorraine's shrill voice as she was. "Didn't you see the BuzzFeed video on Facebook?"

"I run a newspaper," Paige said. "I prefer to get my news from sources other than the people I went to high school with and my racist parents."

Lara didn't know why she was surprised. Paige had always acted like that, haughty, holier than thou, better than everyone else because she thought she was so much smarter. She wasn't. Not really. She and Lara had both gotten into the same college, had both started their own businesses, had both ended up in Perry after graduation. The only difference was that Lara hadn't stayed stuck here.

Lorraine, defeated by Paige's lack of enthusiasm, slapped her phone against her thigh, as if wiping the screen of dirt would also wipe away the cracks. The curls of her hair seemed to lose their springiness as she whipped her head around to face Lara.

"It was great to meet you." The hand that wasn't holding her phone stretched out, and Lara shook it with as much of a smile as she could muster after such a shitty morning.

"It was nice to meet you, too." It wasn't, but Lara didn't need to tell her that.

Lorraine looked back at Paige, wiped the smile off her face, and continued on to wherever she had been heading when she'd bumped into Lara. Part of Lara was happy to see her go, but part of her was sad that the girl had left her alone with Paige. Again.

"Sorry," Paige said, apologizing for Lorraine's rude behavior far more easily than she ever apologized for her own. "Interns." Paige rolled her eyes and grumbled in a way she clearly expected Lara to understand.

Lara didn't. "I can show myself out." She started towards the door.

"Wait!"

Lara's feet stalled, despite her brain's insistence that they shouldn't. Paige fished into the pocket of her pant leg and extracted a small stock paper card. She handed it to Lara. "Call me later."

In her palm, the image of Paige's gapped-tooth smile looked up at her.

Her business card. Paige had actually given her a business card. This was the most impersonal thing she could think of, and it took every ounce of willpower not to rip the paper in Paige's face. Wordlessly, Lara slipped the card into her pocket, left the office, and stepped out onto the empty downtown sidewalk.

Chapter 4

The stack of papers felt comfortable in Lara's hands. It was therapeutic for her to organize them, collecting them one by one as they shot out from the printer. Tapping the stack against the side of a nearby bookshelf to align the pages uniformly, it felt like she was chronicling magazines at the back of the library again or helping the local kids print out their school assignments. There was a comfort in the nostalgia. That routine and security of it was something Lara hadn't realized she missed.

How had it already been four years since she'd left her job at the library to move to Oklahoma City and knit cat sweaters full time?

Lara took a deep breath and set the papers on the checkout desk with conviction. "Genie, I need a favor."

Genie was short standing up, but she was even shorter seated behind the counter. Lara towered over the older woman, who rested slumped backwards with her feet up on the desk and an open Cosmo magazine in her lap. Genie tilted her head, lifted her eyes, and let her glasses slip down her nose before taking them off completely. The cat-eye frames swung around her neck like a pendulum from a thick purple string of yarn before dropping onto her chest.

"I'll grant you a wish, Spellmeyer, but, remember, you only get three, and you used your first one to get yourself out of this place." With a groan and a few cracks of her joints, Genie carried her boots back down to solid ground and sat up straight in the chair. "What do you need, dear?"

Lara felt something bump her side. "Excuse me."

When she looked down, a young boy was next to her, standing on his tiptoes and balancing himself on the edge of the counter so he could see Genie over it. A man Lara assumed was his father trailed behind and gave Lara an apologetic smile.

"Do you have any books about monster trucks?" the boy asked.

Genie stared him in the eyes and gave a deadpan "Nope."

The boy and his dad were frozen in space, shifting awkwardly. Neither had prepared for this outcome. "Oh."

"Relax, I'm joking." Genie shot a quick glance of disbelief Lara's way, as if the man and his son were too dumb to notice her searching for solidarity. "Go up to the second floor and make a right. You'll see the sign for the automotive section."

The boy's face lit up. "Thanks!" Once again, he took off without his father.

"Hey!" Genie shouted.

The boy stopped, his expression strained with guilt at being caught.

"If you're going to run in the library, at least put your back into it. Pick up the pace, kid!" She motioned for him to get moving, and he did, footsteps echoing as he stomped his way up the staircase, his light-up shoes transforming the stairwell into an aurora borealis of colors. The father shot a disapproving look at Genie before begrudgingly trudging after him.

"Sheesh, no one has a sense of humor anymore," Genie said. "What did you want, Lara?"

Lara tapped the stack of freshly-printed papers, and Genie stretched her neck to look at them. "My friend April is hosting a knitting club. I figured this would be a good place to put up a few flyers and spread the word."

"Sounds boring. What do you need me for?"

"I just need permission."

"Permission granted. You worked here for six years. Do you really think I care if you hang up ads for your knitting circle? Or that you need my permission?"

"Figured I'd be safe rather than sorry. I didn't think you'd have a problem with it. I was just worried about —"

"Ah. I see. You want someone already in your corner in case Sanchez doesn't like it.

"Well…yeah, to be honest."

"She's not going to mind. She's disappointed in how you left, but she doesn't hate you, you know. Well." Genie paused to think. "Okay, maybe a little bit. If you want to talk to her, though, you're out of luck. She's not in today."

Lara knew that. She'd been scheduling her library trips around Sanchez's old schedule and raking the parking lot for Sanchez's car before she came in. She and Sanchez hadn't talked since Lara had quit. Or been fired, rather. It was complicated. If it was up to Lara, she'd *never* talk to Sanchez again.

"Thanks, Genie."

"No problem, hun."

Genie settled herself back in the chair, recovered her place in the magazine, and got to work memorizing the latest celebrity gossip, while Lara took her flyers and set off. If Paige wasn't going to help April, Lara would. It was the least she could do.

The receptionist at the front desk of the nursing home smiled at Lara in recognition. The cafeteria din called to her, enticing her with a slice of blueberry pie, but Lara instead boarded the elevator that opened as soon as she stepped in front of the doors, as though it had been waiting for her. Everything was becoming a little too familiar. Especially room 319.

"Hey, Gam Gam."

Grandma Betty was in another flower-print dress, her signature style these last few weeks. This one was a deep red patterned with pink cherry blossom petals that fluttered as she moved.

Betty's smile was huge. "I thought you'd forgotten about me, Lara."

"I moved back to Perry for you. I'd never forget you."

Lara sat down in her favorite spot, an armchair directly bedside with scratchy fabric and a cushion half an inch thick. Everything in the room was bland, cold, only a small step up from the hospital. The white walls were replaced by a somehow more boring shade of rusted brown. The uncomfortable assembly-line furniture was replaced by just as uncomfortable antiques. It wasn't the kind of place that Lara could imagine living in, but Betty had made it as much like home as possible.

When Lara and her parents had first brought her over here, she had such a Betty reaction: one look at the place and she'd told Lara's dad to get a pad of paper from the nurse's desk and then proceeded to dictate of list of things she'd wanted from home, over her son's protests that she wouldn't be here that long. She'd replaced the blankets with one Lara had watched her knit herself over the last few weeks. The candles from her living room were working hard to rid the room of the sterile smell seeping in from the hallway. Pictures decorated the walls, both family portraits and photos taken long before Lara was born of Betty as a young woman visiting vacation sites across the globe. A stack of library books that Lara had borrowed for her on everything from crocheting to Gothic architecture towered on top of the dresser.

Lara loved those personal touches. They were the same details she had loved about visiting her grandmother's house since she was a kid. But this wasn't her grandmother's house. The nursing home was supposed to be a temporary residence until Betty was feeling well enough to go back home. Lara was worried that Betty was starting to feel too complacent here. She wouldn't let herself feel the same way about Perry.

It wasn't until Lara fully settled in that she realized the items from home weren't the only thing different about the room today. The dividing curtain was drawn back, and the second bed was empty.

"Where's Stella?"

"Gone."

"They released her?"

"That's one way to put it."

The clock clicked a steady, stable rhythm. That and the humming of the air conditioner were the only sounds in the otherwise silent room.

"Let's talk about something else," Betty said. "How have you been doing?"

"I've been better," Lara admitted.

"What's wrong, dear?"

"There's this journalist. He said he was going to write an article about my business, but all he did was grill me over a single bad experience one of my customers had. He completely blew everything out of proportion and caught me off guard, and now I'm a media punching bag. People keep telling me to relax, but I can't. I guess it's my own fault for talking to him and not watching my words."

"It sounds like he was going to twist your words no matter what."

"Probably."

"Take it from me: when people decide in advance that they're going to be negative about a situation, nothing you say can change their mind."

"I feel useless not trying, though," Lara reasoned. "I might not be able to change things if I try, but if I don't try, then I know nothing will change."

"If the outcome is going to be the same either way, you might as well not waste your time. Life isn't as long as it seems."

"But what if it doesn't turn out to be a waste of time?"

"Do you know how many decades I spent trying to defend your grandfather?" Betty asked. "No one wanted to hear it. He could have cured cancer, and they still wouldn't have seen him any differently. You can't let people like that bring you down."

"How do you not feel down about that?

"You get used to it. The secret is to stay positive. Look at me. Just because no one lets me forget that my husband drank too much, it doesn't mean that I'm not living the life." Betty sprawled out her arms as if her room was truly something to behold. She coughed slightly.

Lara laughed. If only she could have her grandmother's sense of humor.

Maybe other people were part of the problem, but Lara certainly wasn't helping her own cause. She couldn't seem to do anything right anymore. Not her orders. Not her interviews. She couldn't even convince Paige to run an ad that she had been paid to put in her newspaper.

But wallowing in her misery just made her feel selfish. Her grandmother was in the nursing home after a series of hospital visits, and here was Lara complaining about her petty drama with Paige and Roger Feldman? That was what April was for. Betty deserved good news.

"Well, one thing I am feeling positive about is my friend April and I are starting a knitting club." Betty's eyes lit up, and Lara knew it wasn't a reflection of the fluorescents overhead. "You taught me everything I know, so I figured I should do some good and pass on the knowledge."

"Any star pupils?"

"Well, we haven't officially started yet." Lara thought of Paige and tried not to let her anger bleed into her deliberately cheerful tone. "We're having some issues getting the word out, but I've been trying to put up flyers and get an ad in the newspaper. Things like that. Our first meeting is this weekend."

"I used to have a knitting circle," Betty said. Her eyes flicked towards the ceiling as she recalled the memory. "We met every week for twenty years. Then, well, couple of us died. Couple of us got arthritis. Just fell out of touch at some point." Betty took a moment to reminisce in silence. "If you need help, I know a few people who would probably be interested."

"Gam Gam, you know Dr. Barnes said you can't come home yet. He's not going to let you out early so you can knit," Lara teased.

She almost didn't feel the playful slap that hit her arm. It was more of a touch than anything, too weak to really be called a slap, but Lara knew when she was being chided. "I didn't mean me, silly. You're not the only one that visits me. I have friends, you know."

Of course she did. Even in a town full of people who hated her for the man she married, Lara's grandmother still had more friends than Lara did. Not that Lara could fault her. Betty was an awesome woman.

"Do you think they'll come?"

"Of course. I'll give them a call tonight. They'll love being there just as much as you'll love having them there." Betty coughed, then shivered. "Maybe if all of you make me some scarves, I'll have enough layers to stay warm." She said the words as though they were a joke, but Lara watched her rub her hands together to trap a bit of warmth between them.

Without thinking, Lara took off her cardigan and laid it across Betty's chest. It *was* cold in the room. An army of goosebumps rose up from her arms that stretched from her shoulders to her wrist. "I'll talk to one of the nurses about it and see if they can up the thermostat."

"Thank you," Betty said, her throat finally clear. "I swear, it's like they try to give you pneumonia so that you have to stay in here longer and give them more money."

"Don't you have insurance that'll pay for everything?"

"It's not *that* good."

Betty coughed again, and Lara reached for the glass of water at her bedside. Beside it was an earmarked book on holy sites in Israel and a newspaper that looked just as worn. It was that morning's copy of *The Daily Page*, and Lara couldn't help but take a peek.

Hometown Heroes!

We'll review all submissions carefully and select only the very best to represent Perry. The winner will be chosen through several rounds of voting, available to those who sign up for an account on *The Daily Page* website. Frontrunners will be profiled individually after each round, and the winner will receive an article submitted to the Oklahoma News Organization covering their invaluable contributions to the community and will be invited to attend the award ceremony in Oklahoma City. The deadline for nominations is October 21st.

In the margins of the page were several hastily scrawled names. Bob Piotrowski. Luna Glenson. Lara recognized a couple as her grandmother's friends. Circled amongst all of them was Lara's own name. She couldn't help but smile. The thought was sweet. Silly and stupid, but sweet.

Betty handed the glass back to Lara after a long sip. "Thank you, dear."

"You're welcome." Lara was still absently skimming the article, and Betty was keen enough to notice.

"Haven't you read the paper already?" she asked.

"No. You know how I hate the press." Lara tried to make a joke of it, but she came off sounding as bitter as she felt.

"I submitted your name to that contest."

Lara was stunned; she had thought the markings in the margins nothing more than thoughtful scribbles. "I appreciate it, Gam Gam, but why? Out of all the people in Perry? I haven't even been here the last few years. I should put your name in the running. You've done more for Perry than I ever could."

"No." Betty was matter of fact. "Everything I've done is in the past. The winner should be someone young—like you."

"Gam Gam—"

"No, I mean it. I am so proud of you, Lara. Nothing has ever held you back. When you lost that science fair in fourth grade, you went to space camp over the summer so you could win it in fifth. When you got stuck in a dead-end job you didn't like, you started your own business. When your grandmother got sick, you dropped everything to move back home and spend time with me. I am so proud of the woman you've become, Lara Spellmeyer."

There was no way Lara would win the popular vote for that Hometown Heroes contest, but all those Hallmark cards were right; it was the thought that counted. Lara felt so many things all at once. Sympathy. Guilt. Love. Mostly she wished there was a way to pay Betty back for the kind words. Being here in this moment was a start, right? Moving back to Perry was the most selfless gesture Lara had ever performed for another human being, but it still didn't feel like enough.

A comforting hand found Lara's. Betty's smile calmed her.

"How's your father doing?"

"He's coming over for dinner tomorrow, so I'll let you know." The implication of Betty's words hit Lara a little late. "Wait, hasn't he been to see you lately?"

"Eh, once or twice."

Once or twice? Lara had assumed he was visiting just as often as she was.

"I'll tell him to come by soon."

"I'd like that."

"He should be here." Lara had packed up her life to be here for Betty. Her father lived less than a mile away and he couldn't be bothered to visit his own mother? That wasn't like him.

"It's alright, Lara. I know this is hard for him, and I know he's busy. I'll be here when he's ready. It's not like I'm going anywhere just yet."

That was exactly what Lara was afraid of.

A nurse came by and rapped on the door to get Lara's attention. "Visiting time's up in a few. Say your goodbyes."

It was that late already? God, it had been a long day. Lara had done so much, and yet it felt like she'd accomplished nothing. The entire day had felt like a waste of time, one fruitless pursuit after another.

"I guess I'll see you tomorrow, Gam Gam."

"I look forward to it."

The drive home was short, but the drive from anywhere in Perry to home was short compared to the traffic of the city. It wasn't a big town, though it felt that way sometimes on days like today, when Lara had visited nearly everywhere there was to visit. She was exhausted when she stepped in the door, eagerly taking off her shoes and padding barefoot to the kitchen to finish her nightly chores. She fed the cat, put the dishes in the dishwasher, and made sure the back door was locked. When she finally sat down on the couch, her entire body breathed a sigh of relief along with her lungs.

She emptied her jacket pockets onto the coffee table. A tube of lip balm. Car keys. The wrapper from the tuna fish sandwich she'd picked up on the way home. The only thing left was her phone. And Paige's business card.

Lara weighed the card in one hand and her phone in the other. Somehow the stock paper felt heavier than the metal. With a flick of her wrist, she tossed the card on the coffee table. The numbers stared up at her, mocking. She opened the call screen on her phone and hit dial.

April answered on the first ring. She'd be so excited about Betty's plan for Tight Knit.

Chapter 5

Lara had a bit of a hoarding problem, but April had a full-fledged craft store in her house. Her ex-husband's office space had been converted into a sewing room, and it took both her and Lara all morning to unpack and set out supplies for the inaugural Tight Knit meeting.

April had more needles than a hospital and more wool than all the sheep in Oklahoma could produce in a year. Bins of supplies circled the coffee table like a moat, and the castle in the middle was decorated in sweet treats. April's world-famous peanut butter fudge sat alongside store-bought brownies that had suspiciously lost their original packaging and been placed on a large serving platter. Lara had skipped breakfast to gorge herself, and at this point she barely cared if there were any snacks left for the rest of the guests. Between her and Cynthia, there wouldn't be. April's youngest was seated beneath the coffee table, her wide smile and grabby little hands just a bit more chocolatey than normal.

As soon as they had a moment to rest, Lara fell into the couch cushions. That's when April brought up the one thing Lara had hoped she'd forgotten about.

"Thank you again for talking to Paige."

Lara took a moment to slip off her shoes and compose her thoughts. It left her with cold feet, in more ways than one. "Yeah, about that…"

"I really appreciate it. I know you didn't want to do it, especially with your… history," April settled on saying. "Oh, let me go grab the newspaper!"

This was not how Lara envisioned this conversation going. April was reaching forward before Lara could protest and brandishing a days-old copy of *The Daily Page* from the coffee table. Excitedly she flipped through the pages, looking for something that Lara knew wasn't going to be there.

"Right here, look."

She turned the paper around for Lara to see, and if April wasn't there to back up the claim, Lara would have thought she'd gone crazy and started imagining things.

There was the ad, right there in the center of the classifieds. Paige had run it after all.

"It's even bigger than I paid for. In color, too!" April let Lara soak in the images for a moment longer before taking the paper back. "Paige was so sweet about it when she called me."

"She called you?"

"Yeah! Apologized for the mix-up and the delay. Said she wanted to make the situation right and was sorry she hadn't gotten in contact with me sooner."

Lara held the paper in her hands in disbelief. Apparently insulting Paige's ability to run her business had hit a stronger nerve than she was willing to let Lara realize.

"She even said she was going to come to the meeting and do an interview! She's thinking of running a piece on it."

Oh. Or she just wanted to use the opportunity for her own gain.

Yeah, that sounded more like Paige.

"That's…great." Lara had never worked so hard to force herself into what she assumed was a smile. She had to see Paige again? Not only see her but spend an entire afternoon with her during a special event that Lara had been looking forward to for weeks? This was so far beyond Lara's idea of a good time. She felt like she was floating in outer space with an empty oxygen tank.

But this wasn't about Lara, and this wasn't just Lara's group. If April wanted Paige there, then so be it. Lara would just have to suck it up.

Easier said than done.

The doorbell chimed at the exact moment the grandfather clock sung out 1:00 p.m. Their first guest was so punctual that it made Lara feel late.

"I'll get that," April offered, as if this weren't her own home. "Can you grab the drinks from the kitchen?"

It was more scut work, but it was easy scut work. "I'm on it." Lara peeked her head beneath the fort Cynthia had made of the coffee table. Her walls of carefully arranged plastic bins weren't strong enough to keep Lara out. She scooted one out of the way. "Want to help me carry cups, Cynthia?"

"No."

Who knew a four-year-old could be the most honest person in Perry? Lara respected that.

Alone, Lara made her way to the kitchen. With all the red Solo cups and two liters of pop, one would think April was throwing a party. The noise from the living room made it seem like one too. From the din of conversation, it was obvious that more than one person had shown up on time, and the doorbell rang a couple more times as Lara decorated the dining table with fizzy drinks and bags of ice.

"Need some help with that?"

Lara was so anxious to get back into the living room to see what the turnout was like that she would have accepted help from anyone.

Except for Paige.

Lara didn't bother to turn around at the sound of her voice in the kitchen doorway. "No, thanks. I'm good."

Instead of hearing feet shuffle away onto the living room carpet, Lara heard them squeak closer to her on the kitchen tile. Paige started laying out cups beside her like she was preparing for a stacking contest.

Lara couldn't decide if it was best to pick a fight or completely ignore her.

Paige decided for her. "You didn't call me."

"You didn't tell me you were planning on writing an article about the meeting," Lara snapped.

Paige shrugged. "I would have if you'd called me."

"Not in a million years, Paige."

If Paige wanted to help set out drinks so badly, fine. She could do it. Lara set off for the living room, leaving Paige to finish the job without her.

April's living room wasn't big, but it felt significantly smaller when it was packed full of people. It wasn't the biggest crowd that had ever gathered in Perry, but at least a dozen people had shown up. It was calming to see such a turnout: A couple of elderly women that no doubt Betty had called, accompanied by younger women Lara guessed were either their daughters or caretakers. A few women Lara recognized as either working in the craft store or spending so much time there that they might as well be getting paid for it. A couple of April's friends. Even a couple of kids, though most of them were closer to April's son Tommy's age than Cynthia's. They were all women except for one younger boy, but Lara had expected that. This was Perry, after all. Men would only work with yarn if they were doing it on one of the factory lines.

Several people had brought their own half-finished projects. Hats and sweaters and strange pieces of loosely woven together fabric that Lara couldn't yet see the finished projects in. The scene took her right back in time. All of a sudden she was sitting at the foot of a rocking chair in her grandmother's house, clumsily mashing together knitting needles half the length of her body while all the women around her talked about their husbands and their kids and the new recipe books they had ordered out of a catalogue. Five minutes in, and Tight Knit was everything that Lara had hoped it would be.

Lara took a seat on the couch next to April, where she had set up her supplies earlier. "April, this is great! Look how many people showed up!"

"You sound surprised."

"Well, yeah, I guess I am." The realization hit Lara as she said the words. "It's one thing to have an idea to do something, but it's another to actually pull it off."

"It's all thanks to you," April said. "This was your idea anyway. Frankly, I initially assumed that knitting circles were a bit outdated and that no one would be interested, but you were right! This was something Perry needed."

Lara blushed. "You're the one who offered to host and organize everything."

"Don't be so humble. This wouldn't have happened without you either.'

April was right. Lara had helped, at least a little bit. She deserved to enjoy the day that she'd helped create. Even if Paige was here too.

Instinctively, Lara surveyed the room for the threat. Paige was chatting with a woman whose infant child sat at their feet, tugging on Paige's shoestrings. She was ignoring the baby in favor of her notepad. Good. As long as Paige was busy getting interviews from everyone else, Lara would be free to enjoy herself. And she would enjoy herself that much more if Paige happened to trip on her untied laces when she stood up. She kept her fingers crossed.

"Oh." April stood from the couch. "I'm going to find my friend Kerry. I told her you'd show her how to do a rib stitch. I would have taught her myself, but you're way better than me, and she should learn from someone who actually knows what they're doing."

April was gone before Lara could say anything. Normally Lara wouldn't be too enthusiastic about being asked for knitting advice—she got messages every day from people wondering how she'd pulled off a specific pattern or fitting. But in this context, she was happy to do it. This circle was all about meeting new people and sharing techniques and life stories.

April wasn't slick, though. Lara knew exactly what she was doing. Kerry was the woman April wanted to set her up with, and apparently, she wasn't taking Lara's no for an answer.

April returned with a lanky woman in a tight red cardigan by her side. In her hands was a ball of fabric and needles too small for the type of yarn she was working with. She settled in next to Lara on the couch, and the first thing Lara noticed was the scent of cheap candles and potpourri. It reminded Lara of an antique store. It was a nostalgic feeling, and not an unpleasant one.

"Kerry, this is Lara, the woman I was telling you about the other day. I'm leaving you in good hands, I promise."

Lara rolled her eyes. Of course April had talked to Kerry about Lara too.

"I know this is a mess." Kerry gestured to the ball of yarn in her hands. It wasn't all wound together. She had turned the end into the start of something, but that something was definitely not a proper rib stitch. "I'm more of a sewer than a knitter," Kerry admitted. "I'm trying to 'expand my skill set and improve my marketability.'" Kerry accented the words and made air quotes around them as if she was reading from a template.

Lara chuckled. "You said that so clinically."

"My boss has been on me about my 'professionalism' and 'productivity.' I'm a tailor down at Taylor Made. Not as glamorous as cat sweaters, I'm sure, but fitting suits pays the bills. I'm Kerry, by the way."

Kerry already knew her, of course. This was basically Lara's worst nightmare. "I'm Lara," she said with slight unease.

"I know."

"So, uh, did April tell you what I do, or have you seen the BuzzFeed video?"

"Who hasn't seen the video?" Kerry asked. "I don't know you from either of those, though." She paused, as if waiting for something. Lara silently prayed she wasn't about to bring up the *Daily Page* article. "We went to school together," she finally supplied.

Oh! Lara's eyes wandered as she scoured her memories, scrambling to recall something familiar about the woman in front of her.

"It's okay," Kerry said with a cheeky grin. "I didn't really expect you to remember me. I was a couple years under you."

Then suddenly Lara found what she was looking for in those unmistakable dimples. "*Kerry Redshaw?*"

"The one and only."

"I do remember you! You were the cute girl who sat in the back of the music room so Mr. Reed wouldn't see that you weren't actually playing your flute. I'm so sorry I didn't recognize you. You look really different."

Kerry had cut her hair. Once upon a time it had been *my-parents-are-freakishly-religious* long, and Kerry had worn nothing but beige skirts that went down to her ankles. Now her hair was cropped short at the back with bangs that stylishly swooped just above her eyes, and she was wearing clothes from this century that actually fit her.

"I was definitely not cute in high school," Kerry said, "but I will take that 'different' comment as a proper compliment. 'Different' is very much what I was going for. Not all of us had the guts to come out in high school and break our parents' hearts. Some of us had to wait years before we built up the courage."

It was a bit stunning to hear Kerry out herself so openly. This was Kerry Redshaw, the goody-two-shoes religious girl. She never would have been this vulnerable back in high school.

"You know, I always did peg you for a lesbian," Lara said, feeling a bit brave herself. "Around here, though, it's sometimes hard to tell the difference between a bull dyke and a farmer's wife, so I'm never totally sure."

Kerry let out a hearty chuckle. It was a nice laugh. Lara couldn't help but ride its contagious wave. Her chest bubbled, and it was the best she had felt in days.

"Well, you weren't wrong. I always thought you were cool for being out. And now I think you're cool because you get to knit cat sweaters for a living." She paused. "And I'd think you were even cooler if you taught me how to do this damn rib stitch."

"Oh, right, sure." Lara had forgotten all about the knitting. Clearing her throat, she got her thoughts back on track and fell into teacher mode. "Well, first of all, you're using the wrong needles. Here." Lara rummaged through one of the bins surrounding the coffee table. She found a pair of larger point needles for Kerry to use. "These will help quite a bit."

Kerry accepted the gift with reverence. "Thank you. Again, no idea what I'm doing."

"It's pretty easy once you get the hang of it. The first step is always the hardest part."

Lara picked up her own set of needles and tried to show Kerry the starting stitch. She took it slow, because it was harder to focus once she noticed Kerry's blue eyes boring into her. Lara's cheeks burned with the start of a blush, and she felt the hair on her neck prick up slightly. She wasn't used to being watched this closely or this intimately.

She made a mess of the stitch, if she was being honest with herself, but Kerry was clueless enough that she still seemed genuinely impressed. Kerry tried to mimic her movements on her own project, and Lara was relieved to be the one doing the watching for a few moments.

"Like this?" Kerry asked.

"Close. More like…" Lara tried to mime the proper motion with her hands, but Kerry was still having trouble repeating it.

"Help me?"

Tentatively Lara placed her hands over Kerry's, trying to guide the needles through Kerry's fingers rather than her own. Within a few strokes, Kerry got the hang of it, and Lara gradually lifted her hands away and back into her own lap.

"Awesome! Thank you."

Kerry's excitement made Lara smile, but Lara couldn't ignore the bubbling in her stomach. Why she felt so nervous, she didn't know.

Yes, she did. April had been right. Again. Kerry was awesome, and if this was who April wanted to set her up with, maybe she shouldn't have been so quick to judge.

"April actually told me a bit about *you*," Lara said.

"Oh yeah?" Kerry asked. "Only good things, I hope."

"Actually, all she said was that we would be good together and I should ask you out."

Kerry looked just as surprised as Lara felt when the words came out of her mouth. Lara was impressed with how quickly the woman pulled herself together.

"Yeah? Are you assuming I'm single?"

Heat crawled up Lara's neck. She *was* assuming. April knew most things, but it was possible that she didn't know Kerry was already seeing someone. Lara thought the two of them were hitting it off, but if she'd been misreading Kerry's advances, she'd like to know it before she made a complete ass out of herself. Lara didn't want to ruin her prospects of them becoming friends by being too forward. "Sorry. Are you single?"

"Well, I've got a wife back home, but she doesn't like my knitting, so I'm here looking for a steamy affair. She'll never suspect I'm cheating on her at a knitting circle, and she'll never bother to come check on me here herself."

Lara snorted. Was Kerry this funny in high school? They would have gotten along great. Lara should have given her more of a chance, freaky Jesus-girl or not.

"You've committed the perfect crime."

"I don't think cheating on your wife is a crime, necessarily. Just a really good grounds for divorce."

"I'd sure dump you for that."

"Oh no. Have I ruined our relationship before we agreed on that first date?"

"If we haven't been on a first date, then we don't have a relationship, do we? We better go through with the date. Then I can decide whether you're a home-wrecker I should dump."

Kerry's eyes lit up, and she pulled out her phone. "You should give me your number. I could get it from April, of course, but then she'd ask why I wanted it and she'd try to plan our entire date."

A laugh ejected out of her. Kerry wasn't wrong. "April is pretty good at that. Maybe we should let her."

"She'd probably be more than happy to."

That warmth in Lara's chest turned to heat as she typed her number into Kerry's phone. Kerry's laughter was so nice. As bad as things were lately, nothing could ruin this moment.

Except the sound of a third voice interrupting their conversation.

"Mind if I steal her for a moment?"

Lara looked up to see her least favorite person hovering over them, looking out of place with a pen and pad of paper instead of yarn and knitting needles. It wasn't Lara she was talking to. Paige eyed Kerry, waiting expectantly, and Kerry glanced back and forth between her and Lara, seeming more confused and startled than anything.

"Uh, yeah, sure." Kerry collected her things and turned to Lara. "I'm gonna go show this to April and prove to her I'm not completely useless. Thank you again." She put a hand on Lara's thigh, then pulled it away almost as quickly.

Awkwardly, she stood and tried to shuffle out of the way. Paige blocked her exit and refused to move, forcing Kerry to sidestep through the narrow opening between Paige's body and the couch. Lara couldn't tell if she was being rude on purpose or if she was so caught up in her own quest that she couldn't bother to think about anyone else's well-being. As soon as Kerry was gone, Paige plopped down in her seat with an excitement that Lara did not mirror.

"Paige, I was busy."

Scouring the room to where Kerry was now sitting with April and a few other women in a small group in the corner, Paige scowled slightly. Was she actually jealous?

"What do you want?"

"I just want to ask a few questions." She clicked the end of her pen and poised it at the face of the paper, waiting to tear into the page and make it bleed with ink.

"Paige, you are not interviewing me."

"Come on, just a couple of questions."

"No. This is April's thing. Talk to her about it."

"I did talk to her. She says the knitting circle was your idea."

Lara sighed. "Semantics."

"You really aren't going to talk to me?"

"No."

Paige sighed again. She tapped her pen against the page. It reminded Lara of late-night study sessions before exams. Back then, Paige's nervous ticks had been cute. Now they were annoying, and they were more annoying because Lara's natural instinct was still to find them cute. Paige tapped out the rhythm to some imaginary song, and Lara tried her hardest not to guess what tune was stuck in her head.

"Come on, you've given interviews before!"

"Exactly! I'm tired of talking to journalists. I feel like I'm constantly repeating myself just so every stupid news site can get its daily dose of content. I'm done."

"It'll only take a few minutes." Paige was practically begging. It helped Lara's confidence.

"No, I mean it," Lara said. "It's draining. I started a business about knitting because it was supposed to be something I enjoyed, but all the interviews and news coverage just suck the life out of me. That's exactly why I started Tight Knit. I want this to be something fun for me again. Knitting used to be how I relaxed, and now it's so stressful I barely want to do it anymore. I don't want to talk to you about this, Paige. Talk to April. Talk to any of the other women here. I'm sure all of them would be more than happy to give you whatever you need. Now, can you leave me alone and let me have this?"

A tense moment of silence hung in the air.

She had already pushed it this far. She might as well cut deeper. Paige had no power over her now. "I was talking to that girl, by the way. It was rude of you to run her off like that."

Paige's scowl was back full force. "You can talk to your friends any old time. I'm only going to be here for today. Then I'll be out of your hair."

"I have no obligation to talk to you, and I'm not going to. So kindly fuck off."

Lara stood to leave, but Paige grabbed her arm.

"Don't touch me." Lara yanked her arm away, and Paige didn't try to grab her again. "Why are you so hung up on this story? It's a knitting circle. I promise no one cares. I know Perry is boring, but I'm sure you can find something more interesting to cover."

Paige thought for a moment, then sighed. "Fine, you want the truth? I'm not just here for the knitting circle. I'm here for you."

For the briefest of moments, something in Paige's eyes made Lara reminisce about a time when she'd said things like that and meant them.

"There's this contest," Paige continued. "All the local papers in Oklahoma are set to write columns on their hometown hero. Winning that award could be great for *The Daily Page*. And for Perry. We're such a small town. Something like this could show that we have valuable people and resources to offer the world. I know I can write a killer article, and you're one of the people who's been nominated for it. Your grandmother submitted your name."

Unbelievable. For the second time in only a few short days, Paige was trying to profit off from Lara's story. Had she felt no remorse the first time?

"You think I'm a hometown hero?" It was cute that her grandma had nominated her, but Paige doing it made it real, and Lara was not about to accept the title.

"Yes. After I saw the way Lorraine treated you, I looked you up. She wasn't kidding. You really did take Festive Feline Fashion way further than I thought you would. You turned it into a great, successful business. You're exactly the kind of person I want for this contest to show what Perry has to offer. You're out there achieving the success and recognition that the great people of Perry deserve You're a role model for the rest of us. Some might say a hero, even. Betty isn't the only one who nominated you."

Her delivery was so stiff. She was treating this like some kind of job interview.

"That's too bad," Lara said. "I'm not doing it, so I guess you'll have to find a new subject."

"Is this because of the other day?" Paige asked.

"What do you mean?"

"Are you only turning me down because I was mean to you at the office? Because I didn't want to help you with your ad and I ran that article you didn't want me to?"

"Those are two of the many reasons I wouldn't work with you, yes, but they're far from the only ones."

"Look, I'm sorry." Paige took a deep breath, and for a second Lara thought she might actually be genuinely apologetic. "I shouldn't have been rude to you." Lara opened her mouth to speak, but Paige said the words for her. "And I'm not just saying that because I want you to do something for me now. I thought about it, and it's stupid to keep holding a grudge against you after all this time."

Another thing they disagreed on. Lara was more than happy to hold onto her grudge forever. Her spite knew no expiration date.

Paige continued, "It's been four years, and we're both adults. I was petty and in the wrong the other day. I want to move forward. I think this project could be a good way to do that."

"And if I have no interest in moving forward?"

Paige sighed and stared down at the notepad, seemingly incapable of looking Lara in the eye. "Then I guess I can't really blame you, can I?"

Really? She was going to make it that easy? It was a surprisingly hollow victory to see Paige so despondent. Lara was still geared up with adrenaline pumping through her system. It told her to keep fighting, and the fact that she couldn't—or rather that Paige would no longer engage her—felt unfair and bittersweet.

Without a reason to throw more ammunition at an already-fallen Paige, Lara didn't know what to say. So she didn't say anything.

"This was stupid," Paige filled in the silence matter-of-factly. Her demeanor had shifted. She tried to brace her shoulders and regain some air of confidence, but it only made her look slightly less pathetic. "Sorry to bother you. I'll do a piece on April and Tight Knit, and I'll leave you out of it if that's what you really want. Forget I mentioned the contest."

Before Lara could process the words, Paige was up from her chair and halfway across the room.

Great. Now she felt out of place at her own get-together. *Thanks, Paige.*

But then someone called her name from across the room. Not April or Kerry, but an elderly woman in a rocking chair, about Betty's age. Lara didn't know the woman well, couldn't place her name, but there was something familiar about her. She cradled a giant purse in her lap like a newborn, the size of it making her look even smaller and frailer than she already did. The woman was dressed nicely, a wide-brimmed hat adorning her head and a floral print dress folding around her legs. Lara walked over to meet her.

"You're Hank's daughter," she said. "Lara, right? Betty talks about you all the time. She has ever since you were born. We used to work together at Harrison's old law office, and I'm pretty sure she showed me every one of your baby pictures at least a dozen times."

Sometimes it amazed Lara how old ladies were capable of remembering not only every face they had ever seen but every person that face was related to as well.

They had trouble remembering their own children's names, but they never forgot a kind stranger.

It was incredible how hearing someone speak and looking into their eyes as she now looked into these eyes could trigger a memory long forgotten. "Glenda." The name came out with a small smile. Lara still couldn't recall exactly who she was or any specific interactions she'd had with the woman, but the name felt right. She was someone in her grandmother's circle, and all of those women had a fond place in Lara's heart.

"Have you seen your grandmother recently?" Glenda asked. She gestured to the women seated around her. "The girls and I like to make a couple trips a week down to Cherry Oaks to make sure she has company."

Lara nodded. "I try to go every day."

"You're a good kid for coming back here to help her."

The comment would have been patronizing from someone closer to her own age, but being around elderly women made Lara feel like a kid again. She was happy to please.

"Are you having fun?"

"I'm having a blast." Glenda's brown eyes flashed. She meant it. "We haven't had a group like this for a while in Perry. Your grandmother would love it, too."

"She would. She wanted to come, but the doctors wouldn't let her."

Lara's chest ached, and she felt like she might start to choke up further if she kept talking about it. She let the moment pass, bracing herself to make her excuses and gracefully exit, but Glenda intervened before she could open her mouth again.

"Some of the girls and I were brainstorming. We can't imagine how awful it is to be cramped up in that room all the time. When Betty gets back home, we want to do something nice for her. Throw her a surprise party. Give her a few gifts. Something to let her know that we're all here for her and thinking about her." The women surrounding Glenda nodded and smiled at Lara expectantly.

A welcome-home party was a fantastic idea. Everything about Betty, every mention of her name, every visitation with her had been tainted in a layer of sadness. Nothing could prevent what was happening to her or make anyone entirely forget about the reality of the situation. Betty was getting frailer, and she wasn't going to live forever, as much as Lara would like her to. But something like a party was exactly what everyone needed to lighten the mood and make the best of a bad situation. It would be great for Lara and Glenda and anyone else involved, but, most importantly, it was exactly the kind of thing her grandmother would love.

"That's a great idea," Lara said. "She'll love it, and I'll definitely be there. If you need me to help plan anything, just let me know."

Glenda waved the hand that wasn't trapped in her purse dismissively. "We can take care of the mechanics. You just worry about showing up and keeping the secret. And making sure you find a good gift."

Glenda's other hand finally emerged from her purse. Gripped proudly in her grasp like an artifact retrieved by an explorer, a tube of blood-red lipstick appeared with it. Glenda unscrewed the lid, applied a generous coating, and tossed the tube back into the purse to be lost and found again later. "Well, I better get home and make supper for the Mister." She stood, rising slowly but surely to her feet. "It was nice seeing you, Lara."

"You too, Glenda. You'll be here next time?"

"Oh, you can be sure about that."

Chapter 6

"Where *is* everything?" Denise repeated for the fiftieth time since she'd entered the house. Lara was already a pro at tuning her out. An entire childhood of ignoring her mother's nitpicking made for good practice.

To be fair, Lara had expected the criticism. Her living room looked like a sweatshop, but that was better than the alternative. Without the knitting supplies everywhere, the room was threadbare. It hosted no more than a couch, a clock, and a television on the floor that she hadn't bothered to hang up on its wall mount. Lara had hoped the clutter would distract from the fact that everything else in the room was, well, nonexistent. No pictures. No coffee table books. No DVD collection. After weeks of living like this, Lara was starting to forget what her living room back in Oklahoma City had once looked like.

The kitchen was no different. Lara was cooking out of a cardboard box of loose pans and skillets. The few items she had in the cupboards were things like oatmeal and an ancient bottle of barbecue sauce that had come with the house when she rented it. She'd been living off of Saltines and canned goods, trying to avoid the fact that she'd have to go to the grocery store and stock back up on actual sustenance. She'd finally caved for the dinner party with her parents, splurging on steak and fresh asparagus.

Denise rifled through the cabinets, scoffing at their emptiness. "No, I'm serious, Lara. How do you live like this? Are we really going to have to eat steak off of paper plates?"

"It's not that big of a deal," Hank said from the dining room. Denise had instructed him thirty years ago to stay as far away from the kitchen as possible, and he contributed now as usual: by setting out Styrofoam cups and cutlery on the dining table.

A frown highlighted Denise's wrinkles. "It's just not classy." She opened a few more cabinets, her motions growing more frantic as she crossed the kitchen. Lara was afraid she'd rip one of the doors off its hinges.

"I don't know what you're looking for," Lara teased. "The cabinets haven't grown china since you looked last."

"We need something to make the table look nice. Do you have any candles?"

"Not in my kitchen cabinets."

"Well can you get them, wherever they are?"

Lara groaned. They didn't need candles, but if it got her away from her mother's griping, then so be it. The meat sizzled in the pan, and Lara gave it one last prod. "Fine. Watch dinner for me."

Lara left for the bedroom so fast that it didn't give either of her parents time to follow her. If Denise thought the living room was messy, she hadn't seen anything yet. Lara's entire life was crammed into her bedroom. Boxes of office supplies, knickknacks, and all the miscellaneous things Lara had collected over the years were stacked from floor to ceiling. Her clothes were folded neatly into her suitcases. Even her toothbrush was packed in a toiletry bag she kept by the bed, which held only a single pillow and a comforter on top of a bare mattress. The room itself was claustrophobic, holding onto a breath it couldn't release as it waited for Lara to give it space. All of her things were ready to be unpacked, but Lara wasn't ready to unpack them.

After a bit of digging, she found a candle in a box labeled *Why Do I Have These?* Also buried in the box was a small lighter with the image of a hot blonde in a bikini suggestively straddling a motorcycle. It was in the wrong box. Lara knew exactly why she had it. It wasn't hers. She checked her impulse to throw it away. It was the only lighter she could find in this chaos on such short notice.

As Lara closed the box and rose to her feet, she realized that the only noise around her was the creaking of the floorboards beneath her as she moved. It was blissfully quiet, something it hadn't been since Denise and Hank had set foot in the house that afternoon. Lara was so thankful for the two seconds of peace that she couldn't resist sitting down on the bed. She pulled her laptop off the nightstand, intending to double check the instructions on the asparagus recipe, but mindlessly her fingers opened a new tab, and Instagram reared its ugly head.

She had posted a new photo earlier, an orange and black calico wearing a pumpkin sweater stretched out lazily atop a pile of leaves. Most of the comments were simply things like *Cute!!!* or wishes for Halloween to come sooner, but a few less-innocent ones stuck out: *Cute photo. Sad to hear the owner's a bitch.* And: *Almost bought one of these from the store, but I'd rather my money go to a creator who actually cares about animals. I'll find something cuter on Etsy.* A few people had also posted the link to Roger Feldman's article. Some were directed at Lara by concerned fans. (*Have you seen this?*) Some were replies to other commenters who still had the audacity to be supportive. (*I love this!! How did you get so creative, Lara?* Followed by: *She's not. Look at this.*)

Lara's fingers hovered over her trackpad. She could delete the rude comments, but that didn't feel right. Erasing the hate meant she was actually threatened by the article. She couldn't give Roger any more fuel or attention. All she could do was ignore it. Boy, did that make her feel helpless.

"Lara? Did you find the candles?" Denise's voice echoed from the hallway, her words becoming much clearer as she stepped into the room. "Jesus. If I had known your place was going to be this much of a mess, I would have asked you to come to our house."

"You're the one who insisted on coming over here."

"Well, I thought you were taking better care of yourself. Honestly, Lara, it looks like you moved in yesterday, not a month ago."

A month already. A month of being stuck here. A month of Betty being in the nursing home.

Lara tried not to think about it. She held up the candle for her mom to see, but Denise's interest quickly faded.

"What are you doing?" she asked, pointing to the laptop at Lara's thighs.

"Oh. Uh." Lara shut the computer and laid it on the pillow beside her. "Nothing."

"Hey." Denise's voice softened, and she floated onto the bedspread like a fallen angel. "Are you alright, honey? You seem…" she gestured to the mess around them, "out of it."

"I've just been stressed," Lara said, knowing full well her issues with Roger and twelve-year-olds on Instagram had nothing to do with why she hadn't unpacked. "Work problems."

"You should have told me." Denise wrapped Lara in a hug. She pulled Lara's head into her chest. "You could've come home. Let Mama make you dinner."

Lara leaned into the hug, comforted even if all of her problems remained the same. "Thanks."

"I could come over sometime and help you get settled," Denise offered.

That was not going to happen, but Lara appreciated the concern when it wasn't hiding between Denise's usual nagging. She let her mother rub the small of her back. "We'll see," she said.

Footsteps trampled down the hall, diverting their attention. Hank poked his head in the doorway, the few tufts of hair left around the crown of his scalp a bit more frizzy than normal. His eyes bounced wildly between the two of them. "Sorry to interrupt. I think dinner might be burning."

Had she been in here that long? "Shit."

The blaring of the smoke alarm filled the house as Lara rushed to the kitchen, bringing the candle and lighter with her and setting them quickly down on the counter. She pulled the asparagus out of the belly of the oven like a body out of a cremator. A wave of smoke choked her, forcing her to cough in a way that she hadn't since she'd been around Paige's smoking on a daily basis. With both hands, she used her oven mitts to fan the tray as her father opened the smoke alarm to take out its batteries and silence its distress signal. Her ears pulsed as her heart rate returned to normal, but that was the least of Lara's problems.

As the smoke cleared, she surveyed the food like a crime scene. The asparagus was definitely overdone, but not burnt to a crisp. It was salvageable. Mostly. At least her mom had taken the steaks off the stove before coming to look for her.

Leaving the food to cool, Lara lit the candle as a centerpiece. A light lavender scent filled the space surrounding the table, but Lara wasn't convinced that it would be enough to mask the smoky smell.

Despite everything, Lara expertly played the role of host. Her mother seemed pleased enough, slicing into her steak and taking several hearty bites. Her father, however, did little but stare at the candle.

"Is the food too burnt, Dad?"

"No, dear, just thinking." Hank made a show of picking up his fork and knife and toying with a spear of asparagus, but none of the food actually made its way to his mouth. After a moment, he asked, "Have you seen your grandma lately?"

Lara hummed around a mouthful of meat. "Of course. I go every day."

"How is she?"

Lara shrugged. "About as good as a woman stuck in a nursing home can be, I suppose."

Her father let out a sigh of relief so big he finally had room in his body for food. He took a bite of steak. A small one, but still a bite.

"Why haven't you been to see her?" Lara asked.

"It's…hard."

Lara scrunched her brow. "I imagine it's hard for her too," she said reproachfully.

Hank grimaced. "It's one thing when your grandmother is in the hospital. It's another when it's your mother." Another bite. "God, I hope you never have to see me in one of those beds."

A knot clogged Lara's stomach. Now she wasn't feeling so hungry either. She reached across the table to take her father's hand in her own. "Hey, it'll be alright. You're fine, and Gam Gam will be too. I said she was doing good, remember?"

Hank gave a small smile, but it was thin and disingenuous. "She's not, though, honey."

The fork stopped halfway to Lara's mouth. "What do you mean?"

"The doctors say she hasn't regained the lung function they expected. Even after the surgery."

Lara's heart pounded in her ears. It made Hank's words that much harder to hear. "Could they go back in?"

"They could, but they don't expect it will help much more." Lara had taken Hank's hand to comfort him, but now she was the one being comforted. Her dad gave her fingers a gentle squeeze. "Remember how they gave her a year? Maybe two?"

Lara nodded. Of course she did. She'd moved back to Perry as soon as she'd heard.

"They changed it to six months. Maybe a little more. Maybe a little less."

"But I was with her yesterday. She was doing fine."

Denise laid her hand on top of both of theirs in silent support.

"Then maybe we'll get those few months," her father said. "But we do need to start preparing ourselves."

"Does she know?" Lara asked.

"Yes."

"Why didn't she tell me?"

"She's a fighter. And she didn't want you to worry, honey. She loves you. You've always been her favorite grandkid."

Lara chuckled through the tears. "I'm her *only* grandkid. I didn't get to see her today. I should have gone, but I caught up on work instead." Lara shook her head. It didn't rid her of the guilt.

Denise cleared her throat, her subtle way of butting in without intruding. "Maybe we can go after dinner?" She checked her watch. "Visiting hours aren't over, are they?"

"I'd like that," Lara said. "Are you okay to come, Dad?"

"Yeah. I think that's a nice idea. We'll bring her leftovers."

When Lara pulled into April's driveway, the garage was open and her friend was inside, working beneath the rows of LED lights as the last streaks of sunlight faded outside. Hammer in one hand, she waved with the other as Lara got out of the car and joined her in the garage.

"I didn't expect to see you tonight," April said. "Not that I'm not happy to."

"Sorry to drop in on you. I started working on something and forgot I was out of felt markers. I'd go buy some, but the store is closed by now. Do you have a spare I can borrow?"

"Probably. Check in one of the bins behind you." April looked her up and down, and Lara suddenly felt self-conscious. This was supposed to be a quick late-night trip, but maybe she should have at least changed out of her pajama pants before coming over. April wasn't quick to judge, but she sure seemed aware of Lara's appearance now, and it made Lara wonder if she looked as bad as she felt. "You're working this late?"

Lara shrugged. "I lost track of time. Haven't been sleeping much."

"I can tell. You look tired."

"Yeah. Bad week." Lara turned around to hide the bags she was sure were under her eyes. April's garage was a functional storage unit, with shelves lining the walls and bins lining the shelves. Each section was labeled: *Toys. Winter clothes. Craft supplies.* Lara pulled that one down and focused her mind on sorting through the various shears, tape measures, and needles.

"Is that article still bothering you?" April asked. A metallic ringing echoed in the small space as she resumed her hammering.

"No. Well, yes, but I've got other problems too."

"Do you want to talk about it?"

Lara pricked the pad of her index finger on a loose sewing pin. A small dot of red blood bubbled up from the surface, no bigger than the pinhead. Lara licked the blood away before it stained anything and soothed the wound with her tongue. "There's not much to talk about. My grandmother is sicker than we thought. My dad couldn't even bear to visit her until I made him go with me the other day. Which made her happy, but still. It sucks. We can't do anything to help."

"I'm sorry to hear that. Did you find the markers?"

April's words manifested a fresh pack near the bottom of the bin like a magic spell. "Yeah, thank you." Lara pocketed the package and stood to put the bin back on its shelf.

"You're welcome to stay if you want," April said, her hammer filling the gaps between her words. "You can keep me company. Help if you want to."

Lara was so wrapped up in herself that she hadn't even noticed what April was doing. She was standing next to a flatbed trailer, and while that didn't seem too out of the ordinary, Lara quickly realized that April didn't own a truck, let alone have a reason to keep a giant flatbed stored in her garage where her minivan should be. "What's this?"

"A parade float. The Harvest Festival is coming up."

Jesus. April was such a soccer mom. Lara wished she was organized enough to find the time and the emotional capacity to care about things like parades. April made being happy and busy at the same time seem so easy. "What are you making a float for?"

April pointed, and Lara crossed the garage to read the sign attached to the end of the trailer. *Tight Knit.*

"Tight Knit has a float?"

"Yup! I got it approved and everything. Didn't you hear?"

Lara had not heard. She had a sneaking suspicion that Glenda would bring it up the next time they spoke, though.

"How do you do everything all the time?" Lara asked.

"I wish I knew myself."

That was Lara's favorite thing about April. She *did* things. No matter how much she had on her plate, she never let herself cave under the pressure. Lara couldn't handle criticism. Lara couldn't stand up to people like Roger and Paige. April was a stronger person. Lara would kill to have half of her drive.

"I want to do something for my grandmother," Lara decided. If April could find time to be a mom, counsel Lara, organize clubs, and build parade floats in her spare time, then Lara could give up a bit of her own time to do something special for her grandmother's last days. "I just don't know what."

"She wanted to come to Tight Knit, right?" April asked. "Maybe we could host a meeting in her room."

Maybe. Lara doubted the nursing home staff would even allow that many visitors at once. Plus, Betty would be able to come to all the Tight Knit meetings she wanted once she was back home. "I don't know. That doesn't feel personal enough. Glenda and the other women from Tight Knit are already throwing her a party. I want to do my own thing."

"I'm sure you're gift enough for her, Lara. She loves you. I doubt there's a nicer thing you can do for her than simply spending time with her while you still can."

Lara was planning on doing that regardless. It didn't feel like a gift. "Yeah. I'm sorry I bothered you," she said morosely. "Thanks so much for the markers. I think I'm gonna head home and let you get back to your float."

April's smile was soft. "Come over anytime you need to, Lara."

The one thing Perry had over Oklahoma City was the quiet. At night, the streets were empty, and the sky was clear enough to see stars shining in the periphery, even as Lara kept her eyes locked on the road on the drive home. She could drive forever, back to Oklahoma City or even across state lines, if only she had the time.

When Lara arrived home, she was more aware of the ticking of the grandfather clock in her quiet house than ever. It was a pretty thing, a deep brown mahogany that refused to be bleached by sunlight or dust. The more Lara stared at the face of it, the more she could see her own great-grandfather's face reflected back at her, the hands ticking away like the whiskers of the mustache on his itchy lip. She had been so young when he'd died that she barely remembered him. Would she start to forget her grandmother in a few years too?

She picked up her knitting and tried to resume her work, telling herself it would be a distraction. But work carried deadlines, and the passing of time was something Lara did not want to think about. She didn't want to think of what would happen to Betty in a few months, or less. Or what would happen in a couple of weeks if she couldn't keep up with her orders. Or what could happen in a few days if that article got any more traction. The holidays were coming up, and the negative press was messing with what should be her busiest time of year.

A sudden jerk at the work in her hands made her look down.

"Hey, Rocket."

Rocket head-butted Lara's hand, purring vigorously and plopping his body atop the half-finished cat sweater draped across Lara's thighs. Lara scratched him behind the ears, welcoming the intrusion.

"You don't want me to work tonight?"

Rocket closed his eyes in bliss. His ears drooped back as Lara massaged the top of his scalp.

"Are we calling it an early night? Did you have a long day too?"

Rocket's purring slowly faded out, replaced by the quiet of his deep breathing. The gentle rise and fall of his chest was a comfort, even if his bony feet digging into Lara's leg was not.

As she set her work down on the coffee table, her gaze caught on something. Paige's business card. She had meant to throw that away.

Something compelled her to keep staring at Paige's stupid, smug face. Her stupid, bragging title as the owner of "Perry, Oklahoma's Only Newspaper," named after herself, no less.

It would be so easy to throw the card away and pretend that Paige no longer existed like she'd been doing for the past four years. Except she couldn't. Not when doing the Hometown Heroes contest would be the perfect gift for her grandmother. Not when Betty was on her deathbed.

This time, when Lara picked up her phone, she dialed Paige.

Chapter 7

In a perfect world, Lara would look out at the sea of customers and spot her best friend waiting at their regular table. Instead, when her eyes locked onto their usual spot in the corner, Paige was the one staring back at her. She waved Lara over enthusiastically, as if she couldn't discern whether or not Lara had seen her, despite the fact that Lara was staring directly at her.

Lara nodded her head in the direction of the line, signaling that Paige could wait two more minutes while she got coffee.

Paige responded by holding up not one coffee cup, but two.

There went Lara's chance at two more minutes of peace.

With a sigh, she slowly strolled to the table and took a seat opposite her tormentor, who cheerfully passed her one of the cardboard cups.

"You still like pumpkin spice, right?"

Lara wanted to say no just to spite her, but it wasn't like Paige was wrong. Her addiction to pumpkin-flavored caffeine and her promise to treat Paige with at least a modicum of human decency won out over the instant urge to argue.

She took the cup. "Thank you."

Paige had to shove a notebook aside to make space for Lara to set down her cup. The table was small, and Paige was using its full surface as a workbench. The printed-off pages and notebooks were all upside down to Lara, but she could make out her name on a few of the sheets. Paige was clearly doing her research.

"How many hours did you spend Googling me to find all this?"

"A few," Paige admitted. "What can I say? I'm dedicated to my work. We both have that in common."

Lara took a sip of her coffee. Just the perfect amount of sweet. Paige had remembered she liked two packets of sugar. Somehow, Lara found this supremely annoying. Paige swished a swig of coffee around her mouth. It took her longer to swallow than it should have. This, too, was somehow infuriating.

Lara's fingers itched to curl into a fist, but she gave them something productive to do instead. The cool relief of metal soothed her palm as she dipped her hand into her pocket and gripped the cylinder. "I found this." Lara held up the lighter, a counter offering to the coffee.

Paige's smile of recognition was instantaneous, as if jolted by a spark of electricity. "Cinderella!"

Lara stared blankly as Paige reached across the table to snatch the lighter from her hand. "You named the motorcycle babe on your lighter Cinderella?"

"Yeah. Get it? Cinder. Fire." Paige pushed down on the ignition and stared into the flame like a caveman seeing fire for the first time. With a release of the button, the heat was gone, but Paige's smile remained. She pocketed Cinderella, trapping her in the castle of her coat pocket with old receipts and lint as the evil stepsisters. "I can't believe you kept this."

Great. Paige had missed a half-naked woman on a piece of plastic more than she'd missed Lara.

"I didn't keep it," Lara said pointedly. "I found it in a box of old junk I don't *want* anymore."

"Thanks for giving it back and not throwing it away."

God, Paige was clueless. Lara almost had thrown it out. Clearly, she should have, and she cursed herself for not following her instincts. "You're welcome." The sarcasm was heavy on her tongue. A swig of pumpkin spice washed it away and strengthened her resolve, despite the temptation to grab the stupid lighter out of Paige's pocket and set her stupid mountain of papers on fire before walking out.

Paige sorted through Mt. Daley officiously. "We should get to it, yeah? I have to record you, if that's okay."

A pocket voice recorder came out. Paige pressed a few buttons, and its red light glowed ominously, pulsing as it awaited Lara's words.

"So, tell me about your work."

"Really?" Lara asked. "That's your opening line? Wait. Can you be a little more vague, please?"

Paige scoured her notes, visibly startled. "Lara—"

"Everything you need to know about my work you have in your notes right there. I've said it all before, and you're not going to find out anything new by asking me general questions like that. I thought you knew how this journalism thing worked?"

With a bit of hesitance, Paige set down her paper. "I guess it's been awhile since I've been able to write my own stuff. It seems like all I do is management nowadays. But still..." Her tone grew firm. "Most of my subjects over the years have been more than happy to answer the general questions. It's usually all people prep for. If you get too specific at the start, you catch them off guard, and then you don't get anything good out of them."

"Well, I'm tired of answering the same questions over and over again."

Paige was silent for a moment, chugging her coffee as if it wasn't still molten. Maybe all those years of smoking had numbed her throat to the burning sensation. Or maybe she was just that desperate for caffeine. She did love her morning cup— and her morning cigarette. Lara had always been there to hand her both.

"This is just an initial profile piece," Paige said. "These are the types of questions I'm asking everyone. We'll get into the deeper stuff if you make it to the next round."

The last thing Lara needed was someone digging deeper into her life, especially for a contest publicized across Oklahoma. Although, to be fair, her sense of threat was unfounded. Even Lara's most basic Tweets would get more readers than any Oklahoman newspaper article. It wasn't like she was going to be chosen as Perry's Hometown Hero anyway. She just needed to do this one candidate interview to make her grandmother happy and to restore whatever shred of dignity she had left in the mind of Perry's residents. She could survive a round or two of interviews before happily being voted out of consideration.

"I'll hold you to that. You've disappointed me too many times, Paige. At least make this good."

"Hey, I pulled through for you on the Tight Knit advertisement," Paige said.

"Only so you could get on my good side and use it as leverage to get me to do this article for you."

"Is that why you're doing this?" Paige asked. "I 'got on your good side' that easily?"

"Definitely not."

"Why, then?" Paige asked. She scrunched her brow, genuinely contemplative. With the steam of the mug wafting in front of her face, she looked wistful, engaged, like a poet on the brink of brainstorming her next great line.

Lara didn't owe her any answers. "Does it matter why? I'm doing it. Don't make me change my mind."

Paige held her hands up in defense. "Fine."

"Why are *you* doing this?" Lara asked, feeling a bit more vindictive. She had to admit it was kind of a power rush. Paige was letting her control the conversation. "You want to win some silly contest that badly?"

"No. I'm doing it for Perry."

Why was Lara not surprised? "For Perry? Really? Talk about cheesy."

"It's not cheesy. I mean it. Paige continued, "We hear all this news about the big places in the world, Los Angeles, London, Dubai. Even local news stations are full of the same segments that are on every other national and international news channel known to man. The world is never going to care about places like Perry. We're the only ones who care, and we deserve to celebrate that. We may not have Nobel Prize winners or mass shootings every week, or the world's best basketball team, but we have people like Nancy Carmichael, who sends gift packages to veterans all over the county every Christmas. We have people like Jason McCormick, an eighth-generation locksmith who knows more about the history of lock picking than any other person on this planet. We have people like you, who have turned their passions into businesses that help customers all over the world. Perry has so much to offer. It's right in front of our faces, and we don't even let ourselves see it because we're taught that all we're ever allowed to be is a blank space on a map that's never going to be big enough to deserve a marker. Even you bought into it. That's why you moved away, isn't it?"

"Do you really think that's our problem? That we're anonymous to each other? Everyone who lives here knows *too much* about Perry. That's the problem. The fact that Jason McCormick can trace his lineage back that far is ridiculous. The fact that people know who he is in reference to some ancient relative he's never met is exactly what's wrong with this place. Everyone's been here for so long that it's common knowledge the Jacobsons hate the Mackles, but no one remembers why they hate each other anymore. It's the fact that Nina from the mall cafeteria will forever be known as the little girl who broke her arm trying to climb the McDonald's sign, even though she's, like, fifty now and has lived an entire life apart from that. It's the fact that ever since I was in kindergarten, no one wanted to talk to me because every five-year-old in town somehow knew that my grandpa was an alcoholic who ran over a kid.

"I've spent every single day of my life wishing that I could be anonymous, and the only time I've ever felt like that was in Oklahoma City. And, yeah, maybe Oklahoma City isn't L.A. or London, but it's big in comparison to Perry. There were so many people. There was so much going on that no one ever gave a shit about who I was or what I was doing. Not the people I went to class with in college. Not the people who lived in the apartments next to me for years. News stations cover the big cities because there's so much news happening that no one will ever be able to tell it all. If you want to be a blank space on a map, move to L.A. If you want to feel famous or celebrated or important, move to Perry, Oklahoma.

"That's why you decided to stay here, isn't it?" Lara pressed. "Couldn't make it as a journalist in OKC and decided to stay in Perry because there wasn't any competition? Because you could finally be the best at something?"

Paige clenched her jaw. "I came to Perry because I fell in love with you. I stayed because I fell in love with the city too."

"If you actually loved me, you would've come back to Oklahoma City with me."

There it was. Out there in the open. There wasn't enough space for the truth at their cluttered table, but it shoved its way between them anyway. Paige was quiet.

"I don't know why anyone would love this place," Lara muttered. "You weren't born here. You don't understand what it's really like."

"You take Perry for granted because it's all you've known."

"I know Oklahoma City."

"You only lived there for a few years. I'm the one who grew up in OKC, and even I never fully understood it. Like you said, it's too big to know."

"Well, Perry isn't. I know Perry," Lara stated, "and it's not as great as you think it is."

"I think that's a matter of opinion. There's no right answer to this argument."

Paige was right. This *was* a pointless argument. She wasn't going to convince Paige of anything, and Paige wasn't going to convince her of anything. They were both too stubborn for that.

"Also I can't really use this in the article," Paige said. "The entire point of the contest is to show how great Perry is. The News Organization doesn't want a hometown hero who hates their hometown."

That was exactly why Lara hadn't wanted this role. She wasn't right for it, and she didn't deserve it. Just because Betty and April wrote in to say how worthy she was didn't make it true. Like every other aspect of Lara's life, other people's assumptions did her more harm than good.

"So, what *can* you use in your article?" Lara asked. "What do you want me to say?"

"I don't want you to fake it."

Lara was pretty sure that wasn't meant as a double entendre, but she couldn't help but think of the other connotations.

"I'm not going to be great at this," Lara warned. "I do want to try, at least, but I don't think I'm the right person for this contest, so you might be disappointed."

"If you don't consider yourself a hometown hero, why agree to be a part of this project?" Paige asked. "You never answered me before."

Lara hated talking about her grandmother. It made her too sad, and she was already in a bad mood. She might as well tell Paige the truth, though.

"For my grandma."

Paige scrunched an eyebrow. "Care to explain?"

"She nominated me. She started her family in Perry. She loves this place. I want to make her proud before she…" Lara's eyes welled up. She wanted to blame the assaulting red lights on the voice recorder, or the way the bitter coffee beans bit into her taste buds, but it was useless.

"Hey." Paige sounded panicked. She reached beneath the table to put a hand on Lara's knee, but Lara swatted it away.

"Don't touch me."

"Sorry." Paige took a moment to recover. Lara needed it too.

"She's sick," Lara said, finding the strength to be curt. "I just want to make her feel a little better."

"I'm sure your grandmother is already proud of you."

She was. Lara didn't need Paige to tell her that. "Thank you."

Lara didn't know what else to say. Paige didn't either. The silence was awkward, but Lara was thankful that Paige was giving her the time she needed to collect herself instead of trying to make her feel better or changing the subject.

"That's enough for today," Paige decided.

That was more than enough for the rest of Lara's life. She knew this wasn't going to be fun, but she didn't think she'd have a complete breakdown and end up near crying.

"If you make it to the next round, I'll call you again. With those better questions you want."

"Don't count on it. No one's going to vote for me."

"Sorry to break it to you, and I probably shouldn't be telling you this, but you got a lot of initial nominations. I bet you ten dollars you make it through to the next round."

Wow. What a generous offer. Lara groaned.

"I'd start prepping for another interview if I were you. Do you want to go ahead and schedule to meet up on Friday?" Paige asked.

No. No, she did not. But more importantly, she couldn't. "I have a date."

"Ah." Paige seemed slightly surprised, but Lara didn't care. She had more things to worry about than the thoughts that went through Paige Daley's head. "Next week, then?"

"Fine. But could we maybe not do it here? Mozart isn't the place for this." Lara gestured around the table. Whether she was referring to Paige's mess strewn out around the too-small table or her own mess of a self, she didn't know.

"Sure. Your place or mine?"

This time the double entendre was definitely purposeful. Lara was starting to regret mentioning that date. "Just call me. We'll work out the time and place."

"Are you actually going to answer my questions next time?" Paige asked. Her tone was half-joking, half-insulting. It was punctuated by what Lara had to admit was an elegantly raised eyebrow.

"I'll answer. I'm the one who called you to set this up, wasn't I?"

"You were." Paige's faith seemed to be restored as she began to collect her things. There was no order to that madness. She picked up small pieces of paper, then stuffed bigger notebooks on top of them, then slipped more article snippets on top of that pile. How Paige ever managed to keep anything organized enough to function, never mind be a journalist multitasking several articles at once, Lara never had found out, no matter how much time they'd spent together. Some things in life were meant to remain mysteries.

"I'll do some work. Get ahold of you when I think of some good ideas."

Lara could see Paige's brain working a mile a minute. It exhausted her.

"Do you need a ride home or anything?" Paige asked.

"Don't push it."

"I'm just trying to be friendly." Paige held up her arms defensively, then slung her bag around her shoulder. She'd never been one for purses, but the attaché suited her. She looked professional. Sort of. Her hair was slightly unkempt, and her bag bulged with the amount of stuff she was forcing it to carry, but her outfit looked nice. What little makeup she had on wasn't too smudged.

"We're not friends," Lara said. "We're…" She tried to think of a term that suited them. *Enemies* came to mind, as did *two people who should never interact but are being forced to*. "Business partners," she decided.

"Partners, huh?" Lara knew that lilt in Paige's voice all too well. It made the last bit of sludge in her coffee cup somehow more bitter as she chugged it down.

"Paige, you're pushing it again."

"Sorry." She adjusted her bag and glanced toward the door but made no move to leave. Her weight shifted from foot to foot as she looked back at Lara. "Thank you for doing this. It means a lot to me."

"I'm not doing this for you."

Paige nodded. "Still. This means a lot to me. I promise it won't be as horrible as you think it will."

When Paige was being sincere, it made her voice go soft, as soft as her eyes looked right now. Lara couldn't bear to be too mean to her.

"Yeah, well, we'll see about that."

Chapter 8

Lara's thumbs kept poor time on her steering wheel as she tapped out the drumbeat to some pop song on the radio. She fiddled with the dials, turning the volume up, then down again when it got too loud. The more she played with the radio, the slower its clock seemed to tick. The colon between the hour and minutes blinked back at her like a set of fluorescent-green cat eyes. She was set to pick Kerry up from work at five, but it was only 4:52 p.m. Two more songs and then a DJ bit. That was when Lara could go inside Taylor Made without looking overeager.

The song faded away, was replaced by another, and some minutes later Bobby Berns, the KFZW 98.6 FM DJ, talked over the last strains of Adele's latest. "A chilly but sunny evening tonight. Expect an early sunset and temperatures dropping significantly after nightfall. Things should warm up again slightly at the start of next week. Enjoy these days while we have them, friends." Betty had said something similar more than once.

A knock pounded on the window next to her ear. Lara jerked in her seat to find the clock ticking at 5:02 and Kerry's face smiling at her through the window. Lara rolled down her window halfway, and Kerry leaned against the sunken glass.

"Are you my Uber?"

"I'm getting paid for this?" Lara asked. "This is already the best date I've ever been on."

Kerry chuckled and circled around the car. She let herself into the passenger seat while Lara fidgeted with the radio again, turning it down so low it was almost inaudible.

When Kerry sat down, she seemed unfazed by the disarray of the vehicle. "I gotta say, it's way nicer seeing you here to pick me up from work than the bus driver."

"Next time I ride the bus, I'll tell them that."

"Don't! I'll get banned for life."

"Who needs public transportation anyway?"

"People who care about the environment. And who don't have their driver's license."

"Oh, so you're one of *those* people." That earned Lara a slap on the arm.

"So what if I am?"

"No worries, I like it. So, where is it you're taking me exactly?"

"You'll see when we get there. Just drive."

"Drive where?" Lara looked out at the parking lot for an answer.

"Just go." Kerry waved her toward the main road. "I'll be your personal GPS."

Kerry was so mysterious. It wasn't the same as when April or Paige tried to be secretive or mischievous; Lara could see right through them. But she didn't know what to expect from Kerry yet. They had never seen each other outside of Tight Knit, and Lara couldn't imagine what Kerry enjoyed doing during her spare time other than knitting. It was exciting getting to know someone new. She tried to suppress her smile and kept her eyes on the road to avoid catching any distracting glimpses of her passenger.

Kerry directed her turns, and it wasn't long before they were outside of the town center and driving away from anywhere Lara would have guessed they'd be going. The city turned to country, and Kerry didn't correct her path.

"I'm kind of scared to keep driving," Lara admitted after some time. "I have no idea where we are. Are you sure your directions are right?"

The road they were on was barely paved. It stretched forward endlessly over the rolling green landscape. There were no turns, no exits. Kerry could be leading her out into the middle of nowhere to murder her and hide the body, for all Lara knew.

"We're right on track. You may not know where you're going, but I do."

"Have you been here before?" There was nothing to see out here. Only grass. Not even trees. "Why would anyone come out here?"

"I used to live out here," Kerry said.

Finally a sign of life as they passed a dairy farm. Still no humans in sight, but there were plenty of cows. "Uh, is your family Amish?"

"Shut up. We're Pentecostal." Kerry slapped her again. Lara's hand jerked lightly on the steering wheel, but there were no other cars around for them to swerve into.

The drive wasn't actually as long as the never-ending stretch of nothingness made it seem. Lara didn't quite know where they were, but she wouldn't be surprised if they were still technically within Perry's limits. Kerry had brought her somewhere identifiable only by the sign on its gate: Clandestine Orchards.

Calling the place an orchard was a stretch. It was a small farm, if anything. A stretch of apple trees loomed in the distance, but the highlight of the acre was right behind the gates: A small barn was set up as a market space, and beside it, several families wandered through a pumpkin patch. A tractor loaded up a group of passengers in its hay-baled trailer and slowly set off for a ride around the farm.

"They have the best cider here. I'll buy us some."

By the hand, Kerry dragged Lara into the renovated barn storefront. The old wooden walls blocked out the chilly gusts of wind, and the aroma of spices and fresh fruit filled the space. Fresh jams, candies, and apple butter lined the shelves, and the counters were stocked with trinkets and baubles, key chains, and branded apple corers. Everything was hand-packaged and homey, and Lara let the warmth of the atmosphere settle into her bones. Memories of Christmas shopping in small stores as a child came to mind. There was so much to take in that Lara didn't know where to start.

"Do you like caramel?" Kerry asked, picking up a small package of it. "They make their own here. It's amazing."

Lara nodded. Kerry grabbed a few other things and paid for them while Lara looked around. The first thing to catch her eye was a fresh pumpkin roll. Lara hadn't had one in years. They were Paige's favorite, but she preferred pumpkin pie.

Kerry returned with a tap on Lara's shoulder and a bag full of goodies. She handed Lara one of the two cups fisted in her palms and resituated her plastic bag to grab it by the handles instead of letting it dangle from her forearm.

"What all did you get?" Lara asked.

"Try the cider first."

Lara obliged. The liquid was warm and sweet on her tongue. It was thick and velvety, and left Lara smacking her lips. She hummed her pleasure, and Kerry nodded in agreement. "Right?" Kerry took a sip, and Lara peeked into her bag.

"Jesus, there's like four jars of jam in there. How hungry are you?"

Kerry pulled the bag away from Lara's judgment. "I refuse to eat store-bought jam when this place is right here. I stock up every fall."

"So our date is me taking you grocery shopping?"

"No, our date is you and me drinking cider in the pumpkin patch. Let's go."

The air was chillier as they stepped out of the barn, but it was crisp, not cold. It was perfect sweater weather, and Lara was dressed in one her grandmother had made her.

"Isn't it beautiful?" Kerry drank in a large breath, as if she couldn't get enough fresh air into her lungs, as if she wouldn't be satisfied until the entire sky was inside her. "I love it out here. Especially this time of year. There were a lot of shitty things about my childhood, but growing up out here in the country was not one of them."

This quietude of this place made Perry seem bustling. The buzz of insects preparing for winter replaced the electronic hum of cars and lights. Grass replaced the old brick roads that should have been taken down and replaced a long time ago. It was a whole different world out here. It was peaceful, but strange, and definitely nothing like her life in Oklahoma City. This would be a good vacation spot, a nice getaway if she wanted some peace and quiet. She couldn't say whether she would have liked growing up here. She was a city girl at heart, but then again, maybe living on the outskirts of Perry would have shielded her from its judgment.

"There's beauty in everything if you look for it hard enough," Lara said. "It's all about perspective. Beauty is in the eye of the beholder and all that."

"My eye doesn't have to look very far to see the beauty here," Kerry said.

"This place is nice," Lara said, but she only meant the farm. "I never thought Perry was all that beautiful. I went to college in Oklahoma City and moved back there a couple years ago because I loved it so much." Lara bit her lip and debated whether or not to tell the full story. Something about Kerry invited her to open up. "This girl I knew in college, Paige, is from OKC and lives here now. She was going to move back to OKC after a couple of years, but I guess she changed her mind because she thought Perry was beautiful. I just don't see it."

Kerry scrunched up her face. "I hate the city. There's no green. It's too loud. There's beautiful parts too, I guess—museums and monuments—but it's not somewhere I could live. Oh, here's a good spot!"

She pointed to a bed of hay that had been picked nearly clean of pumpkins. A couple of misshapen gourds were nestled into the haystacks, but plenty of the bales were barren, and there was more than enough room for the two of them to sit down without getting in any anyone's way.

Lara sat first. Her shirt rode up slightly as she leaned back against the haystacks, and a piece of straw dug into her side. "I don't think I dressed for the occasion." She tugged down her sweater and tried to get comfortable, then glanced up at Kerry, who was still standing. "You look great, though."

"Thanks. I tailored the outfit myself." Kerry gave a spin and a wink. Lara tried not to blush as Kerry sat beside her.

"Do you like fashion?" Lara asked.

"I wouldn't say it's the most important thing in the world to me, but I probably like it more than most people."

"I only ask because you always look so great."

"You'd be surprised at the difference between an outfit straight from the store and that same outfit tailored to fit you specifically. When you've got the skill set to alter your own clothes, it's a lot easier to look nice. I appreciate the compliment, though."

Lara blushed again. She hid the redness behind her cup.

"I guess part of it is how I grew up too," Kerry said. "When you don't have much say in what you wear as a kid, you compensate by fixating on your outfits as an adult. You saw me in high school. There aren't a lot of fashion choices when you live in a cult."

Lara felt her eyes grow wide. "Wait, your parents were in a cult?"

Kerry laughed. "No, not really. We didn't drink Kool-Aid or bathe in goats' blood or anything like that. We didn't lead a conventional life either, though. It may as well have been a cult. Just a more socially acceptable one that doesn't lead to murder or jail time."

Lara laughed, but felt a little guilty about it. She had always made fun of Kerry for her religious expression back in high school, and it didn't make it okay that she had done it silently instead of to her face. Now, as Kerry made fun of herself, Lara couldn't help but wonder if it was a coping mechanism brought on by years of torment.

"You're really comfortable talking about all of this." She didn't want to prod, but if Kerry was willing to talk about it, then Lara was willing to listen. Truth be told, she was pretty curious. In high school, Kerry had been the weird kid with the *Little House on the Prairie* calico dresses who didn't talk to people much and said a prayer before lunch in the cafeteria.

"It's part of who I was," Kerry said simply. "It's part of who I *am*, I guess. It happened. It's either talk about it and joke about it or pretend it never happened, even though everyone already knows it did. The former works out better."

Kerry Redshaw was another victim of the Perry gossip vine. She seemed less bothered by it than Lara was, though. Or maybe she was just better at using her coping mechanisms to mask her true feelings.

"Besides," Kerry said. "I can't feel that weird about it. Everyone has to live with the awful legacy of their parents. What weird shit did your folks get up to?"

Lara thought and blanked. "Nothing. It was never about my parents. It was always my grandparents. Well, grandfather on my dad's side. He liked to drink. Not Kool-Aid." Lara tried to joke as casually as Kerry had. It didn't feel natural on her tongue, but it got a chuckle out of Kerry.

"Yeah, I heard. That kid he killed would have been my cousin like eighty times removed or something."

Lara's blood ran cold.

"What?" Her voice came out in a whisper. She hadn't meant to say anything. She wasn't sure if the word had actually come out of her mouth or if her throat had constricted enough to make it feel like she was speaking when she wasn't. Her hands were paler than usual where they weakly gripped her cup.

"It's alright." Kerry scrambled to comfort her, swiftly reaching out and placing a hand over hers. It lingered for only a moment, just long enough to let Lara know that she was there. "I mean, it's awful, but I wasn't born yet, and I didn't know him or anything. We probably would have talked to each other like once a year and forgotten each other's names all the time. I've got a big family. It's part of the religious cult thing."

Lara's grandmother had talked about meeting the boy's family, about how sad they were, and how sad her grandfather was, and how fucked-up the entire situation was, but Lara had never thought she'd have to meet them herself. She'd never thought about how someone else—a whole family of other people—would have had to deal with the repercussions of her grandfather's actions, just in a different way than Lara did. A worse way than Lara did.

If Lara had felt bad before, she felt horrible now.

"Still, I'm sorry. I don't know what to say."

"You don't have to say anything. Or apologize. It wasn't your fault that your grandpa drank too much."

It *wasn't* Lara's fault. At least Kerry got that. Most people didn't.

Lara felt the blood rush back into her fingers. The furious pumping of her heart was harsh but soothing in its own way. "Yeah. No one in my family drinks anymore. Not even wine or a beer with dinner. I guess that's one good thing that came out of it all. We learned from his mistakes."

"I was thinking of taking you out for drinks later, but I guess that's off the table?"

"Yeah, bars aren't really my scene. I don't think I'd ever be able to show my face in one without the bartender knowing who I am and knowing who my grandfather was. They probably wouldn't even serve me."

"Hey, no worries. We'll find something else to do."

Kerry stared off into the distance, and Lara stared down into her cup. It was empty, and it felt like deadweight in her palm. But then Kerry snapped her fingers together. "I have an idea. Come on." She stood and dusted the hay off the back of her jeans, so Lara did the same.

Kerry grabbed her hand and guided them through the maze of the pumpkin patch so easily it was like she had designed it herself. Soon the pumpkins gave way to fields and the fields turned into a dirt trail through a thin tree line, obviously the boundary between farms. While the nature was beautiful, the further they went, the less there was to see in terms of public attractions. Still, the walk was nice. Kerry was a couple inches shorter than Lara. She hadn't grown much since high school, but neither had Lara, who was short in her own right. She'd spent so much time in her life looking up at people like Paige, who towered over her, that it felt welcome to tilt her head down to make eye contact with Kerry.

"Where are we going?" she asked.

"Up there." Kerry pointed to the tree line, and Lara didn't know how she'd missed it. Laced amongst the branches of the thickest trees was a tree house so big that it might as well have been a tree palace. A roped bridge of wooden planks connected several housing compartments like train cars on a rail. It was a whole village of tree houses, and Lara could only imagine the high-society squirrel families living inside.

"How'd you find out about this?" Lara asked. They were so far out of the way, she never would have guessed this was here.

"They used to let people up here. Then some kid broke his leg, and they deemed it too *dangerous*." Kerry made air quotes and rolled her eyes.

Lara eyed the structural integrity. It was fairly shoddy. Surely it had been nice when it was originally made, but now the exterior was muddy and worn, and the ropes of the bridges looked as frayed as an old cable. It was still the nicest tree house Lara had ever seen.

Kerry put her foot on the first rung of the ladder before Lara could protest. "Are you sure we should be going up there?"

"Of course. It's perfectly safe."

"Didn't you just say it was unsafe?"

"Only if you're a five-year-old who thinks wearing a T-shirt with monkeys on it gives you the power to swing between tree branches without falling."

Kerry scampered up the rungs, all ease, no hesitation. Carefree as a child.

"Come on up!" she shouted when she reached the top. She leaned over the railing and beckoned Lara closer. Lara had a sneaking suspicion that it would be best to keep their voices down. She followed Kerry up, if only so she would stop making so much noise.

The view was incredible. Clandestine Orchards was bigger than Lara could have imagined, and from up in the treetops, she could see everything the place had to offer. Children scurried around the pumpkin patch, carrying gourds like ants carrying crumbs to their hill. The entrance gate extended for several yards with a beautiful Gothic fence design. The barn where Kerry had bought them apple cider was lit up like a lighthouse. Even the apple orchards were beautiful with their careful planning and intricate organization.

"I know your family was shitty, but it must've been nice to grow up around here. Thanks for showing me this."

"They weren't completely shitty, just mostly. " Kerry shrugged. "But, yeah, living out here was one perk, I guess. Hey, you can judge for yourself if you want. We can go meet my family right now. I'm sure they're not busy." Kerry swung her feet off the porch of the tree house, ready to climb back down.

"I know we're lesbians, but isn't it a little soon for that?" Lara asked.

"Not at all. They'll hate you. It'll be fun."

Lara guffawed. "Did you miss the part of the conversation when I told you it's basically my life mission to get people to stop hating me?"

"You're the bad girl. It's hot."

Lara had never been described as either of those things by anyone at any point in time. "So I'm basically the equivalent of the stoner high school dropout that you're only dating in order to get back at your parents?"

Kerry shrugged. "I wouldn't say that's the only reason, but it is a nice bonus."

"Call me old school, but I like to make a good impression when I meet my date's parents for the first time."

"I don't think you'll ever get to meet my parents, then." Kerry quickly added, "It's not the Spellmeyer thing. It's the gay thing.... And the Spellmeyer thing Just a little bit."

"Figures." Kerry's family didn't even like their own daughter. Lara didn't expect them to be sympathetic to the Spellmeyers either.

"Seriously, though," Kerry said. "Today's been fun. I want to do this again sometime."

"I don't know how many abandoned tree houses we're going to be able to find around town," Lara joked.

Kerry elbowed her side. "I didn't mean this specifically. I want to take you out again."

Lara wanted that too. This was far from the worst day she'd had in the last month. Looking out over the tree line, Lara's bubble didn't feel quite so small. "It's a date."

She sealed the deal by placing a kiss on Kerry's lips.

Chapter 9

Lara had never heard Paige knock before. Not on her door, anyway. The sound actually threw her off guard as she brewed tea in the kitchen.

Her first instinct was to scold Paige for forgetting her key, but then she remembered that she didn't have one. Lara wanted to shout "come in," but the door was locked. She had to abandon the kettle on the stove to let Paige in.

Paige wore a beanie and a jacket that Lara had never seen before. She looked familiar yet unfamiliar, like Paige's long-lost twin or a coincidentally identical cousin raised on the other side of the world. That gap-toothed smile was the same, though, and it never faltered.

"You gonna invite me in, or are you going to keep staring at me?"

Lara could feel herself blush, but if she tried hard enough, she could blame her red cheeks on the rush of cold air suddenly passing through the doorway.

"You're not a vampire. Just come in." She gestured for Paige to enter and closed the door behind her.

As Paige discarded her bags and removed her hat to reveal a flowing head of brown curls, Lara averted her eyes. In a corner of the room, Rocket peeked his head out from his favorite sleeping spot behind the couch. He observed the scene for a moment and watched Paige shed her winter clothes with wide eyes, taking in the sight of her in a way Lara that wouldn't let herself indulge in. Slowly, he crept forward on silent, white paws. Lara expected him to bolt for the kitchen or the bedroom or anywhere away from Paige, the way he did with all of Lara's guests, but he didn't. Instead he pranced steadily forward, gaining momentum with each step until he was fully rooted at Paige's feet and pawing up at her leg. He gave a questioning meow, and she returned the greeting with a gentle coo.

"Rocket!" Paige reached down to pick him up, and Rocket actually let her. He relaxed into her grip, and Lara could hear him purring from several feet away. She tried not to feel betrayed. Rocket was always a stubborn thing—even Lara couldn't pick him up for more than two seconds without receiving a face full of claws—but here was Paige cradling him like a baby.

"Did you miss me, buddy?" Paige's cute baby voice almost made Lara a little less bitter. Almost.

Rocket purred his confirmation.

"Yeah? Do you miss Roll too?"

"Oh, God. Are you still calling Cosmo 'Roll'?"

"Of course I am. She's fat and tan like a bread roll." Paige punctuated the explanation by jiggling the pool of fat around Rocket's stomach. "Plus she's Rocket's sister. They're Rock and Roll!"

Lara shook her head. "This is why I didn't let you name the cats."

"That cat is all I got in the divorce. Let me call her what I want."

"Don't say 'divorce.'" Lara groaned. "We weren't married."

"It's a figure of speech. And a joke. Lighten up."

The easiest way to get someone to not lighten up was to tell them to lighten up. Even Rocket seemed offended. Finally, he'd reached his attention apex. Ungracefully, he flopped out of Paige's arms and landed with a dull thud on the hardwood. His seat behind the couch was quickly resumed, and he set about licking his paws and running them across his ears where Paige had touched him.

With the absence of Rocket's purring, Lara noticed another sound: the hissing of the kettle. "Shit." She raced to the kitchen and pulled the pot off the burner. Paige followed her.

"'Bout set off the fire alarm with that one," Paige joked. Her eyes shifted to where the alarm hung on the wall. Its face was open, and its empty guts were displayed for all to see. "Or not." She sauntered over to the wall and quirked her eyebrows questioningly after glancing pointedly at the batteries on the counter.

"There was…an incident. Asparagus…" Lara waved her hands in the air fleetingly. The story didn't matter, and she didn't particularly want to remember her disastrous cooking efforts or the conversation that had taken place at the dinner table after that.

"Glad to see you didn't become a four-star chef while I was gone. At least I'm not missing out on that." Paige picked up the batteries and fit them into their slots. The alarm beeped with signs of life, and Paige closed its lid. "There. Good as new."

"Do you want some tea?" Lara asked. The water made bubbling sounds in her ears as she poured it into her morning mug.

Paige scrunched her nose. "Do you have coffee?"

Lara stared pointedly at the empty coffee pot. "I mean, I *have* it. There's none made at the moment, and I'd prefer not having to make some when I've already made tea."

"Come on, I got you coffee last week."

Bribery. Low blow. Paige's pleading pout reminded Lara of Rocket pawing at her slippers every morning to get her to fill his food bowl. "I didn't ask you to get me coffee."

Paige groaned.

"Come on, you used to like tea." Lara fiddled with the string as her tea steeped, and Paige eyed the wet tea bag as if she had never seen anything more disgusting in her life.

"I didn't like tea," Paige said. "I drank it because my doctor told me it would help with my stress and anxiety."

"And are you still stressed and anxious?"

Paige looked away. Her shoulders peaked in a half-hearted shrug as she crossed her arms. She looked as nervously guilty as Rocket did every time he knocked something off a counter.

"That's what I thought."

Paige huffed and uncrossed her arms. "Fine." She drew the syllable out as wide as her steps toward the cupboards. When she opened the cabinet door she was greeted with nothing but empty shelves.

"Did you break all the mugs and forget to replace them?" She took it upon herself to search every nearby cabinet, finding nothing but almost empty shelves. Lara had been using the same single set of utensils every day. It was easier to wash one bowl as soon as she was done with it than it was to unpack all of her cookware. "I get that you live alone and you don't have a lot of visitors, but I know there were other mugs and plates in that set when we bought them."

"I didn't break them," Lara said. "They're in the bedroom. Hold on, I'll get you a cup."

"Hold on" meant "don't follow me," but Paige either didn't have the social skills to pick up on that or didn't have enough courtesy to care.

"You keep your dishes in the bedroom?"

Lara's footsteps echoed with Paige's in the hallway. Her bedroom door creaked open ominously. Letting Paige see the mess that was her life wasn't exactly on the agenda, but there was no avoiding it at this point. "Sorry about the clutter. Watch your step."

Paige danced around a rogue box as she entered the room, then let her eyes shift from box to box. She analyzed the scene like a connect-the-dots portrait. "This isn't clutter," she said after a moment. "You're moving again."

She could tell that Lara was planning to get out of here for good. Again. Lara could tell by the flash of worry in her eyes and by the way her lips pouted into a quivering frown.

But why was Paige so concerned? She certainly hadn't cared this much when Lara had walked away from her the first time.

"Not for a while," Lara said. "I came back for my grandmother. She got sick. They originally gave her a year, but now it's only six months." A lump formed in her throat.

"I'm so sorry," Paige said. "That sucks."

"Yeah. So I'm only back until…" Lara couldn't finish the thought, but she didn't have to.

Paige was silent for a moment before she said, "It hurts just as much when people leave you while you're alive, you know."

The insight caught Lara off guard. "What's that supposed to mean?"

"You left me to run off to Oklahoma City." Paige's words played into their typical dynamic, but it was clearly a muscle memory reaction. Lara could tell she wasn't in the mood to fight. She was still sad, visibly disappointed. Although, why she cared about Lara leaving was impossible to guess. "And why do you want to leave at all?" Paige continued. "The rest of your family will still be here."

Lara wanted to get away from Perry, not her family. She'd call them. She'd come back to visit.

"I haven't been happy here since…" No. She'd be damned if she was admitting *that* to Paige. She wasn't about to give her more ammo in this fight. "I've been happy in Oklahoma City."

"How do you know you'll still want to go back in a year? You know what they say: 'We all go looking for paradise, then we go back home.'"

"That's an Ani DiFranco lyric."

"So what?"

Paige had some nerve—and Lara was laying more of her soul out than she needed to. "So when is your vacation in Perry ending?" she asked, sarcasm coating her tongue. "You must be eager to get back home to OKC and leave this place behind if you believe in that philosophy "

"And leave Perrydise?"

Lara rolled her eyes at Paige's shit-eating grin.

"Right now I like it here. I like my friends. I like my job. But maybe someday I'll go back," she said seriously. "Maybe we'll be neighbors in the same apartment complex."

God, Lara hadn't even thought about both of them ending up back in Oklahoma City. Lara could move away from her family and her coworkers and her city, and it all felt so easy. But when it came to Paige, Lara felt like she could never escape her. Even after they had broken up, it felt like she'd been haunted by Paige's ghost. Locks of brown in her hairbrush. Photo albums full of their couple photos. Memories attached to places they'd visited during their college days. Paige had always been there somehow. Reconnecting with her now felt like Lara was finally giving up trying to fight the inevitable. If Paige ever did fall off her Perrydise kick and move back to Oklahoma City, they probably would end up being neighbors. Lara wouldn't put the universe past that.

"You wish." The comment was more playful than Lara meant it to be. She'd spoken without thinking. She cleared her throat and changed the subject. "Anyway. Why don't you go set up in the living room? I'll get the mug."

Paige nodded silently. The bed creaked as Lara climbed over it, and the floorboards echoed its groans as Paige padded away.

The privacy was nice. Lara relished in it. She used the quiet to collect herself. What was it that she was even supposed to be looking for? The mug. Right. Lara opened a box labeled *kitchenware* and fished a ceramic mug from its cocoon of bubble wrap and copies of the newspaper so old that Paige hadn't taken over the company and renamed it yet. Lara had fond memories of reading *The Perryodicals* when she was younger, and she took a moment to skim a few headlines. It was another aspect of her life that Paige had tainted for her.

A quick stop by the bathroom to check her makeup and Lara was pouring tea in the kitchen. Her own cup was cold now, but she wasn't much in the mood to enjoy it anyway, even if it probably would help her feel a little calmer.

When Lara returned to the living room, it looked lived in for the first time in months. Paige had brought her usual clutter and had taken over Lara's coffee table as the base of her operation. A hefty camera sat poised on a tripod facing the couch, and a strobe light washed the space in white.

Lara had given plenty of interviews before, but the ones that turned into something as serious as this were still intimidating. "You didn't tell me you were making a big production out of this."

"We're low-budget, not low quality. All of the finalists are getting video interviews for the website."

"You actually care about the website?" Lara asked. "I thought you were all gung-ho on good old-fashioned print journalism."

"I'm also gung-ho on keeping my business alive with ad revenue. I do as little with the website as I have to. The interns mostly take care of that aspect." Paige fiddled with the settings on her camera. "Maybe you could grab some of your work and show it off?"

Lara rolled her eyes. "You could have told me that before I left the bedroom."

"Didn't want to ruin the mood."

Lara hummed and practically shoved the mug into Paige's chest. She took a half-hearted sip, and Lara let herself enjoy the bitter grimace that twisted her face as she swallowed. From the bedroom, she grabbed a box of old knitting projects. In the box were prototypes of Festive Feline Fashion designs as well as milestone pieces like the first scarf she'd made as a kid and the first pair of baby booties Betty had knitted her when she was born. Lara settled into the couch with the box at her side and looked pointedly toward Paige.

"Ready?" Paige asked.

"As I'll ever be."

The camera's red light flipped on, and Lara tried not to squint with the brightness of the lights around her.

"I've read a lot of your interviews, and it seems like people always ask you how Festive Feline Fashion started. What they don't ask is how you got into knitting in the first place. What piqued your interest in the hobby?"

Paige had done her research again, and this time Lara appreciated the effort. It was actually a question that made her think and reminisce. The answer came out easily, not forced or preplanned.

"My grandma started to teach me before I was even old enough to remember it. It's in my blood. Just something I've always done. We'd knit while we watched cartoons. She'd take me to her knitting circles on weekends. I got good at it early on, and I loved it, so I kept doing it. I never really thought to stop."

Paige smiled at her from behind the camera. Lara lost herself in the story. It wasn't as hard as she'd thought it would be. After about fifteen minutes of questioning, Lara was feeling pretty good about herself. She couldn't believe she was sitting in the exact same spot where she'd so recently botched that interview with Roger Feldman.

"That was good," Paige said, "but I think I know how we can make it better."

Or maybe it hadn't gone so well after all. "Oh? How so?"

"Let's go visit your grandmother."

"What?"

"She's such a big inspiration to you. I want to see you guys together."

That wasn't a horrible idea. Maybe sharing it with her grandmother would help Lara enjoy the journey.

"Let's do it."

When Lara walked into Room 319, her grandmother was the same as ever, and Lara considered it a victory that she didn't look worse. Betty didn't need to look up from her needlework to greet her. "Hi, Lara."

"Hey, Gam Gam. I have a surprise for you."

"Oh?" That caught Betty's attention. She looked up as Paige walked into the room behind Lara and gave a polite wave.

"Grandma, this is Paige Daley. She's the chief editor of *The Daily Page*."

Betty dismissed Lara's introduction. "You act like we've never met. And like you never dated her."

Lara rubbed the back of her neck. "I wasn't sure if you remembered."

"Remembered? She brought me green bean casserole last week."

Lara whipped around to confront Paige and was greeted by smug grin. "What?"

Paige shrugged. "Just because we broke up doesn't mean I had to stop being friends with your grandma. She's nice. She lets me borrow books and tells good stories about the history of the town. Who did you think told me you were back in Perry again?"

Of course. Of course Betty would still be friends with her ex. Of course Paige would put more effort into her relationship with Lara's grandmother than with Lara.

She looked between them, unsure of what to say, unsure of how to process any of this.

"It's nice to see you two together again." Betty's face was stone-cold unsurprised, and that might have annoyed Lara more than Paige's smugness. There was a clear implication to her words, and a protest formed on Lara's tongue, but Paige beat her to the punch.

"We're not back together, Betty," Paige said. "I'm actually here because Lara has some other good news."

Lara hated the way Paige said 'other.' As if she and Paige getting back together would be good news instead of a sign that Lara had officially lost her mind.

"Let me guess: you're going to be writing my obituary?" Betty smiled, but the room went quiet. The air was suddenly colder.

Paige looked as flushed as Lara felt.

"Relax," Betty said. "I know I'm going to die. I'm having fun with it. If I can laugh about it, you should be able to too."

Like hell Lara would laugh about that. If Betty was okay with dying, Lara would bear the grief for both of them. "It's not that, Gam Gam. It's better. I'm a finalist in the Hometown Heroes contest."

Betty clasped her hands together in a swift clap. "I knew people would vote for you, Lara."

"We were kind of here to talk about you too," Lara said.

"Me?" Betty asked.

"Yes, you. You're the whole reason I started knitting. Without you, I never would have started my business. Paige wants to talk about how we used to work together when I was a kid."

"If you have time," Paige added, ever the professional.

Betty smiled. "You two better sit down. I've got all the time in the world."

Lara wished that were true.

Chapter 10

More than anything, Lara was looking forward to a Tight Knit meeting without Paige.

The universe did not let her have nice things.

Paige wasn't there in person, but if anything, she had even more presence at this meeting than she'd had at the first one. She was on everyone's lips, and her name was everywhere Lara looked. Several ladies had brought copies of the *Daily Page* article. Paige had given it decent space. The writing took up more than half a page, and the grainy black and white photo of the group gave the column ever more presence. It was certainly more pronounced than April's advert, and Lara had been impressed by what Paige had done with that.

She had to admit—the article was good. Paige knew how to write, and she hit all the key points: The sense of community knitting provides. The heritage of it. The blending of generations. All her quotes were great, and Lara was surprised by how sophisticated some of the members sounded in print. April especially sounded like a real community leader. Of course, it shouldn't have come as a surprise to Lara, but seeing the fruits of their labor documented in print like that made everything feel that much more real and validated.

Lara was tempted to frame the picture herself. It was a grainy, blurry, smudgy, black-and-white mess of ink that would never compare to the original digital image Paige had stored on her camera somewhere, but it was them. The whole group—young and old and everything in between, posed and smiling in the center of April's living room, proudly displaying works in progress. Lara was right there in the center, smashed between April and Kerry. When she looked at the smile on her own face, she could almost believe that she was happy.

The first ten minutes of the meeting were filled up with people pointing to themselves in the photograph and lamenting their crooked smile or mid-blink eyes.

They pointed to each other and complemented the way their friends' hair looked or how cute so-and-so looked with little Bobby in their lap. The room was giddy with excitement, possibly even more so than it had been during the first meeting. It was a refreshing relief to have good press for once. It was like seeing the first few big articles written about Festive Feline Fashion. Reading that first bit of good press for her business had been out-of-this-world incredible, but the Tight Knit exposure was better. The publication might be smaller, and the buzz might be buried in the back of a local newspaper, but this time, Lara had people to share the excitement with.

While talking to April about the spread, she felt a tap on her shoulder.

"Hey, stranger."

The voice that greeted her was familiar, but it wasn't until Lara turned around that she placed it. "Hey, Kerry."

She sat next to Lara. "Your friend wrote a really good article."

"She's not really my friend."

"Oh." Kerry seemed taken aback. Perhaps she'd been a bit too defensive. "April said you knew her, so I just assumed."

One part of Lara was upset with April for saying anything about her and Paige. Another part was extremely thankful that April hadn't gone into more detail than "they know each other." A third part was intrigued that Kerry had been talking to April about her. Although, with the way Paige had run Kerry off like a hissing cat marking her territory, Lara shouldn't have been surprised that Kerry would ask around about who she was.

How much of her history with Paige did Lara want to give away?

"We used to be friends," Lara said, because that was technically true. Once upon a time, she and Paige had been in an albeit brief friendship before deciding to date. "Not anymore, though."

Kerry nodded thoughtfully. A moment passed before she spoke. "So, ex?"

Lara's throat constricted with a stammer that no doubt gave away everything. No sense in denying it now. She was caught. "Well, yeah."

Kerry smiled. It wasn't the sheepish smile Lara was used to. This one was smug, tilted at one side as if a fishing hook had caught the edge of her lip. Lara had never seen Kerry so confident. It was a good look on her. "Well, it was a good article. And it's so cool seeing the pictures. The last time I was in the newspaper it was for winning a spelling bee in second grade."

"That's impressive. I was always bad at spelling bees. Stage fright."

"If you think that's impressive, wait 'til you see the work I've been doing." Kerry got up and disappeared into the crowd. When she came back, she was holding a nearly-finished scarf that was the same coral blue color as Paige's eyes.

Lara had almost forgotten they were here to knit.

"I've been practicing," Kerry said. "I'm basically a pro now, all thanks to you." She elbowed Lara lightly in the side. "When I start my own knitting company, I'll give you some credit."

"You gonna put me out of business?"

"Hey, that's the capitalist dream, isn't it?" Kerry looked down at the scarf thoughtfully. "I've been waiting for a week to show you this. I could have called and talked to you about it, but I didn't want to be too clingy. I know I've always been awkward at the whole dating thing, but I figured I'd try to have more game than that. So instead I waited until we both came to a knitting circle. Clearly that's the epitome of game."

Kerry was so direct. Lara was taken aback, but, for once, in a good way. She wished she could be that open about her own insecurities.

"I happen to think knitting circles are pretty cool," Lara said. "And I'm pretty impressed with your stitch. Still needs a bit of improvement, but not bad for a beginner."

"I'll take that compliment. I was hoping for a bit more, but I'll take what I can get. It's, admittedly, deserved." Kerry tugged lightly at the scarf, and a loose thread instantly came undone. "Yup. Could use more work."

"If it makes you feel any better, I don't sew much. I kind of remember what they taught us in Home Ec. class, and my grandma showed me how to sew a button back on if need be, but I'm definitely not a professional tailor."

Kerry perked up. "Maybe I can teach you a thing or two then, Spellmeyer." Kerry elbowed her in the ribs, and Lara cringed at the jab and the name. "You'll have to come down to Taylor Made some time."

"Yeah? I may need a suit tailored."

"Sounds perfect. It's a date."

Was it? Visiting Kerry at work hardly felt like a traditional date, but at the same time, it didn't *not* feel like a date. Their trip to Clandestine Orchards had been fun. There was something there with Kerry. They were two snips of thread from the same ball of yarn, and Lara hadn't felt the buzz of infatuation like this in a long time. Kerry made her feel like a schoolgirl again, crushing on pretty girls in magazines and in the upper classes, ones she knew she would never have. Only, Kerry was right here next to her, not bothering to hide her own schoolgirl crush.

Lara deserved to have this little bit of fun, right?

They fell into a comfortable silence. Kerry worked on her stitching, sighing every so often as she twisted the fabric into an awkward angle and was forced to undo a part of her work. Lara watched her with amusement. Kerry was focused and concentrated. Her forehead had more knots than her thread. Lara offered to help once or twice, but Kerry shooed her away, insistent upon doing the work herself. Lara eventually gave up and went back to her own work, which actually was work this time: a red and white sweater with a zigzag pattern for a Maine Coon in Minnesota.

Lara was in a room with more than a dozen people, and attention shouldn't have surprised her, but she couldn't shake the feeling that someone was staring at her. Lara tore her gaze away from her work and found Glenda smiling at her from a loveseat on the opposite wall. Lara relaxed—relieved—and smiled back. After a moment, Glenda set aside her work, got up, and came over. She sat on the arm of the couch, near eye level with Lara despite the fact that she was sitting higher up.

"Hi, Glenda. How are you?" Lara put on her most polite tone. It didn't take much forcing. She was happy to see Glenda back here.

"I'm great, dear. In the paper and everything." She flashed Lara a knowing grin, dentures glowing a pearly shade of white. "Have you heard anything new about your grandmother? I haven't been in to see her for a few days."

"She's about the same," Lara said, deciding to be honest. "The surgery scar is healing up nice, though. They don't need to monitor her quite as much. She's able to move around a bit more with the oxygen tank. They might even let her go home soon with hospice."

There was joy in her words, but it was a hopeful premise that was ultimately false. When Betty finally did come home, it was only temporary.

"Oh, that's wonderful," Glenda said. "Let us all know her release date as soon as the doctors tell you."

The only person Lara would have to tell was Glenda. Word would spread instantly after that. Sometimes the gossip chain in Perry could use its powers for good. "I will. Don't worry. And if you find out before me, make sure to let me know."

She chuckled. "I'll do that too. Do you happen to know Betty's measurements by any chance?"

For the first time, Lara really noticed what Glenda was working on. The sweater in her lap was gorgeous. Neater than anything Lara had ever produced; it sported a complex laced pattern that hurt Lara's brain to think about recreating. Glenda was working on it like it was nothing, and she was working fast too. She certainly hadn't brought the same piece with her last meeting; Lara would have noticed. Glenda was good, better than Lara could ever hope to be in her wildest dreams.

Betty would cherish a sweater like that for the rest of her life.

"I can get them for you."

Chapter 11

"Does your grandmother do anything but read?" Genie asked as she scanned the fifth book in the stack.

"She knits," Lara said, "but she also reads while she knits."

Genie continued scanning through the pile one by one like a grocery store clerk, stopping only to give the occasional comment. "A medical encyclopedia? Really? She must be bored out of her mind, Spellmeyer. Get her some trashy romance novels or something. What kind of grandkid are you?"

"This is what she told me to get. I'm not going to risk her wrath. If she pummels me with that medical encyclopedia, I'll never make it."

Genie's chortle was masked by the beeping of the scanner.

"Yo, Lara!"

It took Lara a moment to realize that the voice behind her was calling out to her. She had no plans to talk to anyone this afternoon that wasn't Genie or Betty, and she really wasn't mentally prepared to come face to face with Paige as she turned around.

Paige was smiling. Lara definitely was not. "What are you doing here?" Paige asked, as if they exchanged polite pleasantries on a daily basis.

"It's a library. What are you doing here? Are you stalking me?"

"No."

"The surveillance equipment says otherwise." Lara pointed towards the camera in Paige's hand.

"Oh." Paige raised the equipment to give Lara a better look. "I'm interviewing Rita Sanchez. She's one of the finalists for Hometown Heroes."

Rita Sanchez? The same Rita Sanchez Lara knew? "How exactly did you decide that?"

"People voted for her."

"Uh, I think you mean she voted for herself using a bunch of pseudonyms. Paige, she's awful. You know how awful she is. I complained about her to you for *years*. Or were you not listening to me?"

"I know, I know," Paige said defensively. "But it's not my choice. The people want to see her interviewed."

Lara didn't want to win, but the idea of Sanchez winning over her boiled her blood. She didn't want to think about it. She wanted to get out of here as quickly as possible. If Paige was here to interview Sanchez, that meant Sanchez was here, and the last thing Lara wanted was a run-in.

She started to pick up her books, but Paige didn't get the hint that she wasn't in the mood to talk longer.

"Wow," she said, eyeing the number of books on the counter. "I didn't know people were allowed to check out that many things at once. Or are you getting your library buddies to bend the rules for you?"

Library buddies? The library was nice, and it maintained a generally friendly environment with the exception of Sanchez, but Lara's relationship with her coworkers had been far from office camaraderie. Lara had spent most of her time working by herself. The only person she could maybe say she was friends with was Genie. Anyone else was a loose acquaintance at best.

"I don't have library buddies," Lara said. "I have ex-coworkers who wouldn't bend the rules for me even if I asked them to because they want to keep their jobs. I doubt any of them want to get fired like I did."

Paige stopped in her tracks. They were only halfway to the door. "Wait. You got fired? You told me you quit." An odd mix of disbelief and amusement flickered across her pupils. Her voice had lowered, and she leaned in close, thoroughly entranced.

Lara shouldn't have brought it up. Of course Paige would want to know more. "Yes, I got fired. No, I don't want to talk about it."

Paige's feet shuffled forward, but her smile never faltered and her eyes remained fixed on Lara. "You have to tell me more. I didn't think you had it in you, Spellmeyer. How does a good girl like you get fired? Did you shelf Chekhov under Dostoyevsky? Did you spill your morning coffee all over the return cart? Wait—" She put on an overdone expression of shock. "Did you put a Bible in the fiction section?"

"Drop it, Paige."

"So you *did* drop your morning coffee all over the return cart. Was it by accident or on purpose?"

Lara glared at her. "You know what I meant."

"If you don't tell me, I'm going to turn the camera on."

"Please." Lara rolled her eyes. Paige followed through on the threat.

She took a step back and surveyed the lounge area, where a few other people were stationed. A group of students was studying at a large table, and a man Betty's age sipped out of a Starbucks cup and stared down at the book in his lap. Paige fit as much of the scene into the backdrop as she could, then turned the camera on Lara.

"If you won't answer that question, then tell me about the library," Paige said.

"Well, it's a big building with a lot of books." Lara smiled at her own joke, not for the sake of the camera.

Genie had gone back to her magazine. Subtly, she tore her eyes away from the pages to watch them, but she snooped with fascination, not an intention to intervene.

"Come on," Paige coaxed. "Be serious. What was your role here?"

Instantly, everything came back. Once upon a time she had really loved this job, before Sanchez had ruined it for her. She'd been passionate about the programs she'd helped start. She loved the quiet environment. She loved helping people who were genuinely appreciative of her assistance. It was almost as special to her as knitting had been. Remembering the good parts of her job almost made her forget how shitty Sanchez had made it seem sometimes. She could talk about it all day. It was only a matter of where to start or if she should. Did she risk indulging Paige? Maybe. But only because it would be fun to relive the memories.

She opened her mouth to speak, but something glued the words to the inside of her throat.

Sanchez's distinctive top bun appeared over Paige's shoulder.

Lara's jaw went slack. Every positive thought in her mind disappeared, and the more Sanchez's figure came into view, the more Lara's brain turned to mush. She was a phantom, a devil over Paige's shoulder, but she was real, and she was coming closer. Her brown eyes were almost black as they locked onto Lara's. Her outfit was as dark as her eyes, and her posture was as unwelcoming as her stare. Arms crossed and foot forward, she kept just enough distance between herself and Lara that Lara was forced to look slightly up at her. Sanchez always knew how to make her feel small.

Sanchez paid Paige and the filming equipment no mind. There was no hesitance in her interruption.

"For someone so eager to get kicked out of the library, you sure spend a lot of time here, Spellmeyer." Her tone was whimsical, but her words were dipped in a coating of malice. She nursed a snake's smile, deceiving and venomous.

Lara's heart dropped. Somehow she found the words to speak because she had no choice but to say something. "Hi, Rita. It's nice to see you again." Lara tried to stop her voice from shaking, but she could feel it wavering with each syllable. Her heart pounded in her throat.

"Is it?" Sanchez's arms lay trapped across her chest. "Kind of seems like you've been avoiding me." Sanchez raised an accusatory eyebrow. "Not that I can blame you. I'd be too embarrassed to show my face around here too."

Paige pulled her face away from the camera. She looked back and forth between Sanchez and Lara, hesitating a moment before she held the camera back up and angled it in Sanchez's direction.

Lara sighed. "Look, I'm sorry, Rita. The way I behaved was out of line, and I know that. I don't know how to apologize to you any more than I already have. I'm not here to start trouble."

"That's good to hear," Sanchez said. "It's hard to know sometimes since I'm— what did you call it—'unobservant and out of touch.' I thought you might be here to blow up at me again. Maybe you forgot something you wanted to say the first time?" She glanced around the library, eyeing the shelves and the entryway and the checkout counter. "There's a few people around. I'm sure our patrons would love to hear about how much of a bitch I am again."

Paige's eyes widened. She glanced toward Lara quickly, as if Lara's face would give her context. Lara regretted not telling Paige why she'd gotten fired now. Sanchez's side of the story didn't paint her in a positive light. Not that it should. Lara had blown up at her in the middle of the library in the middle of the day. She'd made an ass of herself and Sanchez, getting all of her grievances off of her chest in the hopes of cutting all ties with the woman. It had worked. A few days later, Lara had escaped to Oklahoma City, never to see Sanchez again or face the repercussions of her actions. Or so she'd thought.

Pissing off Sanchez had seemed like a good idea at the time, when she'd thought she would never see anyone at the library ever again, but now that she was stuck back in Perry, she didn't need to make any more enemies than she already had. She felt childish, and she was just as scared of Sanchez as she'd always been, even if her former boss no longer had any power over her.

"I'm sorry about that," Lara said again. "I shouldn't have said those things about you, and I shouldn't have done it in front of the patrons. I regret being so crude, and I'm not going to do it again, Rita. I was under a lot of stress, I was frustrated, and I didn't handle it well. That's my fault."

"Yes, it is," Rita said. "But don't blame yourself. It was partially my fault for hiring a Spellmeyer in the first place."

Lara's heart stopped. It was a phrase she'd heard a million times before in a million different variations. For the past thirty years, Lara had been searching for a response. She'd never found one.

"Hey! Don't talk to her like that." Paige's voice was booming, way too loud for the library, but Lara wasn't sure if the volume shocked her or if it was the very existence of the words.

Paige backing her up? Unexpected.

Paige's eyes darted back and forth between Lara and Sanchez, and she tried to calm down a little. She seemed to recognize she was crossing a line. Her shoulders shifted from arched to tense, and her height seemed to drop as she visibly released a breath and let her chest deflate.

"I don't know the whole story here," Paige started, choosing her words deliberately and trying to regain some semblance of civility. "But there's no reason for you to talk to her that way. I don't know exactly what Lara did, but you don't need to drag her family into it like that. If you have a problem with Lara, then you have a problem with *Lara*."

Sanchez sized Paige up before replying. "I didn't realize you'd gotten back together with your girlfriend, Lara." Her gaze shifted back to Paige. "You should have heard the stuff she told us about you." She grimaced and *tsked* in an unpleasant, exaggerated way. "Yikes. I wouldn't have taken her back after that."

Paige didn't stand down, but Lara could see the way her eyes flickered with something vulnerable.

"You said it best yourself," Sanchez said. She stepped forward just slightly, bringing herself closer to Paige. "You don't know what happened, so you should be minding your own business."

Sanchez was tall enough to intimidate Lara by getting in her personal bubble, but Paige was much taller than Lara, and whatever moment of hurt she'd felt had passed. While Sanchez was still doing an impressive job being threatening by Lara's standards, Paige towered over her, staring her down.

"I know that this isn't the place for this." Paige's head tilted, pointing toward the other side of the main lobby where a small boy and his mother approached Genie at the checkout. She scanned their books, but did so more quickly than usual, keeping one eye on Lara and Sanchez. "You have no right to yell at Lara for making a scene in front of patrons if you're willing to do the same thing."

Sanchez's eyes followed Paige's. In silence, she watched the boy and his mother thank Genie and walk past the three of them on their way to the front doors. She gave them a small, tight smile.

Not so subtly, Paige stuck the camera in Sanchez's face. This couldn't be the kind of interview Paige was expecting, but the camera wasn't the audience Sanchez was expecting either.

"Point taken," Sanchez hissed and uncrossed her arms. She took a step back. "At least your girlfriend has a sense of decorum, Spellmeyer. Looks like you spread a bunch of lies about her as well."

Paige stepped closer to Lara, practically standing between her and Sanchez. Lara could see the tension in her jaw. She was biting her tongue.

Sanchez took another step back. "Get that thing out of my face." She turned around completely and stalked away, disappearing into a back room. Behind the camera, Lara could see Paige's jaw relax. Her own heart started to slow down.

"Thank you," Lara said. The words were hard for her to say, especially to Paige, but Paige deserved to hear them. "You stood up for me."

Paige's eyes widened. Her gaze shifted to the ground, then to the wall, basically everywhere but directly at Lara's face. She finally settled on her feet.

"Hey." Paige hesitated, clearly thinking her words over before speaking. "Don't worry about it. I know how you hate people bringing up your family like that."

"Yeah."

Lara was staring at her own feet now. It was easier than looking at Paige or Genie or the door where Sanchez had disappeared. It was easier than looking at the library that had given her so many good memories, but so many bad ones too. She could feel herself breaking down, and she wanted desperately to get back in control of herself. She stared at the creamy beige tile and took a few deep breaths.

Paige's hand slipped into Lara's view, then hovered there hesitatingly. She was reaching for Lara's arm, but stopped herself. Lara had pushed her away before, and she couldn't blame Paige if she thought the same thing would happen if she tried to comfort her now.

"It's okay," Paige said. "She's gone now."

Lara kept her arms tense at her sides.

"Come on, let's get out of here." Paige hit the *stop* button, popped the lens cap on her camera, and let the machine hang loose around her neck.

Lara frowned. "'We'? You didn't even get your interview."

Paige shook her head. "It doesn't matter. Sanchez clearly isn't going to talk to me today. It's not worth staying here."

"Right," Lara said. "Sorry I ruined your video."

Paige's eyes searched Lara's, quizzical. "I don't care about that." Lara could hear the concern in her voice. "I just don't want you to have to stay here when that's clearly not something you want to do."

The words were exactly what Lara had needed to hear, and she didn't even know it until they were out there in the open. Her shoulders relaxed. "Thanks," she said again, and she meant it just as much the second time.

"Do you need help with those books?"

Lara had forgotten she was carrying the stack.

"I can help you carry them to your car if you want." Paige tucked her camera under her arm, hands clearly as full as Lara's, but still somehow willing to help. She grabbed a couple of books from the top of the pile before Lara could answer. "Just get the doors for me."

Lara obliged, backing out the door and holding it open for Paige as they walked out together. Paige followed her to her car and gave the books back only after she'd opened the passenger's side door. Lara restacked the books into two even piles in the seat, then shut the door. She expected Paige to walk away, but as Lara made her way to the driver's side of the car, Paige stayed in place. Her arm rested against the hood of the car, and Lara knew she couldn't drive off with Paige standing in her way.

"Did you forget something?" she asked.

"This is probably going to sound weird," Paige said, "but there's a new ice cream parlor around the block. I've driven past it a couple times. It looks nice."

Ice cream? What did that have to do with anything? "Ok? What's your angle here?"

"There is no angle. I just want ice cream, and I figured you could use some too since you've had a bad day."

"You want me to get ice cream with you?" Lara was torn. Paige was a woman of ulterior motives. But Lara also knew Paige well enough to know that sometimes she was simple to a fault. Sometimes she got her sights set on little things like ice cream, and she did what she had to do to get what she wanted.

Also, ice cream *did* sound pretty good. And she *had* had a shitty day

"Is that okay?" Paige asked. For someone who was blocking her ability to drive off, Paige seemed genuinely concerned about Lara's consent to the trip "I figured you could use some company."

She wasn't wrong. If Lara went home now, all she'd do was replay the conversation she'd had with Sanchez in her head over and over again. That did not sound like Lara's idea of a good time, and it probably wasn't healthy for her to spend so much time alone with her thoughts. In comparison, ice cream didn't sound so bad.

"I guess that's fine," Lara said. "But you're driving us there, and you're paying."

Paige's eyes lit up. "Deal." She smiled in Lara's direction, and it was so genuine that it was almost contagious. "Come on, my car's over here." She tossed Lara her keyring as she led them to the other side of the parking lot. "Unlock the backseat for me."

Holding Paige's keys in her hand was eerily familiar. Paige still had the same beat-up SUV. Blindly, Lara chose the car key on the ring and unlocked the doors.

Paige tucked her equipment into the backseat like it was a toddler, and Lara resisted the urge to climb into the driver's seat as she waited for Paige to finish. Paige was as frantic with her driving as she was with everything else in her life. She was capable, but when the two of them had been together, Lara had almost always driven, if only because she trusted herself to keep a cooler head and therefore keep them alive.

It was tempting now to do the same, but that didn't feel right. This was Paige's car now, not her and Paige's car. When the keys exchanged hands, Paige's fingers brushed Lara's—a brief connection, but noticeable. It reminded her of helping Kerry with her stitches.

Kerry. They had another date, of sorts, tonight. That thought alone forced all of her anxieties about Sanchez to the back of her mind. Well, almost.

When she rounded the car to slip into the passenger's seat, Lara was happy to put distance between her and Paige again. The car roared to life, and Lara kept her hands clasped in her lap, far away from Paige's hand on the gear shift between them.

Lara wondered if Paige had learned to drive more carefully in the four years they hadn't talked or if she was driving more safely because Lara was in the car with her again.

Even going the designated speed limit, it wasn't long before they pulled up to a quaint shop. Lara recognized the building. It used to be a franchise in a fast-food chain, but it had been so many years since Lara had driven through this part of town that she couldn't recall which one.

The shop itself was nice. It was clean, new, brightly lit, and refreshing. It was styled like an old-fashioned ice cream parlor with red counters and chrome stools, but the ice cream selection itself was much more modern. The line was self-serve, with flavors ranging from vanilla to raspberry, and the counter hosted a selection of toppings so expansive that Lara couldn't identify all of the crumbled cookies and candy pieces.

Seeing it all made Lara feel like a kid in a literal candy store. She spared no expense, loading her bowl with a little bit of everything in an attempt to taste test as many of the flavors as possible. Her helping was massive, way more than she could eat in a single sitting. She'd definitely end up taking the bowl home and putting it in the freezer.

"Did you get enough?" Paige asked, eyeing the plastic container weighing down the scale. In comparison to her own cup of chocolate vanilla swirl, Lara's serving looked particularly chaotic.

"I figured if you're paying, I'd get my money's worth."

That earned her a chuckle. "You're an evil genius. I shouldn't have trusted you."

Paige paid for her mistake in actual money, and Lara picked out a couple of free seats for them at the counter. A window rested on the wall at eye level, and Lara watched the cars go by on the street. It wasn't a particularly scenic view, but Lara had always liked the warm tones that fall gave to the leaves and the sky and the people who were enjoying the cooler weather after the oppressive summer heat.

When Paige sat beside her, Lara glanced over to see a pink spoon dangling from the corner of her mouth. She was eating and walking because of course she was. Paige wasn't one to wait.

"Okay, that was expensive, but it was worth it."

Paige licked her spoon clean as Lara dug in for her first bite. The sugar melted on her tongue like an exploding rainbow fireworks display. She had packed so many flavors into one bowl that her second bite was completely different than the first. The dish was a chameleon of flavors and colors, all of it absolutely delicious. Lara hummed lightly.

They ate in comfortable silence for a moment, staring out the window and watching the occasional passerby. The outing was working as Paige had intended it to. It was a childish fix— going out for ice cream to distract from one's problem, but as Lara shoveled sugar into her mouth, she was barely thinking of Sanchez.

It wasn't long before Paige was scraping the bottom of her bowl and licking her spoon in that loud, obnoxious way that Lara had always hated when people other than Paige did it. Somewhere over the course of living together, she'd gotten used to the sound of Paige eating. Or if not gotten used to, she had liked Paige enough that she forgave the pet peeve.

"There's no way I'm going to be able to finish all of this." In lieu of scooping up another bite, Lara used her spoon to gesture to the still massive mountain of slowly melting ice cream in her cup.

"That's your fault for getting so much." Paige tossed her own empty bowl into a nearby trash can. "If you need help finishing the rest, I'll be glad to take it off your hands."

Lara shielded her bowl from Paige's threatening advances. "Back off. It's mine. You don't want my germs anyway."

Paige rolled her eyes. "I've had your germs before, Lara."

Good point. "Still mine," Lara said. "I'm saving the leftovers."

Cup in hand, Lara headed for the doors with Paige on her trail. Once in the car, she balanced the cup between her legs and decided that if an accident occurred and she got ice cream all over Paige's interior, she'd only feel slightly guilty about not grabbing a lid.

Paige climbed in after her, in no hurry, the small smile on her face aimed at nothing in particular.

Lara buckled herself in and let Paige maneuver them out of the parking lot. Paige's tire cut too close to the curb as she pulled onto the main road, but it didn't bother Lara as much as it usually would have.

"Hey, do you want to get dinner?"

Lara blinked back her surprise. "I just ate a pound of ice cream." She eyed the cup in her lap. The longer she looked at it, the more her stomach churned at the thought of eating more food.

"I meant later," Paige said.

"I've already got plans tonight. Sorry." Lara was not sorry. After their little ice cream outing, Lara was actually in a decent mood for once, and that mood was only going to get better when she saw Kerry tonight.

"You have plans?" Paige asked. "With who? Rocket?" Lara shot her a death glare. If Paige had been looking at the road like she was supposed to, she wouldn't have seen Lara's expression, but Paige did see it, and she did not look happy about being scowled at. "Not that you don't have friends." Paige scrambled to cover her trail, but neither of them were convinced.

"I do have friends," Lara said. "And a girlfriend. Sort of. Maybe. Don't worry about it," Lara said, deciding that Paige didn't need to know the answer anyway. "Just take me back to my car."

Paige gave a sigh so small that Lara didn't know if she was supposed to hear it. The car gave a tired sputter, a little more run-down than Lara remembered, but it chugged ahead.

"This was fun," Paige said, and Lara quietly admitted to herself that maybe spending time with Paige wasn't the worst part of this day. Maybe the nice weather was putting her in an extra-good mood. Maybe she was just excited to kill time until her date.

"It wasn't bad," Lara said.

"Want to do it again sometime?"

Lara felt the chill of the cup between her thighs, the warmth of the sun against her cheek. "We'll see."

Chapter 12

Lara had never been inside Taylor Made. Any clothing adjustments she'd ever needed she could easily take care of herself or by asking Betty to help her, but that had been for simple hems on outfits that were inexpensive and easily replaceable. Lara didn't trust herself to fit an entire suit, which was why this one had never fit right.

She made sure to show up exactly when Kerry had told her. They might be dealing with fashion, but Lara didn't do fashionably late. She didn't want to risk coming too early and seeming desperate or interrupting Kerry's work either, though. She approached the front door at exactly six and caught the store hours listed on the sign posted to the door. Nine to five. Kerry must have stayed late for her.

Lara felt herself smiling when she walked in. Kerry smiled too upon seeing her. She was sitting near the front of the shop at her work station. She had a measuring tape wrapped around her neck like a boa, and pencils tucked behind each ear like horns. She looked like something out of a variety show, and Lara wondered if she herself looked this eccentric when she was surrounded by her knitting equipment.

"Hey there, stranger." Kerry stood, and her stool squeaked across the linoleum floor. "Welcome to my domain." She held out her arms like a queen presenting her kingdom.

Lara took a brief look around. It was a nice little shop. Quaint, but not too small, considering the number of customers they probably had. There was Kerry's messy work station, another cleaner sewing station on the opposite side of the room, and rows of shelves and fabric in the back that were harder to see. Only the front lights were turned on.

"If you're looking for cats, you won't find any, I'm afraid," Kerry said, her tone teasing. "We only serve humans here, and having pets in the shop seems like an allergy hazard. Wouldn't want to kill anybody."

"Please tell me that you're secretly all of the Internet trolls who go around calling me The Cat Killer, and that it was a fake prank all along."

"I'm afraid not. Unfortunately those are real idiots," Kerry said.

"Yeah, I had a bad feeling about that."

"Is this the suit?" Kerry asked, pointing to Lara's garment bag.

"Yep."

"Let me see."

Lara handed her the bag and Kerry unzipped it. She assessed the fabric carefully. "I like it. Get changed."

"Uh." Lara shifted self-consciously. "Right here, or?"

"Yes, right here."

"Oh." Getting half naked within the first five minutes of the second date wasn't exactly something Lara made a habit of, but in hindsight she probably shouldn't have agreed to a suit fitting if she wasn't prepared to take off at least some of her clothes.

Hand on hip, Kerry tapped her foot on the tile, stared Lara down, and waited impatiently for her to start undressing.

Sheesh. Talk about lesbians moving quickly.

Slowly, Lara dropped to one knee, prepared to make a fuss of untying her shoes to stall for time. Intently, she focused on the dirty gray laces, hoping the more tunnel-visioned she became towards the task, the less she'd feel Kerry's eyes burrowing into the top of her skull.

A sharp bout of laughter caused Lara to look up into Kerry's mischievous grin. "Lara, stop. I'm messing with you. We have a changing station." Kerry walked to the corner of the room and pulled back a curtain to reveal a small, sectioned-off room with a mirror and several hooks. It reminded Lara of the dividing curtains in Betty's old hospital room.

"Right." Embarrassed, Lara stood up, took her suit, and entered the room. She'd forgotten how long it had been since she'd tried the outfit on. It smelled like musty mothballs, and that only reminded Lara of Betty's hospital room even more. What was the point of wearing a suit to impress your date if you smelled worse than your grandmother while you were wearing it?

Oh well. If the smell of her was enough to scare Kerry away, Lara didn't want to be with someone so shallow, right? Still, it was a bit unnerving to walk out in the oversized thing to be directly inspected for flaws. She pulled the curtain open and bent her voice into a sing-song tone. "Okay, I'm coming out!"

It was a stupid joke she already regretted. But she stepped out and spun around slowly, showboating in an ironic way for Kerry, who, to her credit, gave a couple of faint cheers and slow claps and generally papered over Lara's insecurities with what seemed like genuine enthusiasm.

"You look great!"

Lara blushed at the compliment. "I'll look a lot better once you make it actually fit." Lara held her arms out and let the fabric drape out around her to show how loose it was.

"Yes, you will. Stand over here."

Lara let herself be directed onto a small podium. Kerry invaded her personal space, and Lara let her. She quickly wrapped Lara in the tape and jotted down her measurements.

"This is a quality suit," Kerry said, unfolding the tag from around Lara's neck. "Cat sweaters must really bring in the bank."

Lara had bought the outfit long before Festive Feline Fashion, but she played along. "It did until Roger Feldman ruined my business and made people think I was a serial cat killer."

Kerry shrugged. "A little bad publicity never hurt anyone."

"Tell that to my sales."

"You just have to own it." Kerry tightened Lara's tie. Her fingers lingered at the nape of Lara's neck, making the most miniscule adjustments to the fabric. "Everyone loves a bad girl, remember?"

Lara tried to ignore Kerry's breath against her cheek. Her eyes flicked to the ceiling. "I'm not sure that applies when you're selling cat sweaters on the Internet. I want to be the good girl for once."

A car passed by outside. The floorboards creaked. Kerry's body pressed into hers, and Lara instinctively closed her eyes for the kiss. Only it didn't come.

"Shit." Kerry's whispered hiss made Lara's eyes shoot open again. When she looked at the woman in front of her, Kerry's face was draped in shadow. The store was pitch black. Kerry's hand pulled away from the light switch to wrap around Lara's wrist and yank it hard. "Hide!"

Before Lara could register what was happening, Kerry was pulling her towards the changing booth. When Lara's back collided with the wall of the small space, her hiss of pain drowned out the sound of her spine slamming against the plaster. Kerry pulled the drapes closed and enclosed them in the makeshift room.

"Why are we hiding?" Lara whispered.

"Taylor is back. I'm not supposed to be here."

"What? You do work here, right?"

"Of course! But employees aren't allowed to be here after he locks up for the night. He's the only one with a key, but he keeps a spare under the ficus out front. I found it once when I was sweeping."

It took Lara a moment to process what was happening. "So we're breaking and entering?"

"I prefer to think of it as trespassing."

"That's so much better."

"Shh!"

Kerry's hand clasped Lara's mouth shut. Her palm was sweatier than Lara's had been the first time they held hands.

Lara could hear rustling just outside the room. She cursed herself for asking any questions at all. He was close.

"He must have forgotten something. He can't be here for too long," Kerry whispered.

Now it was Lara's turn to do the shushing; she bit down softly on the meaty part of Kerry's thumb.

Outside the changing station, Lara could hear footsteps. First they were close, then they were too close, and Lara held her breath. The lights flicked on, and Lara could see them shining through the slit between the curtain and the floor. She was acutely aware of everything, from the tightness in her chest to Kerry's breath on her palm to Kerry's nails digging into her waist. They were bundled up closer together than Lara had first realized, and she hated herself for noticing it at a time like this. Everything was suddenly hot, and Lara couldn't tell if it was Kerry's body on hers, the adrenaline in her system, or the lack of oxygen in her brain.

The footsteps tread lighter, and the light switched off. The two of them pulled their hands away, and Lara finally released her breath. She didn't risk taking in another until she heard the creak of the front door and the rusty twist of the lock.

"Is he gone?" Lara asked, making her voice nearly inaudible even to herself.

"I think so."

Lara let out a sigh of relief. Kerry stepped away from her to peek her head out of the curtain, and Lara was glad for the space, even if part of her missed Kerry being so close.

"He's gone," Kerry said, her voice returning to normal volume.

Lara followed Kerry's lead and stepped back out into the store. Through the front windows, they watched Taylor drive away. Behind the wheel of his car, he looked so nonthreatening. He was nothing but a small old man, hunched over and barely tall enough to see over the steering wheel.

"I wouldn't have pegged Taylor to be so mean," Lara said. "Would you really have gotten in that much trouble if he'd caught us?"

"He isn't *that* scary," Kerry said. "I probably could've sweet-talked my way out of trouble. But where's the fun in that?"

Apparently Kerry thought that re-enacting the hide-in-the-closet scene of a horror film was fun. Good to know. "You could have at least warned me that we weren't supposed to be here."

"I didn't think he'd come back," Kerry admitted. "My bad."

"Yeah, your bad," Lara agreed. She lifted her arms as Kerry moved to resume her work and cringed. "Your punishment for scaring me half to death is having to smell my sweat."

Kerry laughed. "I deserve that." She picked up a needle and got to work. "When I get done, you'll look so good that I won't even care about your sweaty pits."

At least Lara couldn't say the date was boring.

Chapter 13

April's garage was by no means small, but the float she'd built was so big that it left no room for her minivan, which was parked in the driveway when Lara pulled up. The float wasn't massive, but it took up enough space that Lara was forced to hover by the door, leaving April with barely enough room to maneuver around the edges of the float and pick up a hammer to resume her work.

The float was still incomplete, but April was making thorough headway. Where it had been a blank slate before, now blue streamers lined one side like doilies around a table, and a papier-mâché ball balanced at the back of the float with two giant papier-mâché sticks in front of it.

"Is that a skull and crossbones?" Lara asked.

April threw a loose streamer in Lara's direction. It did a loop in the air and barely grazed her left leg. "It's a ball of yarn and knitting needles!" April gave her work a critical once over. "It's not finished yet. You'll see." As she went back to hammering, her pace was even more determined.

"I completely forgot about the parade," Lara admitted. Her life had been so busy that the idea had fallen onto the backburner.

"How do you forget a parade?" April's eyes stretched wide. Forgetting parades was apparently the only thing that could shock April Helm.

"There's so many of them, they all blur together." It was true. Why did small towns have so many goddamn parades? It seemed like everything from Homecoming to Arbor Day deserved its own all-out Macy's Thanksgiving Day-style celebration. Oklahoma City was not nearly as festive.

"All the more reason to keep track of them, if you ask me," April said. "I write them all down in my calendar."

Of course she did. Lara didn't even own a calendar.

"What is this one again?"

"The Harvest Festival!" April pointed the head of her hammer towards the wall where a puppy calendar was tacked next to the tool rack. It took Lara a moment to see where April was leading her eye. *Harvest Festival Parade* was jotted inside the November ninth square, but it was the monthly image that caught Lara's eye. Four dogs sat around a dining table like it was a poker table and passed gravy boats to each other like poker chips. A dachshund wore a pilgrim's hat. A boxer wore an over-the-top and historically inaccurate Native American headdress. Lara was missing out on a huge market here, apparently. She'd never been much of a dog person, but holiday sweaters for dogs might be a good way to expand the business someday. Cute Canine Clothes could be the sister company to Festive Feline Fashion.

"Is 'Harvest Festival' a fancy way of saying Thanksgiving?" Lara asked.

"No, the Thanksgiving parade is on Thanksgiving." April pointed to that date as well. The parade was indeed written in.

"We have too many parades in this town."

April was not the person to be having this conversation with. She pouted, and Lara instantly regretted saying anything.

"I like the parades. They're fun. And we get to be in this one!"

"Who's we?" Lara had a sneaking suspicion that "we" somehow included her, even though she had spent a combined five minutes of her life thinking about this parade.

"Anyone from Tight Knit who wants to join us on the float. Not everyone from the group. I don't think we could fit that many. But I'm going to let everyone know next meeting. The kids should get a kick out of it, although they might want to be in the crowd getting candy instead of throwing it away on the floats. Tommy's going to stay with Cynthia and his dad. He says he's doing it to help watch over her, but I think he wants candy too. He may be a teenager, but he's not that mature yet." A small smile graced April's lips as she pounded a nail into the side of the float to hold a new streamer in place. "This would probably be easier to staple. Can you grab the staple gun for me, Lara?"

Lara surveyed the tool rack and found what she was looking for. This was the kind of helping that someone who'd been part of exactly zero high school extracurriculars could do. Retrieving tools was about as helpful as she was going to be.

This project reminded her how many tools April had, everything from screwdrivers to saws. They had started appearing one by one after her divorce.

Who knew April would ever look so comfortable swinging a hammer around in her paint-splattered overalls, a thin layer of sweat gluing her bangs to her forehead? But there was always a project to be done, whether that was repairing the house, building something for one of the kids, or creating something for one of her own craft projects. It had been impressive, really, how April had been determined to take matters into her own hands. She didn't need a handyman husband if she could learn the trades herself.

She accepted the staple gun from Lara with a gracious nod. The hammer clacked against the float as she tossed it onto the bed.

"That's better." April mumbled to herself as she worked happily. The steady click of the staples and rustle of the streamers formed a comforting rhythm. Lara took a careful seat on top of a storage bin labeled "Christmas" and watched, waiting for April to give her more orders.

"How's it going with Kerry?"

"What?" Lara fidgeted, transferring her weight from one hand to the other so as not to put too much pressure on the less than sturdy bin beneath her.

"You guys are still dating, right? How's it going?" April glanced up from her work briefly, and her smile was mischievous.

Lara groaned, but flashed April a smile to let her know she wasn't totally annoyed. Should she tell April about Kerry? Part of her wanted to talk about it, but April was enjoying this far too much.

"It's nice," Lara said. That was the official statement so far. "It's only been two dates. I don't know what to tell you."

"What did you guys do? What'd you talk about?" April took a seat on the unfinished edge of the float and looked at Lara expectantly, as giddy for the details as Lara's mother had been when she'd gone on her first "date" with Josh Finny when she was twelve.

April's excitement was infectious, and Lara supposed she might as well spill the details.

"We went to Clandestine Orchards. Walked through the pumpkin patch, drank fresh apple cider. She told me about growing up in the country. We talked about our crazy families. It was fairly standard." Lara decided not to mention last night's breaking and entering. God forbid anyone find out that another Spellmeyer in town was a criminal.

"Did you have a good time?"

"Yeah, I did. It was a nice break from the routine."

"That's good." April abandoned the stapler. She picked up a can of pink spray paint and gave it a few vigorous shakes. "Kerry said she had a nice time too."

Lara squinted her eyes. "If you already talked to Kerry about it, why are you asking me?"

"I'm getting both sides of the story. Isn't that what they do in journalism?"

Lara scrunched her nose. "Why ask me about journalism? I answer interviews, not give them."

"Well, you dated a journalist for a few years."

"We kept the journalism out of the bedroom."

April laughed and nodded. She wiped a sliver of stringy hair behind her ear. "How are things going with her by the way?"

"You mean the project? Good, I guess. I gave another interview. Paige says she really likes what she has so far. She's working on the video we made."

"I didn't mean the project."

Lara picked a string of yarn off her jacket. She felt like a spider spinning silk. "What did you mean?"

"You've been spending a lot of time together."

"Yeah, for the project."

"And that time you went out for ice cream? That was for the project?"

Lara really regretted telling April that story.

"If you're insinuating that I might get back together with Paige, I'm going to accuse you of huffing too many of those paint fumes."

April laughed again and shook the spray can once more for good measure. "Okay, okay, I get it. But don't act like it's *that* ridiculous of an assumption."

"It really is," Lara promised.

"Is it?" April was serious now. She sat on the edge of the float and took a greedy swig of water. She pondered carefully, water bottle cap in hand. "You have history, you were together for years, and you're getting along again. You're both single, and you're clearly back in the dating game if you were willing to give Kerry a chance."

"You think I'd pick Paige over Kerry?"

April shrugged. "I don't know. I'm not saying that you would, or even that you should, but if David came to me tomorrow saying he wanted to try again, I can't be sure what I'd say. I loved him once, and you loved Paige once. Feelings like that don't ever go away. Not fully."

Lara crossed her arms over her chest. She'd thought April was teasing her, not making a serious accusation. "That's ridiculous."

"Don't be dense, Lara."

"I'm not being dense! Maybe you feel that way about David, but I've been over Paige for a long time."

"Look, I'm not the biggest fan of Paige either," April said. "She obviously hurt you, and I think you're better off with someone like Kerry. I'm just letting you know what it looks like from an outside perspective."

The thought made Lara's head hurt. She didn't know if this was actually about her and Paige or if this was April's way of talking about David. April could talk her head off about anything, but never about her ex-husband. It was a sore spot, understandably. Lara never pestered her about the subject.

"Things aren't always what they look like, April. I thought you of all people would know that."

"I just noticed that you were spending more time with her," April defended. "When she came to that first Tight Knit meeting, I thought she was interviewing you for the newspaper article, but when it came out, I saw that she hadn't used any quotes from you. I figured you must have been talking about something else, and I figured that meant you were on speaking terms again. Kerry said you mentioned her a couple times too. I thought maybe you guys had made up and become friends again."

"We haven't. We were talking about the project that day at Tight Knit," Lara explained. "She did try to interview me, but I told her I didn't want to be a part of the article. I didn't think anything of bringing Paige up to Kerry. I was telling her about my work." Lara kicked at an oil stain on the concrete. "Did Kerry seem jealous or something?" Lara tried not to sound too interested in the answer, but her voice betrayed her, rising a little.

"Oh, I don't know, maybe a little." April's tone was taunting. "If you go on a date with someone and they bring up their ex, it's hard not to feel a little jealous, I'd imagine."

Lara blushed. "I didn't mean to make her jealous. I don't think I even realized I mentioned Paige."

"Doesn't that make it worse?"

Lara quirked her neck. "How so?"

"That means she's on your mind."

"Because of the project, April."

April raised her hands in defense. "If you say so." She took the spray can and added the first stripe of pink to the ball of yarn. One thread down, a million more to go. "I'm just saying, you're obviously thinking about her more than you're letting on. You're acting like talking to her is the worst thing in the world when it's probably actually a good thing."

"Why is that a good thing? Aren't you implying that it upset Kerry?"

"Not upset her, just made her wonder. And I'm not talking about Kerry. I'm talking about you. If you're thinking of Paige, that means you have a chance to patch things up." Lara opened her mouth to interject, but April beat her to it. "I'm not saying you should date her again, but it'd be nice to see you let go of some of your anger and forgive her."

"Why is that nice? You're not friends with Paige."

"I'm not friends with her, but you used to be. You could use a little forgiveness in your life, Lara Spellmeyer. You hold grudges like a sloth holds a branch. It'll feel good to let go. I promise. If I can forgive David, you can forgive anyone."

Cheating was definitely worse than anything Paige had done, but April was the type of person who forgave. Lara wasn't. She rarely had reason to be. Most people showed their true colors the first time they messed up, and it was rare for anyone to genuinely change, especially drastically.

Holding grudges took its toll, but so did trusting people and getting hurt.

"Do you want to help me with this?" April asked, cutting the tension with the distraction.

Lara grit her teeth. If she got too involved with this parade, April might expect her to go. Lara had liked the parades when she was a kid, but the older she became, the more she saw them as nothing more than traffic jams. Still, Lara welcomed the change of conversation. She didn't want to argue anymore.

"I've never built a float before," she admitted.

"You ever spray paint?"

"No. The graffiti under the Charleston bridge is really pretty, and I can admire a good tag, but spray painting is not something I ever picked up. I'm not that creative."

"You create art for a living," April countered. "And painting papier-mâché isn't as difficult as tagging a bridge. You'll do fine."

April held out a second can of spray paint and crooked an eyebrow like Lara was one of her children trying to get out of their daily chores. Lara sighed and grabbed the can, not seeing a way out of this one.

April's smile was triumphant. "Just help me get the first layer on. I'll add the details later."

After a quick tutorial of how the spray can worked, Lara was standing beside April on the float. She had a sneaking suspicion that this wasn't the last time they'd be standing here together. The work wasn't abysmal, though. Aside from an annoying splatter on the first few sprays and the nozzle clogging up with paint a handful of times, the process was therapeutic and admittedly kind of fun. They had to open the garage door to air out the paint fumes, but the chilly fall wind that came with it wasn't as bothersome as the questioning stares from the neighbors. Even that, Lara eventually blocked out as she worked.

"What are you going to do with the float after the parade is over?" Lara asked.

April stared at her work. The look in her eye was something Lara didn't see in her often: confusion. "I didn't think that far ahead."

A surprised laugh left Lara's body. Maybe April was human after all.

Chapter 14

Lara had never visited the *Daily Page* website before. She knew it existed, but she had spent the last four years avoiding it. But to her surprise, she didn't immediately feel a pang of disgust as she clicked the link to the site Paige had attached in her email.

Your video is live! It should get people excited. And maybe help your image a little.

She had read the email first thing that morning but hadn't been able to bring herself to look at the website without a bit of caffeine encouragement. An impromptu trip to Mozart got her out of her stuffy house and into a new environment, and she'd picked a different table and a different drink than usual. She sat alone in the middle of the cafe with her laptop open and a caramel cappuccino at her side. The noise of the cafe drowned everything out and comforted her, making her feel invisible and insignificant. Crowded places were always Lara's favorite.

The website was simple and well organized. Whoever had designed it clearly had no input from Paige, which was probably for the best.

It wasn't hard for Lara to find her video. It was right there on the front page, highlighted as part of their weekly most popular segments.

The video had almost two thousand views, which meant that basically everyone in Perry had seen it. Lara's Instagram stories got fifty times as many views, but somehow these numbers surprised her more. The video must have been decent. Or horrifically bad. Those were the only two reasons people would watch.

Lara's mouse hovered over the play button. The thumbnail was Lara on her couch with a title card beneath her displaying her name. It was fortunately not unflattering. The title ghosted over the image like a silhouette. "Hometown Heroes Candidate Lara Spellmeyer Talks the Heritage of Knitting."

Her fingertips raked against the track pad of her laptop. Could she bring herself to watch it? No. She didn't want to. She already knew what the interview was about, and she remembered everything she'd said. And if Lara's message had been butchered by whoever edited this video, she didn't want to see that either.

But the comments section intrigued her.

She scrolled down to the bottom of the page, not expecting to find much. Commenting required that someone cared enough to sign up for an account, and Lara couldn't imagine who would bother taking the time to do that. To her surprise, there was more than one comment.

D. Baker replied, *My mom liked to knit! Never got the hang of it myself haha. Didn't do so great as a Girl Scout.*

Pamela P. said, *I know Lara from the library. Nice lady.*

The last comment was the first chronologically. *That's my girl.* Lara didn't have to read the name to know it was Betty.

Lara's heart fluttered, and it wasn't from chugging too much of her cappuccino in one sip. She didn't know how her grandmother had seen the video, much less commented on it. As far as she was aware, Betty barely knew what the Internet was.

Lara had almost forgotten she was in a public place, even though the subconscious reminder was the only thing keeping her from crying on the spot. Her hand reached out to close her laptop, and as soon as the screen lowered, she saw a figure slink into the seat opposite her.

"This seat taken, Spellmeyer?"

Lara was so taken aback that she forgot to answer the question, not that any answer she gave would have stopped Genie anyway.

"I don't think I've ever seen you outside of the library." In her daze, Lara managed to find the words. She racked her memory for a single instance where she'd run into Genie at the grocery store or the bowling alley or anywhere that wasn't the checkout counter or the break room of the library. She couldn't come up with anything. Genie was the only person in Perry that Lara didn't bump into on a regular basis. She was just like her name, elusive and mysterious. The library was her magic lamp, and the rest of the earthly world was off limits for her mystical form.

"My coffeemaker broke or else I wouldn't be here." Genie lifted her mug in a toast and gulped half of it in one drink. When she slammed the cup back onto the plate, the noise was so loud that Lara heard it clearly over the rest of the busy atmosphere. The liquid that sloshed violently in the cup was dead black. There wasn't a single grain of sugar or drop of cream anywhere near that brew.

"Actually, you know what?" Genie said. "My coffeemaker didn't break. My husband broke it by thinking he suddenly knew how to cook anything other than ice or cereal. I'm only here because he's a dumbass, and if he thinks I'm getting him a cup to go, he's dead wrong." Genie somehow lifted the cup more aggressively than she had slammed it down, and she downed the rest of the liquid like a shot. This time she set the cup down with conviction. Nothing was left but a murky black residue swimming in the bottom of the ceramic like a sea monster.

"Do they do refills here?" Genie asked casually, as if she hadn't just chugged enough caffeine to restart a corpse's heart.

Lara shook her head.

"Damn." Genie grabbed the empty cup by the body and tilted it towards her, apparently hoping that if she stared at the bottom long enough it would magically refill. After a moment she let it clink against her plate again. "This place sucks. They don't even have magazines. The only thing on the news rack was newspapers." She made a gagging sound, and no noise had ever so closely encapsulated how Lara felt about newspapers.

"You hate *The Daily Page*?"

"You ever seen me read a newspaper? They're boring enough as is, but, Jesus, the one we have is written by third graders." Genie leaned forward in her chair, indignant. "Do you know how many spelling errors I find in that newspaper every time my husband leaves it lying around? They misspelled something in the crossword once. Did you see that?"

Was it that bad? Lara had spent years shitting on *The Daily Page*, but now that she was tangentially involved with it, it didn't seem as awful as it used to. Betty enjoyed it. It helped advertise Tight Knit. It offered dream jobs to people like Paige and Lorraine. It had given Lara bad press, but it had given her some good press too.

"No," Lara said. "I don't really read it either." Her cappuccino turned lukewarm in her hands. "My ex-girlfriend is in charge of the paper, so I tend to avoid it."

"Oh, yeah, I forgot," Genie said, looking at Lara instead of her cup for once. "The lady you were with the day Sanchez got in your face, right?"

Lara was trying to block out that day. Or at least that moment from that day. She nodded.

"I've been meaning to talk to you about that. This Genie granted your wish." Genie nodded toward her with raised eyebrows, expecting something that Lara didn't think she had to offer.

"Uh, what?"

"The wicked witch is dead, Spellmeyer. She got you fired by reporting your unprofessional behavior, and I got her fired by reporting hers. It was about time. She was starting to get on my nerves."

Lara had to put her cup down to ensure that she didn't drop it. Did Genie say what Lara thought she'd said? Sanchez got fired?

"Are you telling me some kind of joke to cheer me up? Because it's working."

Genie smirked. "I'm a librarian, not a comedian."

"How?" Lara asked. "It's your word against hers. The board loves Sanchez."

"Loved. Your friend recorded the whole blowout. She sent me the video, and it was her idea to show the disciplinary committee. Sanchez was out of line, and even they couldn't deny it once they had the physical evidence."

"Holy shit." Paige had done that? It was one of the nicest things anyone had done for Lara, and Paige hadn't even mentioned it.

"If you ever want your job back," Genie said. "I'm pretty sure the new manager will give you a second chance."

"The new manager?" The library was always understaffed to say the least. There was Genie, the woman who'd replaced Lara, a couple of pages, the guy who oversaw the DVD collection, and a rotating group of high school volunteers looking for a gig to put on their college resume.

"You're looking at her!" Genie smiled and leaned back in her chair like she owned the place. "It's more work than I set out for, but worse things have happened to better people. Now I can take ten-minute bathroom breaks, and no one can yell at me for it."

Lara didn't need the job. Festive Feline Fashion was still hanging on, if only by a thread. But if things kept going as they were, maybe the library wouldn't be such a crappy place to go back to work to pay the bills. Not that Lara would entertain staying in Perry for a job anyway. Who was she, Paige?

"That's awesome, Genie. I'm so happy for you."

"Thanks. I'd drink to the good news, but…" Genie pointed to her empty cup.

"Have mine." Lara's cappuccino was that awful state of not yet cold but not hot anymore either. She didn't want it. She certainly didn't need the caffeine to boost her mood anymore.

"You know me well, Spellmeyer. Bribery like this will get you far if you decide you want to interview for your old job again." Genie reached across the table, and the cup exchanged hands. Genie took one short sip and grimaced. "Jesus, kid, are you *trying* to give me diabetes? There's an entire bag of sugar in there."

"Sorry." Lara packed up her laptop and slid her chair away from the table to stand. "Thanks for telling me about Sanchez."

"Yeah, yeah." Genie waved dismissively. "Don't think I'm going to be this nice to you *all* the time. You got lucky I was feeling generous."

Lara *was* lucky, and she knew just the person she wanted to share that luck with.

When Lara stepped into her grandmother's room, she was surprised to find herself interrupting someone else's visiting session.

"Paige? You're here again?"

Paige was sitting in the chair beside her grandmother's bed. Lara's chair. She had pulled up a TV tray as a makeshift desk, and she balanced her pen against the notebook on top of it. A tripod was set up on the other side of the bed. Paige's camera flashed red in Betty's direction.

"Paige is interviewing me," Betty said.

"Your grandmother's also a finalist for the Hometown Heroes contest. I think she's winning."

Betty placed an appreciative hand on Paige's arm, enjoying the hammed up compliments; and Lara couldn't even be mad to see Paige. Betty deserved this. Hell, Lara had written in her name, too.

"I guess I can come back later when you guys are done."

"No, no, sit," Betty said, motioning to a chair on the other side of the room. A chair that was most certainly not Lara's favorite chair.

"I don't want to intrude."

"You can stay," Paige said, as if Lara needed her permission. "I won't be too much longer."

How could Lara say no to that? It would be nice to observe and make sure Paige was giving Betty the interview she deserved. And if Betty was happy to be doing this, then Lara wanted to watch her eyes light up as she told her stories. She sat down.

Lara spent her time working on a knitting project she kept in her purse while Paige asked questions and took occasional notes. Lara had never seen Paige so focused, and it was nice to see Betty get the recognition she deserved.

It was some time later before Paige shut off her camera and began packing up her gear. With Paige distracted, Lara figured now was her best chance to squeeze in a few words with Betty before visiting hours were over. "Gam Gam, do you remember my old boss?"

"The awful one?"

"Yep. She got fired."

Paige continued packing, but a small smirk lifted the corner of her mouth.

"They offered me my old job back," Lara continued. "I'm not going to take it, but it's still nice to see her gone."

"I'm glad to hear it."

"I have more good news too."

"Oh?" Betty quirked an eyebrow.

"I'm going to be in the Harvest Festival parade this weekend. We pass by the nursing home, so you might be able to see us. Tight Knit has its own float."

Betty grumbled. "I hate parades, but, for you, I'll watch."

"Why do you hate parades?" Paige asked.

"They remind me of motorcades. I was in D.C. when JFK was shot. It was a horrible time. Everyone was in a panic."

"You lived in D.C.?" Paige asked.

Lara couldn't tell if this was part of the interview or not.

"I'm from Virginia, right outside McLean, where all the rich people who want to live in D.C. but don't want to deal with city life live. I went to a women's college in the capital, and I met everyone there. Young artists, politicians, musicians. It was lovely for the most part. That's where I met my husband. He was visiting on a business trip and we happened to be in the same bar. That's when I should have known he'd turn out to be a drinker. But we were young, and it really didn't become a problem until later."

"What did you study in school?" Paige asked.

"A bit of everything. Once I graduated, I went to law school. I was the only girl in my class, and I thought that was hard, but finding a job once I graduated was harder. No one took me seriously. I had to move to Roanoke just to find a firm that wanted me. Eventually I got to run my own practice in McClean for a couple years. I hired all women. I was the first in town to have an all-female staff. Dan followed me everywhere. No complaints. That's when I knew I was going to marry him. And that I'd travel anywhere for him too."

The two of them had led such an exciting life together in the beginning. Lara's own parents were so square and uninteresting, and Lara blamed that on the fact that they were forced to grow up in Perry. How her accountant father was directly related to someone as exciting as Betty, Lara didn't know. The older Lara got, the more she vowed to end up more like her grandparents than her parents. Minus the alcoholism part. But Lara blamed that on her grandfather getting stuck in Perry.

"Don't you miss Virginia or D.C.?" Lara asked. "You were practically forced to settle down here. Why didn't you ever go back?"

"No one forced me to stay in Perry. I loved my husband very much, and I wanted to move here with him. He's from here. He liked it here. Hank liked it. I raised my family here. It was home for me as much as McClean was. Home is where you make it, Lara."

"But you're from D.C.! How do you come from a place with so much excitement and not crave that when it's gone?"

"Everywhere is exotic at first. Even Perry was exciting and different when I first moved here. I still love to travel, of course. You don't lose your sense of adventure just because you start a family. Dan and I had plenty of fun traveling after Hank was born and after he went out on his own. We flew to Panama to see the canal. We walked on the Great Wall. I still take a cruise every year. Well." Betty coughed. "I did until this year anyway."

"Why not stay in any of these places? Why did you guys come back?" Lara hated vacations. Her own parents never took her anywhere too exiting—the Grand Canyon, Nashville—but all the trips ever did was get Lara's hopes up. Look at this wonderful place full of excitement and opportunity—too bad we can't live here. Vacations just made her feel even more stuck in Perry. If Lara were Betty, she would have gone to China and never come back.

"Because this is home. No one wants to die amongst strangers. Why have a grave if there's no one around to visit it?"

"God, that's a great line." Paige dug her notebook out of her bag and scribbled frantically. Lara couldn't help but chuckle at her enthusiasm.

"Did you get everything you need for your interview, dear?" Betty asked.

"I think so," Paige said. She chewed on the end of her pencil like Rocket chewed on the end of Lara's phone charger.

A soft rap rocked the wood of the door. A nurse stood in the doorway, smiling. "Visiting hours are over soon."

That was their cue to leave. Paige repacked her notebook and Lara stuffed her knitting supplies back into her bag. "I'll be back soon, Gam Gam."

"You better."

"Me too, Betty," Paige added.

"You better too."

As Lara and Paige stepped out into the hallway, Betty's voice boomed out louder. "Oh, Lara! I have one more thing to say!"

Lara peeked her head back into the room. Paige remained by her side. "Yeah?"

"I'm getting out of here."

Lara's heart skipped a beat. She'd thought Betty was going to say she'd forgotten one of her knitting needles, not tell her the most important news she'd had in two months. "What? When?"

"Two weeks."

Two weeks. That was so soon. She needed to talk to Glenda. She needed to get Betty's house ready. Lara had never had such a happy reason to pile a million things on her plate.

"Gam Gam, that's great! I'm so happy for you."

"Believe me, nobody is happier than I am."

The nurse strolled by, "We're just going," Lara said without further ado. "Bye again, Gam Gam." Betty waved, and off Lara and Paige went, for real this time.

It wasn't a long walk to the parking lot, but it was long enough that if Lara didn't say something, their side-by-side stroll would turn awkward. "That was really nice interview, Paige."

"Thanks. Just doing my job."

Lara bumped her side playfully. "No, really. Gam Gam's going to love it when it comes out. You were good today. Although I guess you did lie about how long the interview was going to take."

"Betty's a great subject. I couldn't help myself." Paige tucked her hands into her pockets and stared sheepishly down at her shoes as they turned the corner into another hallway. "So, uh, did you see the video we made yet?"

"I read the comments," Lara said, choosing to be honest rather than lie about watching it.

"People seem to like it so far," Paige said. "And you. Think of it as my apology for running that article on the Roger Feldman scandal in the first place. I know you're still unhappy with me about that."

"I was pretty mad, but most of the buzz from it has died down by now, at least. Thank you for apologizing."

"Thanks for accepting my apology. It means a lot." Paige held open the front door for her. Lara thought this was where they'd go their separate ways, but Paige lingered. "Hey, I was wondering something."

"I'm not getting ice cream with you, Paige. I have plans tonight."

"Another date?"

"No, I'm helping plan a welcome home party for Gam Gam."

"Oh." The news seemed to make Paige as happy as it did Lara. "That's great! Also, I wasn't going to ask about ice cream."

"What, then?"

"I heard you say you were going to be in the Harvest Festival. I'm going too, to cover it. I was wondering if maybe you wanted to carpool with me?"

Lara wasn't sure she heard that correctly. "Why would we carpool?"

"My car's been acting up lately. It'd help me out a lot. Maybe I can give you a sneak peek at Betty's article during the car ride or something."

Paige was trying to sweeten the deal, but Lara didn't understand why she wanted the deal in the first place. "But why would you want to go with *me*?"

"I want to be friends." Lara definitely needed to get her ears cleaned. "Or, you know, just be civil with each other. It feels like we're starting to patch things up, and I'd like to keep it that way."

Could Lara be civil with Paige? There was a time when she couldn't, but now the idea didn't seem so impossible.

"You know your grandmother made me do the interview when she knew you were going to show up. She told me to talk to you and try to work things out. I told her I would, and I want to honor that."

Betty would. That wasn't surprising. What was surprising was Paige honoring her promise for once. Lara couldn't turn it down if this was what Betty wanted.

"Alright. Yeah. I'll pick you up the day of the Harvest Festival."

Chapter 15

Paige's entire house was the equivalent of Lara's bedroom.

Lara had never seen so much junk in one place, and she'd grown up down the street from both a flea market and an antique store. How had Paige managed to accumulate so much stuff? Where had she gotten it? It certainly hadn't come from her parent's place in Oklahoma City, and it also hadn't been there when they were living together.

Lara had to kick an umbrella off the doormat as soon as she stepped inside. In fact, she had to watch nearly every step. Trinkets and baubles were all over the place, and if Lara made one wrong move, she would certainly trip over something, which would only cause her to stumble over something else. The whole place was a war zone, and Lara wanted to avoid the domino effect of explosions that would come from tripping the first mine.

"Jesus, Paige. You could have cleaned a little before I came over."

"I did, actually." She kicked a pair of exercise weights beneath the couch after checking to see if Lara was watching her. She was.

Paige seemed as preoccupied with the mess as Lara was. Her eyes roamed the sea of junk like an old lady at an antique store rummaging for a lost family heirloom.

"What are you looking for?" Lara scoured the mess more analytically, looking for something particularly out of place that Paige might need. More than once while they were dating, Lara had been the one to heroically locate a pair of lost keys or a misplaced television remote.

Paige ignored Lara's question, stalking to another corner of the living room to finish her quest alone. "Don't worry about it. I'll find it."

"Jeez, just trying to help. No need to get snippy." Lara's toe banged against a tilted stack of magazines avalanching from the bottom shelf of the coffee table. "There's also no reason to live like this." Without thinking about it, Lara bent down to restack the magazines into a neat pile.

"I'm enjoying the bachelor lifestyle."

Paige's house looked like she had five kids, not like she was single and living it up.

"Bachelorette," Lara corrected.

Paige rolled her eyes. "The point is, I don't have a nagging wife to tell me to clean up."

Was that a jibe? If being nagging meant not living in filth, then Lara wouldn't take it as an insult. "Maybe you should get one. Although I don't know what girl would date you when you live like this."

"You dated me when my dorm room looked like this." Paige raised an eyebrow.

Fair point. "Young love is blind. And naïve. If I had been smarter and less distracted by that pretty face of yours, I never would have asked you to be my partner on that English project."

"Then how would you have gotten an A?" Her lips twisted. "You thought I was pretty, eh?"

Lara remembered everything about that project: meeting with Paige after class; finally getting her phone number after staring at the back of her head all semester; being alone with Paige in her trashed dorm room; kissing her on that stupid old futon Paige had refused to throw away when they'd gotten their first apartment together. They'd worked for hours on that project, giving it more long nights than it actually deserved, mostly because they spent more time flirting and hanging out than doing actual work. She especially remembered falling asleep on Paige's bed and waking up to her portion of the project already done. Back then, Paige's ridiculous work ethic and her obsessive drive to complete tasks as expertly as possible had seemed admirable and romantic. And it hadn't hurt her grade either. If only it hadn't hurt their relationship later on.

"I was naïve, not stupid. I would have managed."

"You weren't stupid," Paige agreed. "You weren't blind either. Which is why you still think my face is pretty."

Lara stammered incoherently and struggled to find a rebuttal that wouldn't immediately follow with Paige twisting her words again. Damn those shady journalism skills.

"Okay, whatever, you're pretty, yes. I wouldn't have dated you if you weren't. But you're also pretty annoying, which is why you're single again." A thought crossed Lara's mind as she said the words. She didn't actually know if they were true. "You *are* single, right?"

"Why do you want to know?"

Paige was definitely flirting now, but she was also definitely doing it just to be an asshole.

"I don't really want to know." She huffed. "It's just small talk, Paige."

"That's a big subject for small talk."

"Not really. It's a pretty standard question." Lara kicked at a hat that had fallen off the coat rack.

"Fine, yes, I'm single," Paige conceded. "Married to work, as you put it. Not much going on in the love life department. How about you?"

"What?"

"You still seeing that girl you mentioned?"

"You could say that."

Lara couldn't place the flash of recognition in Paige's eye or the way her cheeks suddenly looked a little paler. Mostly because Paige wouldn't let Lara look at her. She turned her head away and acted like this was the moment she turned serious about finding what she was looking for.

Her voice lost all its playfulness. It sounded like she needed a drink of water when she said, "Do I know her?"

"Her name's Kerry Redshaw. She's a tailor."

Paige's face was unchanging. The name meant nothing to her.

Lara could have dropped it at that. It *was* just small talk. Unimportant. Who cared if Paige didn't know Kerry? But Lara found herself somehow disappointed by Paige's reaction. Lara had moved on from their relationship and was on her way to finding someone else. Shouldn't Paige have some reaction to that news beyond a shrug?

"Actually, you probably remember her from Tight Knit," she pressed. "She's the woman I was talking to when you came over to ask me to do the contest."

Paige was quiet for a minute, remembering, Lara presumed. "Yeah. I remember. How's it going?"

How was it going? It was refreshing and fun and one of the best times Lara had had in a long time, minus the almost getting caught breaking and entering part. But it was also a little silly, wasn't it? Lara was leaving—eventually. Kerry was nice, but was she reason enough to stay in Perry? Whatever fling they were having was bound to implode in the face of reality at some point. Lara couldn't be sure they would both survive the explosion.

"It was nice," Lara said, deciding that *nice* was the best description she was going to be able to come up with. It wasn't bad. It wasn't phenomenal. It was pleasant, if nothing else.

"Rave reviews." Paige's usual sarcasm was undercut by a hint of bitterness.

"Why do you need the details?" Lara asked. "You planning on asking her out yourself?"

"Definitely not."

"You jealous?"

"Please. You're the one that dumped me over a sweater and moved a hundred miles away." Paige stormed off, heading for one of the back rooms. "It's probably in my bedroom," she called over her shoulder.

"What's probably in your bedroom? What are you looking for?" Lara followed her. There was nothing else to do. If she stayed in one spot too long, the dust bunnies in Paige's apartment would start nipping at her ankles. They reached Paige's bedroom door. "It wasn't about the sweater, you know."

"Really?" Paige asked as she shoved the door open with two hands, pushing aside a stack of boxes hindering its full range of motion. "Because you kind of made a big deal about the sweater."

"It wasn't the sweater. It was what the sweater meant." Lara shook her head. "Just forget it. It's my fault. I knew better than to knit you a sweater in the first place, and I did it anyway. It's that stupid fucking sweater curse."

Paige's tone shifted from angry to confused in an instant. "What?"

Lara rolled her eyes. "Of course."

"'Of course' what? What curse?"

"Did you ever listen to me?"

"I listen to you a lot. Because you're practical. Smart. Rooted in the real world. You're not the superstitious type. If you had mentioned a 'stupid fucking sweater curse,' I think I would have remembered that."

"It's the curse of the love sweater," Lara explained. "Gam Gam warned me about it growing up. It's the idea that if you knit a sweater for someone you're in a relationship with, the relationship becomes destined to fail. You'll break up right after the sweater is finished."

Paige seemed to consider the story for a minute. "That's silly. It's an old wives' tale."

"It's not." Lara took a deep breath. "Well, it is, but that's no reason to dismiss it. Yeah, a lot of that stuff isn't exactly scientifically accurate, and a lot of it is superstition, but there's always some kernel of truth to old wives' tales."

"And what's the truth about magical, relationship-ending sweaters?"

Lara sighed. "You aren't listening. I already told you that it's not about the sweater. It's about the time it takes to make something for someone. It's all of the effort and all of the emotional value invested in the creation. You pour your heart into making something, and then once you give it to the person, they say 'thank you' and shove it in the back of a closet. They don't wear it. They don't appreciate all the time and love and care that went into the gift, and then the knitter doesn't feel appreciated. They realize that they value their partner more than their partner values them. Their expectations fail them, they get disappointed, and they leave. The sweater dooms the relationship."

"Is that why you left me?" Paige asked. "You felt like I didn't care about the sweater?"

"I felt like you didn't care about *me*. You didn't care about the sweater, but you also didn't care about coming home every night. You stayed late at the office. You worked on weekends. You missed dinners. You missed vacations. You missed dates. The time you spent with me was less valuable to you than the time you spent at work. The things I could give you weren't enough in comparison to the things your career could give you. *The Perryodicals* wasn't even supposed to be a permanent job. You promised you'd move back to OKC with me after you finished your internship. You said you wanted to work for a big publication in the big city. Then you changed your mind without talking to me about it. You decided you wanted to stay here and turn *The Perryodicals* into *The Daily Page*, and you expected me to just go along with it. I wanted to do more than be a librarian for a boss I hated in a town I hated. Festive Feline Fashion was taking off, but you were too caught up in yourself to notice. I couldn't fully invest myself in my career because I was too busy pandering to yours."

"I never stopped caring about you," Paige said. "But I guess I can see why you felt like that. I wish you had told me."

"I did try to tell you. You never listened."

Lara sat down on the bed. Paige kept talking while she searched. "I never thought you'd actually leave, you know. Even when you left. At first, I thought you'd come back. But then you didn't. I was so comfortable with you. I felt so secure. I loved that about our relationship. I felt like you were there to support me one hundred percent. I guess I didn't realize that I wasn't there to support you as much as I thought I was. I should have paid more attention."

"Yeah, you should have."

"If it makes you feel any better, you were right. I shouldn't have spent so much time with work anyway. It was fun for a while, at least as fun as work can ever be, but then it was just… stressful. The more I accomplished, the harder everything got, the more responsibility I had. I wasn't as cut out for it as I thought I'd be."

Lara could relate to that. Festive Feline Fashion used to be fun. Even when it first took off on social media, the increased demand was a welcome change of pace for a while. But lately Lara felt as burnt out as Paige sounded.

Was Paige doing that poorly, though? On the surface, everything seemed to be going well for her. She had taken control of the business. Her employees respected her as their leader, even if it was out of fear. But Lara supposed she knew what it was like to look composed on the outside when she wasn't on the inside. Festive Feline Fashion probably looked as successful to Paige as *The Daily Page* looked to Lara, but under the surface Lara was still struggling to bounce back from the negative publicity. Meanwhile, Paige was a scattered mess. If she was truly capable of doing her job well, Lara never would have ended up in her office asking for answers about the Tight Knit ad.

"I was happy when Bransom trusted me with the newspaper, but, man, sometimes I wish he had never retired. I never feel like I'm doing a good enough job. For me or for him or for the paper or for anyone I work with. It's hard." Paige paused. "If I could get a redo, I'd go back, spend more time with you, and stick to writing whatever drudge work Bransom let me have."

"Good to know that you think having a successful career and a functional relationship are mutually exclusive."

"I didn't mean it like that. I just wish I'd found a better balance. Too much of one thing is never a good idea."

"Do you think you've found a better balance now?"

"Considering I'm still overworked and have been on approximately one date in the last four years, probably not. Maybe if I could go back, I'd follow you. Truth is, I was stressed out back then, too, but I had you to help me, and that made it better. I probably could've handled a bigger job in OKC with you too."

Paige took a deep breath. "You know, we never actually talked about this. After you broke up with me, you just….left. And I don't blame you for abandoning me or ignoring me or whatever you want to call it. You obviously didn't want to see me or talk to me, but I'm glad that we're talking about it now. It feels good to clear the air and get everything off my chest."

"You're right," Lara said. "About all of it. I don't think I was ready to talk to you back then. I don't think I was ready to talk to you until recently, actually. But I'm glad we're talking now, too. And about your problem, it sounds like you need a change."

"What kind of change?"

"That's up to you. Maybe run away to OKC. Worked for me."

"Did it?"

The question was more profound than Lara expected it to be. The more she thought about it, the more she *had* to think about it. "I don't know," she said honestly. "I liked it there. I liked having a new job and new friends and no one to take care of but myself. But it got lonely sometimes, too. Life wasn't as easy as when you weren't around to help me."

Paige nodded. "I don't know if moving would solve my problems. I guess it would force me to quit my job. That would make me less of a workaholic, but that would also make me homeless, and I kind of like surviving, even if I have to slave away to do it."

"You could get a new job."

"And overwork myself there?" Paige asked.

"Get a less stressful job."

"Less stressful usually means less money."

"Money isn't everything," Lara said.

"Maybe you're right."

"I'm always right."

Paige chuckled. "I don't know about that."

The sounds of Paige's shuffling were starting to get repetitive. If this took any longer, Lara was going to lie down and take a nap. "What are you looking for?" she asked. "If you tell me, I can help."

"Hold on, I can get it."

Lara groaned. Paige was so stubborn. If Lara was helping, they could have found what they were looking for ten minutes ago and been out of here already. At this point, they were going to be late for the parade.

Paige ransacked her room, looking in dresser drawers and under piles of clothes. Lara looked around for something that might seem important, trying to guess what Paige was searching for, but the only thing that caught her eye was her own eyes staring back at her.

"You still have pictures of me up?"

"Not still," Paige said. She stared at the photo in Lara's hand, gathering her words. "I was mad at you for a long time. Years. I was still mad at you the day you came into my office. But I'm tired of being mad. It's exhausting, and my life is exhausting enough. I'm not mad anymore, and I'm glad that you're back in my life and that we're, for the most part, I guess, getting along again. You're my friend. I like keeping pictures of my friends around."

Were she and Paige friends? Lara didn't exactly have much experience in the friendship department, but whatever relationship she had with Paige now was a lot different than any friendship she'd ever had. Lara couldn't meet up with Paige and talk about pointless everyday minutia like she could with April. She couldn't look at Paige and feel a temporary sense of easy, carefree calm like she did with Kerry. If what she had with Paige was friendship, it would forever be flavored by their history. But that wasn't necessarily a bad thing. She could talk about the deep things with Paige. She didn't have to explain how she felt to Paige because Paige already knew. April and Kerry knew Lara on a more surface level. Paige was much deeper under her skin, she realized. Talking with Paige could be nice. Familiar. Intuitive. Sometimes Lara needed someone like that to talk to.

"Why do you have all this junk around?" Lara asked. "This stuff in boxes that you clearly aren't using. Why not have a garage sale? Or donate some stuff to Goodwill."

"I don't want to get rid of it," Paige said. "I just don't have anything to do with it right now. I don't know. Maybe I'm like you. I'm always ready to move, so I keep my stuff packed up. If I don't settle down, I don't get disappointed when I have to move on again."

Lara scrunched her brow. She hadn't thought of it that way. "Do you move around a lot?"

"Eh." Paige shrugged. "Sometimes. After you left, I couldn't afford to stay in the same place. I was living in my office for a while. I kind of already was anyway, which I guess is why you left, but..." Paige trailed off. "I stayed with a couple friends who didn't think it was healthy for me to be sleeping in an office chair while I found my own place. Then I moved through a couple different apartments. I'm not moving because I necessarily *want* to move." Paige stressed the word in obvious reference to Lara's plans. "It kind of just keeps happening. I don't move; the world moves me."

Lara felt like that a lot. When she didn't take control of her own life, the world took over for her. It sent people like Roger Feldman. It made Betty sick. It kept

Lara trapped in Perry while she waited on Paige to grow into a person she didn't want to be.

Paige groaned and fell to the floor like a tuckered-out child having a tantrum. "Argh! I can't find them!"

"Will you please just let me help you?" Lara asked. "Tell me what you're looking for."

Paige hesitated, but ultimately gave in and let Lara share the burden. "My bags. They have all my camera equipment in them. I need them. They're huge. They're black. I should be able to find them."

"Did you leave them at your office?"

Paige's head fell back, eyes closed in defeat, but the smile on her face was a welcome change. "Yep," she said. "I took my camera in so Lorraine could download some footage. We'll have to stop by the office on our way." After taking a moment to collect herself, Paige rose to her feet and dusted her hands off on her pants. "Thanks. We make a pretty good team, eh?"

Lara rolled her eyes. "Can we go now?"

Chapter 16

"Lara!"

Hearing her name surprised Lara more than it should have. Her eyes settled on a pair of hands waving frantically as their owner tried to get her attention. After a moment, Lara recognized the girl. Lorraine. The redhead who had bumped into her the last time she was here. The intern who had told Paige about the Roger Feldman article.

"Oh. Hey." Lara tried to sound welcoming rather than awkward, but she was too put off to smile. Lorraine gestured for Lara to come closer, and Lara was in no position to decline.

"It's nice seeing you again," Lorraine said. "Ms. Daley talks about you all the time. I'm helping her with the Hometown Heroes contest, and I'm the one who edited that video we put out about your knitting."

Paige talked about her?

"You do the editing?" Lara asked, trying to make small talk. "That's cool."

"Yeah!" Lorraine's eyes beamed. They were so green, they were neon. "That's one good thing about being an intern. It seems like the younger you are in the industry, the more you know than the people in charge about the tech side of things. I do a lot for the website. Well, me and a few of the other interns, of course."

"That's cool," Lara said again. God, she sounded insipid, but there was little else to say. Lorraine was clearly passionate about her work, and Lara didn't want to discourage her. Talking to Lorraine felt like talking to one of Lara's younger cousins, like playing the older sister role she'd always felt obligated to fulfill. She had never been particularly good at it, but she supposed that came from being an only child.

But Lorraine didn't seem to notice. In fact, she seemed quite content to receive praise, too wrapped up in her own world to notice Lara's awkwardness. "Have you seen it yet?" she asked, almost breathlessly.

"I'm afraid not." If she watched the video, then she'd surely find something off about her makeup or her posture or her words. Lara was more than happy to save herself the embarrassment of seeing herself on film. "I was planning on watching it with my grandmother next time I see her." She didn't even feel bad about making up an excuse.

"Oh, come on." Lorraine frowned. "We can watch it now! Maybe you could give me some feedback?"

The cold mahogany slab of wood that was the closed door to Paige's office offered Lara no comfort. What was taking her so long in there? If only she'd walk out and whisk Lara away from this moment. It suddenly occurred to her that if someone had told her a month ago that she'd be dreaming of Paige as her savior, Lara would have laughed in their face.

There was no way out of it. She shrugged helplessly. "Sure."

Lorraine scooted to the edge of her seat as she fiddled with her laptop and waited impatiently for the video to load. A few other workers passed by in the open space, and Lara made sure to keep close to Lorraine's workspace, leaning against the desk so as to not get in any one's way. She had learned her lesson the hard way the last time, and she was not about to repeat her mistakes.

"Here you go!" Lorraine smiled wide, but no matter how hard Lara tried, she couldn't seem to muster even a fracture of the intern's excitement. Lorraine pressed play, and Lara braced herself.

The video started with a voiceover from Paige. A panning shot of the library decorated with autumn leaves and the first inklings of Halloween paraphernalia filled the screen as Paige spoke about Lara's career beginnings as a librarian. The video cut to a shot of Lara standing at the library checkout counter. Genie made eye contact with camera in the background.

"Tell me about the library," Paige said off camera.

"Well, it's a big building with a lot of books." The Lara on screen flashed a smile that was full of cheese. This Lara was proud of herself. This Lara was…happy?

She barely recognized herself. The Lara standing in the *Daily Page* office blushed. She hadn't meant for that joke to be usable content. She hadn't even meant for that *video* to be useable content. A hand came up to rub behind her neck and soothe the burning skin there. "You kept that part?"

Lorraine paused the video and looked up to meet Lara's eyes. "Yeah, I thought it was funny. It was too good to get rid of. You and Ms. Daley are cute together. I can see why you dated."

Lara's hand froze on her neck. "You know about that?"

"It's a small town, and I've worked with Ms. Daley for almost six months. It's hard not to know."

Of course. Everything was hard not to know in Perry.

Lara's blush was turning into an outright fever. If she didn't try to sway the conversation in a different direction, her entire body was going to be as red as her face must be.

"You've worked with Paige for six months and you still call her Ms. Daley?" Lara couldn't recall the last time someone had referred to Paige so formally. Paige was outgoing enough that even her college professors had gotten to know her on a first-name basis. She couldn't imagine anyone apart from a complete stranger being too timid to call Paige by her first name.

"Uh, yeah." The intern shot Lara the same look of surprise that Lara was sure was reflected on her own face. "I've never seen her joke around like that with anyone. You might be able to bring out that side of her, but around here I am not going out of my way to undermine her authority."

Was Paige that domineering? Lara thought back to the first time she had come to the office. Paige had brushed Lorraine off, and the way she'd said 'intern' meant it was clearly not a respectable title in her book. Lara had trouble picturing Paige as an overcontrolling boss, but she had mentioned being stressed lately. Maybe the work was getting to her.

"I'll talk to her," Lara said before she fully registered that the words were coming out of her mouth. "If she's in a bad mood, she shouldn't take it out on you guys just because she can."

"Y-you really don't have to!" Lorraine was clearly as thrown off by Lara's words as Lara herself was. "It'd probably be better if you didn't, honestly. If she finds out I said something…."

"I won't mention you," Lara said. "I'll just talk to her. See what I can do."

Now Lorraine was the one to blush. She swiped a stray strand of hair out of her face and scratched the back of her scalp. "Thanks again, Lara, but you really don't have to. She's actually been a little better these past few weeks. She let me leave early the other day, which is, like, actually unheard of. And she let me work on this project. I think you've already helped me out."

Had she? Lara doubted that.

"You're the one who's done such a good job on the contest. She's rewarding you for your work."

Behind her smile, Lorraine seemed to consider the thought for a moment. "Maybe, but I don't know. She's been nicer to everyone."

Lorraine was young, excitable, and maybe a bit overwhelming, but the more time Lara spent with her, the more she could tell that this girl was a genuinely good person who cared about her work and the people around her. Lara felt bad for judging her unfairly.

Lorraine pushed play again, and they turned back to the video. On-screen Lara was sitting on her couch, talking to Paige about Festive Feline Fashion. The video wasn't anything unexpected, but it was as clean and professional as Lara could have hoped for. Lorraine had clearly put a lot of effort into the project. She even made Lara look good.

"So did you like it?" Lorraine asked when the video faded to black. "Do you think I should have cut out that banter with you and Ms. Daley? I like it in there. Ms. Daley said it was fine, but if you think that was too personal, I can think about that next time I'm doing a project like this."

What did it hurt? Lorraine was right; it was a personal touch, and it worked. "No," she said, "you've got good instincts."

A broad, genuine smile crossed Lorraine's face. "That means a lot, Lara. Thank you. Hey, you should post the video on your Facebook! I think your fans would like it. Plus it'll help our numbers."

Fans? Lara considered the people who followed her customers and cat enthusiasts. If they were fans of anything, it was her cat pictures. A video of Lara talking about how she changed professions from librarian to knitter was far less entertaining than a cat in a Santa sweater dangling from a Christmas tree like an ornament.

"I don't know about that," Lara said. "I can't imagine why they'd be interested."

"*The Daily Page* readers seem to like it." Lorraine scrolled down to the comments section Lara had read earlier. There were several more now. "If these random people have good things to say, I'm sure your fans will too. They'll get to see a different side of you."

It wasn't the worst point, but Lara still wasn't convinced. "The side that doesn't knit cat sweaters? I'm pretty sure that's the only side they care about."

"It's a more personal side. People will get to know you better. And for who you really are."

Lorraine was using the same tone Lara's mother had used on her after her first disastrous piano lesson as a child. Her mother's assurances had only made Lara feel all the more pitiful. *You did great, and you'll get better with more practice* was parent code for *You were terrible, but I feel bad for you.*

"So you've read the bad reviews?" Lara asked.

Lorraine bobbed her head back and forth. "One or two of them."

Lara groaned.

"Hey, fuck 'em," Lorraine said. The informality surprised Lara. The girl was so afraid of Paige that Lara hadn't expected her to drop the F-bomb in the middle of the office. "They don't know you like we do."

Who was "we"? Lorraine? Paige? The people who had met Lara in real life?

"Thanks." As much as Lara wished she wasn't having this conversation, she meant it. It was nice to have someone on her side, even if the girl was a practical stranger. "You know more about me than I know about me, huh?"

"No one knows you better than you know yourself."

Paige's door finally swung open, and she tumbled awkwardly out of her office, one bag on her hip, one over her right shoulder, and a camera around her neck. She looked like a nature photographer who had packed enough supplies to survive in the Sahara for a week. As she locked the office door behind her, she struggled to adjust her bags into a comfortable enough position that she could walk with them.

Before Lara could say anything about how silly Paige looked, Lorraine spoke up. "I'll see you at the parade," she told Lara, then nodded in Paige's direction. "You should probably go help her."

She was right. Lara grabbed one of Paige's bags, and the relief on her face was tangible.

"Thank you." Paige adjusted the camera around her neck. She looked more comfortable and was standing straighter.

"No problem."

Paige pushed ahead, and Lara followed her towards the exit. "How does it feel to be my subject again?"

"What?"

"You're in the parade, so I'm kind of covering you," she said over her shoulder.

Oh. A suddenly sinking feeling in her stomach made Lara look away until she could compose herself. "Well, *barely.* I'm on the knitting club float. I can assure you that we will not be the highlight of the event. Not even the kids will like us. Most of the group is old ladies who will probably throw out hard candy left over from the '50s."

Paige chuckled. "If you say so, Lara."

It made her feel even more awkward somehow. Avoiding Paige's gaze, Lara held the door open for her as they stepped into the parking lot, then unlocked the car. Having something to do with her hands made some of the awkwardness dissipate.

Now was as good a time as any, and she would probably lose her nerve if she didn't say something.

"I wanted to thank you," Lara said.

"Oh?" Paige fiddled with a zipper as she tucked her equipment into the back seat. "What for?"

"You got Sanchez fired. It was really nice of you to give that video to Genie."

Their gazes locked for a long moment until Paige raised her eyebrows and shrugged. "Eh. It was no big deal. Just felt like the right thing to do."

But Lara could see the smile on her lips. For a moment, she continued to watch Paige fiddle, seemingly without point, then she circled around and pulled something out of the trunk.

"I made these for you and Cosmo."

It was a bad idea. Lara knew it. Every knitter knew it. But she couldn't help herself. Making matching sweaters for Paige and Cosmo was the most fun Lara had had while knitting in months. It was refreshing, doing it to because she wanted to rather than to fill an order. And after their conversation about the first sweater, Lara thought Paige might appreciate the action this time around too.

Paige's head jerked up, and when she saw Lara dangling the set in front of her, her eyes went wide. It took her a moment, but Paige reached out and took the sweater and its miniature gently, reverently. Her smile grew.

"I love them, Lara. Thank you." She laid them carefully in the back seat beside the rest of her stuff and gave Lara a hug that nearly knocked her off her feet.

She stumbled within the hug and just barely managed to not fall over. But once she righted herself, she just stood there, her eyes squeezed shut. Paige didn't seem in any hurry to end the hug, and despite her better judgment, Lara found she wasn't either. When Paige finally pulled away, Lara walked back to the driver's side of the car, her steps light as air.

Paige sunk into the leather cushions of the passenger seat and made cooing sounds of admiration. Lara had never seen someone so intrigued by a scuffed-up dashboard and a faded gearshift. "The car is exactly the same."

"It's only been a couple of years, Paige," Lara said, like those couple of years hadn't felt like an eternity.

"But you kept everything so clean."

This was clean? The spare change in the glove compartment was so old that it was probably collecting mold. Lara was pretty sure a search would turn up several lost French fries beneath the cracks of the seats. She hadn't even bothered to clean anything out this afternoon. She had no appearances to keep up for Paige Daley.

"My car looks totally different than it did a few years ago," Paige said.

"Really? 'Cause it was a piece of junk then, and it's a piece of junk now."

"No, it's definitely junkier," Paige said. "You were the one who made me take care of it."

What was there to say to that? She wasn't wrong. Lara suppressed the urge to smile and started the car.

"I should get a new one," Paige said over the purr of the motor warming up. "I could. I have the money. I just haven't had the time. And it still runs. Most of the time. I'd hate to get rid of it when it's not completely useless."

"I get that. I need a new phone, but I've been putting it off for the same reason. It still works. Mostly." Lara plugged her phone into the car charger. The cracks in the screen glowed like the jagged mouth of a jack-o'-lantern.

Paige eyed the fractured glass. "Oh man, that's rough. What happened?"

"Rocket knocked it off a table."

"Is that a code for you getting angry and throwing it?"

"No, Rocket legitimately knocked it off a table."

Paige smirked. "Rocket's a little shit, isn't he?"

"The worst."

A comfortable silence loomed over them as they set off down the road. Lara had almost forgotten what they were talking about when Paige spoke up again.

"You don't necessarily have to get a new phone. It's not like broken things can't be fixed, you know. You'll be happy with it once it's repaired."

"Or replaced."

Paige was quiet for a moment. "Sure." But she didn't sound convinced of her own answer. "Sometimes that works too."

When Lara pulled into the meeting place for the parade, they were far from the first ones to arrive; the parking lot was full of cars and parade participants looking for their groups. The park was the only place in town big enough to accommodate a couple dozen floats, and emergency personnel were already busy blocking off roads and setting up the line.

It felt like everyone in Perry was here. There was a mix of so many types of people, as if the park had booked overlapping conventions on the same day. In the parking lot alone she spotted a group of men in kilts, a children's gymnastic team in tights, and enough dog walkers to put all the middle school kids out of their summer businesses. The whole scene reminded Lara of the time her parents had taken her to the travelling circus.

Paige's eyes were wide with opportunity the moment Lara finally found a space. She couldn't grab her camera fast enough and undid the manual latch to let herself out before Lara had time to unlock the doors. Lara got out of the car far less enthusiastically, taking time to lock up and make sure their belongings were safe.

Already squatting to her knees in the middle of the lot, Paige was busy taking wide shots, trying to get as many people in frame as she could. She took photos of the floats and the police brigade in front of the park's gates.

Lara couldn't help but laugh at the sight of her. "Jesus, Paige. You look like a photographer, not a journalist."

"Can't I be both?" Paige asked. Lara's mock criticism rolled off her like water off a raincoat. "No one's ever just one thing. Photography's one of the best parts of my job."

Lara envied her confidence. Paige did what she wanted, and nobody stopped her—not posted signs, not gossipy neighbors, not people staring. How many times had Paige's passion for something put Lara in an uncomfortable or embarrassing position right in the middle of downtown Perry?

But seeing Paige now, looking like some kind of khaki-clad wildlife photographer in her element, it was obvious to Lara what she hadn't had the distance to see years before: Paige had never meant to embarrass her. She just approached anything she liked with an unselfconscious gusto that made her completely indifferent to what anyone else thought.

Lara had been that passionate about knitting once. She missed that feeling.

Lightly, she tapped Paige on the shoulder, not wanting to disturb her creative trance. Paige looked up with a smile in her eyes, too happy to be annoyed at being interrupted.

"I'm gonna go find April and the other ladies," Lara told her. "We'll meet up back here when everything is over."

"Sounds good. Have fun."

"You too."

As she moved to leave, Lara realized that her hand was still on Paige's shoulder. She jerked away from the prolonged contact, muttering a small "sorry" that Paige definitely couldn't hear over the din of parking lot conversations and a marching band warming up somewhere on park grounds.

The Tight Knit float was one of the tamer ones. For once, April's efforts didn't look over the top. There were floats with rafters and stands. Floats with giant thrones. Floats large enough to hold entire football teams. A few floats were nothing more than trailers with crude homemade signs and spare decorations, but all of them were impressive and unique in their own right. Still, it wasn't hard to pick out the giant ball of yarn in the middle of the park.

April stood in the center of the float, using it as a soapbox as she doled out instructions to the group of women in front of her. Out of half dozen or so women and one little girl, one person stood out more than the others. Lara claimed a spot next to her and leaned closer to speak in her ear. "April roped you into this too, huh?"

Kerry jerked back in surprise, but relaxed when she realized it was Lara who had snuck up on her. She gripped Lara's arm to stabilize herself, her grip a bit tighter than necessary. "You scared me!"

"Sorry," Lara said, not sorry at all. "I couldn't resist."

"Jerk. And to answer your question, no, April did not rope me into this. She asked me if I wanted to be a part of the parade, and I politely declined."

"If you declined, then why are you here?"

"Because after I declined, April told me that you were going to be here. I then revoked my declination."

Lara's stomach was a buddleia, and she couldn't stop the butterflies from flying into it if she wanted to. In fact, she was pretty surprised at the level of nonchalance that came out of her mouth.

"It sounds like April roped you into it by telling you exactly what you wanted to hear. Face it, she bribed you."

Both of them looked up at April, who was still vehemently giving her rundown of the path of the parade and the floats that would be in front of and behind them. She was a natural-born leader. The other women were eating the words out of the palm of her hand. Even the young child was listening attentively.

"Damn it, you're right," Kerry said. "How is she so good at that?"

"It's a talent unmatched."

Suddenly, April looked Lara dead in the eye, as if she could sense that Lara and Kerry were talking about her. Lara wouldn't put that sort of sixth sense past her.

"Lara! You're here. Good. Come up here. You're going to stand next to me."

It was impossible to ignore her. April was all business. Playtime was over. Or was it?

Lara grabbed Kerry's hand and led her onto the float. Even when they were both standing next to April, Lara didn't let go of the fingers laced between her own.

As April doled out more instructions, Lara forced herself to take this seriously and listen. But the awe factor of it all didn't sink in until the truck pulling their float started moving and they slowly inched their way onto Main Street, passing a seemingly endless crowd of people watching them on the sidewalks. Lara smiled at the kids they passed. Some of the older women threw sweets to the passersby. Lara let them take the glory as they took charge of the float, charming the crowd and entertaining the kids who scoured the streets for candy like ducks racing for bread crumbs in a pond. Beside her, Kerry's eyes glittered in the sun. The way her short hair ruffled ever so slightly in the wind made for a sight almost better than the crowd or the parade lineup.

The crowd was impressive right from the get-go, and the parade didn't even start on the busiest street in town. The early route passed through the area with most of the government facilities, where the few firefighters manning the station instead of participating waved back at the floats. A police officer stood beside his car, watching with a fond expression. The secretary at the post office gazed wistfully out of her window.

Lara was more than content to stand towards the middle of the float, where the crowd wouldn't see her unless they were really looking, but as they approached the nursing home, she stepped forward, eager to see who was waiting on the lawn. Only a few moments passed before she locked eyes with her grandmother, sitting on a bench in a flowery gown with a nurse as her escort.

Lara left Kerry's side to grab a handful of candy from one of the buckets being passed around. She tossed it into the courtyards. A couple of kids who sat with their grandparents on the lawn scrambled to collect the treats, but Betty was able to lean down and grab a piece. She held it up for Lara to see, and Lara kept that view in her sight until the truck pulled them too far away to see her any longer.

Lara returned to Kerry, who asked no questions. Lara would have explained, but as the float pulled onto the busier streets, she couldn't hear her own thoughts, let alone her own voice. The crowd conversed excitedly, children screamed at the floats that caught their attention the most, and the marching band a few spots ahead of them had amped up their playing to a volume Lara didn't know was possible. Her heart was beating fast. She was caught up in the moment, high on adrenaline and the sight of so many happy faces around her. She could do nothing but rake her eyes across the crowd and enjoy the company.

She recognized quite a few faces. It was hard not to. No matter how hard she'd tried to leave Perry behind, she couldn't forget its faces or names. Her hand in Kerry's, she picked out neighbors and old acquaintances and schoolmates in the crowd. Cindy and Tommy were among them, cuddled into the side of April's ex-husband, who looked like nothing more than a devoted father enjoying the day with his kids. Maybe that's what he was. He was a cheater, but maybe he was a good dad too. Maybe Lara could see why April was so willing to forgive him. At least partially.

One face stood out from the crowd in that it was obscured. Phones were held up in the air, recording in every direction Lara looked, but only one face was covered by the lens of a real camera. When Paige finally pulled it away to reveal her face, she was squinting in the sunlight, but it didn't seem to bother her. The camera fell to her neck, and one hand reached up to cup above her brow, shielding her eyes from the light. She stared pointedly at Lara and waved. Her hand flapped in the sky like she was one of the six-year-olds tumbling through the streets on a sugar high. She looked happy, taking photos and letting herself be absorbed in the energy of the crowd

Her lens pointed in their direction for a quick shot of Lara and the Tight Knit float. Lara may have even smiled for the picture, a gut reaction, like the smile and thumbs up Paige gave her as she dropped her camera again. For that one second, Lara and Paige were in their own little world.

Then the hand that wasn't holding Lara's found its way towards her hip, and before Lara knew it, she was being pulled closer to Kerry's side. When Lara turned to her, Kerry's smile was just as wide as Paige's. She was on the same adrenaline high as Lara. There was so much of herself that she recognized in Kerry.

Kerry leaned in for the kiss, and Lara missed a beat, her eyes open wide even after Kerry's lips pressed into hers. Her feet stumbled as she regained her footing, and she couldn't stop her eyes from drifting in Paige's direction before she closed them and immersed herself in the kiss. When Kerry pulled away, opened her eyes, and regained that playful smile, unbelievably, the float had only moved a few feet, which Lara realized when she looked back into the crowd at Paige. She was still in exactly the same spot.

They made immediate eye contact again, but this time, Paige's gaze quickly shifted from Lara to the rest of the float. She eyed the papier-mâché yarn, the rest of the Tight Knit members—every aspect of the float but Lara. And when Paige's gaze finally swung back in her direction, Lara saw it: Paige wasn't looking at her. She stared right past Lara, at Kerry, her mouth sunk into an unreadable expression. And when her gaze briefly did fall back onto Lara's, her smile didn't perk up again.

The float moved on, and Paige drifted out of sight. Mere moments ago, Lara had thought this whole experience was better than she'd ever expected, and better than she would ever admit out loud to anyone—not even April or Kerry. But that happiness was as temporary as everything else in her life. The weird moment with Paige was enough to ruin it, and, for once, Lara was glad that Perry was so small. When the parade ended soon after, she was more than ready to get away from it all.

The rest of the caravan carried their excitement with them, and when all of the floats returned to their starting spots, the park was even livelier than it had been before the parade started. Groups from different floats mingled together, trading leftover candy and complimenting one another on their costumes and designs. April was in the center of the action, as always, with the rest of the Tight Knit ladies, and Kerry started toward them, pulling Lara along by the hand.

"I can't stay," Lara said, planting her feet to the ground and stopping Kerry from dragging her farther. "I carpooled here, and I have to meet someone."

"I could give you a ride later." The suggestion was punctuated by an obvious pout.

Lara looked out over the parking lot and caught a glimpse of Paige, leaning against the car and staring back at her, her fingers clasped around a half-burnt cigarette. She took a long drag, and the wisps of smoke she let out clouded her face.

"I can't," Lara said again. "I'm driving." She yanked her hand out of Kerry's, eyes shifting between Kerry and Paige, her gaze lingering on the latter as she flicked the withered end of her cigarette onto the concrete.

"Alright." Kerry surrendered much more easily than Lara had expected. She made no move to reach back for her hand. "I'll see you around?"

"Yeah," Lara said in relief she hoped didn't show. "For sure."

Lara gave her a quick wave goodbye and was off. She met Paige's eye again as she passed the swing set and navigated her way through the heavily occupied jungle gym. Paige hadn't moved from her spot against the car, and she didn't perk up much when Lara came to stand by her side.

"You still smoke?"

"No." Paige dropped the butt onto the concrete and put it out with her heel. "I stopped last year. I borrowed this from someone in the crowd. It's not even the kind

I like. They're not as good as I remember." Paige let out a deep sigh and kicked the cigarette under the car.

"Stressed?"

Paige shook her head. She wouldn't meet Lara's eye. Her gaze drifted back towards the crowd around the floats. "Just thinking too much."

"About the project?"

"No."

"What, then?"

Paige shook her head again, more aggressively this time. "Don't worry about it. Can we go?" She tugged fiercely several times on the locked door handle.

Lara fished the keys out of her jacket pocket, then put them right back in as she stared at Paige's knotted eyebrows and the tight frown on her face. "No," she said firmly. "Not until you tell me what's going on in your head."

"Lara…"

Lara could sense the rebuttal before it started. Arguing wasn't going to help. Lara softened her voice and laid a hand over Paige's crossed forearms. Paige flinched at the contact, but Lara ignored it. "Hey, come on. You can tell me. What's wrong? I thought we were having a good day. What's bothering you?"

"This."

They were standing close enough that Lara got a perfect view of Paige's throat bobbing as she swallowed. Her eyes softened. Lara had a sense that Paige was coaxing some sort of confession out of her.

Her lips moved in for the kiss.

Lara did nothing to stop it.

Chapter 17

At eight in the morning, Lara's ring tone felt much louder than it did during the day. As she searched for her phone amidst the sheets, she wondered which was worse: being woken up by a bad version of William Tell's Overture or by Rocket pawing against her face demanding breakfast.

"Hello?"

"Lara?" Paige's voice.

Was this a dream? Sensing movement, Rocket jumped onto the bed and dug his paws into her side. Definitely not a dream.

"What's up?"

They hadn't talked about the kiss. They should have when it happened, but they hadn't. Lara hadn't let them. When she'd pulled away, she hadn't been able to look Paige in the eye. She hadn't been ready to listen to what Paige was feeling. She hadn't been willing to admit that she'd been weak. For the past forty-eight hours that was all she had been repeating to herself. The kiss was nothing more than a moment of weakness, and if she stayed away from Paige, they would both forget about it. But here Paige was on the phone, so so much for that plan.

So why did Lara feel…giddy? Why did she want Paige to talk about it so badly? For once Paige was doing what Lara wanted, and for some reason all Lara wanted Paige to do was to go against her wishes and push those boundaries in a way Lara couldn't bring herself to do.

"I normally wouldn't ask this," Paige said, "but I wasn't sure who else to call. My car doesn't want to start, and I have an interview I really need to get to. I was wondering if you can drive me?"

She shouldn't. She'd been asleep. She had plans to see her grandmother later. She had her own rules of avoiding Paige not to break.

"Let me get ready. I'll be there in a few."

The car ride was eerily silent. Under any other circumstances, Lara would have been thankful not to have to talk to Paige, but after that kiss things were different. She couldn't look at Paige's face without seeing her lips and thinking of how soft they had been. She couldn't look at Paige's hands without thinking of how they had felt gripped around her waist. She couldn't look at the phone in her lap without wondering why Paige's phone call hadn't been more than just a request to bum a ride.

Lara wasn't going to be the first one to bring up the kiss, but the silence was making her skin crawl. Small talk was neutral territory, easy, routine.

She eyed the pen and paper on Paige's dashboard. "No camera today?"

"Why? Want me to film you?"

"No. I'm just making conversation."

"You sure? You look great. Did you mean to get all dolled up just for me?"

Lara blushed. Her eyes fell to her lap. Her outfit wasn't that fancy, was it? She had spent longer than usual picking out her clothes, but she hadn't wanted it to seem like she'd been trying *too* hard to look nice. She didn't want to give Paige the wrong idea.

"I need to do laundry," Lara lied. "I ran out of my usual clothes, so I had to wear something nicer."

"Hey, I'm not complaining. You look beautiful." Paige paused. "Not that you don't look good in sweatpants and T-shirts too."

Lara rolled her eyes. "Please. You're just saying that so the next time you need blackmail against me you can film me looking like a complete slob."

"Fine. You got me. Guess I'll just have to deal with you looking like a movie star all the time. How awful."

Lara found herself laughing, and it brought back memories of a time when she'd thought Paige Daley was charming and funny. The moment seemed so long ago, and yet it was right before her, close enough for Lara to grab ahold of if she wanted. She let her fingers brush across it but refused to cling.

Paige cleared her throat and stumbled hastily over her next words. "My camera's in the bag I put in your trunk. Along with some other stuff."

Lara raised an eyebrow. "Do I want to know what else you brought?"

"I'll show you later. Take a left."

Now Paige was acting more like her usual stubborn self. It calmed Lara, if only a little. "This would be a lot simpler if you told me where we were going instead of giving me directions. I know I haven't lived here in four years, but the town isn't big enough for me to forget where everything is."

"If I tell you it'll ruin the surprise."

"I don't know how I feel about your surprises anymore, Paige."

"Hey." Paige reached across the gearshift to put her hand over Lara's. Her fingers held Lara lightly around the wrist. "Live a little. Trust me."

Lara did not trust Paige, but Paige spoke so softly that it was all she could do in the moment. Paige's touch was gone as quickly as it appeared, and Lara resumed ten and two on the steering wheel, letting Paige guide her.

It wasn't long before the route started to look a little too familiar. Perry wasn't big, but Lara recalled far too many bus rides cruising the exact same roads that Paige was taking now. She clung to her doubt for as long as she could, but there was no mistaking the parking lot they were pulling into.

"My high school? Really?" Of all the places that Lara never wanted to set foot in ever again, Marshall High School was pretty high up on that list.

"Yep," Paige said, her tone peppy as she got out of the car, bringing her notepads and recorder with her as she stepped outside. "You should come in with me."

"Have you completely forgotten all the horror stories I told you about going to school here?" Lara spoke to her out the window, her seatbelt still firmly fastened.

"Come on," Paige coaxed. "You're going to get bored waiting in the car. It's cold out here. Come in and be my assistant." Paige didn't give time Lara to rebut. She was already heading toward the trunk.

Lara huffed and clicked her seatbelt free. She threw her door open and tumbled out to see Paige retrieving her bag. "Fine. I'll come in, but only because I forgot to bring something to knit in the car. And I'm not going to be your assistant. I'm not Vanna White."

"You're right; you're prettier." Paige's smile was too smug. Lara wasn't going to feed her ego, even if part of her did enjoy the compliment.

"Who are you interviewing anyway?" Lara asked as they walked inside.

"Principal Hawthorne."

"He's *still* the principal? How old is he?"

"Eighty-six," Paige said, ever the researcher.

At the office, Paige showed her ID to the secretary, who dutifully copied her name onto the guest sign-in sheet. Lara stepped forward to present her own, but the secretary waved her away.

"Don't worry, Lara. I remember you. I've already got you down." Her smile was welcoming, and Lara mirrored the gesture. She remembered this woman too.

"Principal Hawthorne is actually in a meeting right now," the secretary said. "They started a bit late, so you may have to give him twenty minutes or so."

Good thing Lara hadn't chosen to wait in the car.

"Is it okay if we walk around?" Paige asked. "I'd like to take some photos." She held up her camera to prove that she was a journalist, not a predator to avoid letting loose in the halls.

"Sure. Take your time."

"Let's head to the gym," Paige said. "It's over…" She pointed in the wrong direction. "Here, right?"

"I remember where it is," Lara said, and she guided Paige to the shortcut. Within minutes, the squeaking of their shoes on the freshly polished tile was replaced by the cacophony of a whole group of feet sprinting across a basketball court. Lara peered through the windows of the gym doors. The shouts of the P.E. class grew louder as she pressed her head closer to the entrance.

"If you wanted the gym, I think someone's using it already."

"I didn't want the gym," Paige said. "I wanted to show you this."

Paige pointed to a family of gold and purple tapestries hanging from the ceiling in front of the gym door like stalactites. Each banner immortalized the school records for different sports, and Paige quickly singled out the track and field banner. Lara could see why: the second-place time for the 40-meter dash was none other than Hank Spellmeyer.

"How'd you know this was here?" Lara asked. She reached up and stroked the fabric, and the memory of seeing it during her own school days came back to her. She'd half expected his record to be broken by now.

"I've been here a few times. We do a lot of coverage on high school athletes. Your dad must've been someone important back in the day."

Lara shrugged. "I don't know. He doesn't talk about it. I imagine the bullying is worse if your father is a murderer than if your grandfather is a murderer, so I doubt it. He probably got into track because he had to find some way to run away from his problems. Better than drinking."

"Surely he got more out of track than that."

"You know what my dad got out of track? Almost a college scholarship. He was being considered for a couple of schools, but they all went after that guy up there, and others like him who came in first. All my dad got out of running was a good foundation for healthy lifestyle practices and some muscle mass."

"Your school was proud enough of him to hang his name here for everyone to see. He's held the record all these years. I bet the track team still looks up at that and wants to be like Hank Spellmeyer."

"Actually, they want to be like Gary Jones, because he's the guy that came in first and was way better than my dad."

Paige rolled her eyes. "Still, even despite the prejudices against him, your dad was able to achieve something great and be the best that he could be at something that he loved. Just like you."

Lara gave that a moment to sink in. She had built a decent life for herself despite no one but her family believing in her. Her dad had managed the same. It wasn't easy, though.

"Why are you trying to teach me some moral lesson?" Lara asked. "Are you going to write an article about how my dad is a Hometown Heroes candidate too?"

"Hey, maybe. It'd be a good article. It could be about how he raised a daughter so awesome that the sins of your ancestors have been forgiven and you've made the town realize that they were wrong for judging you guys in the first place."

That sounded like a good headline. Unfortunately, it didn't sound like reality. "Yeah, I don't think that that's happened."

"I think it's happened more than you think it has."

Maybe things were better for Lara. She had more friends now than she ever did in high school, and she could go to the grocery store and be greeted by more fans of her work than by dirty stares, but she couldn't be *responsible* for all of that change, could she? Surely it was a matter of time. People were starting to forget about her grandfather. The wounds weren't as fresh, and people had more important things to care about now.

Paige snapped a photo of the banner and walked on, this time announcing no destination. Lara followed her, prepared to take a literal stroll down memory lane.

They were walking through the old social studies wing when a sign caught Lara's eyes. It was a simple sheet of paper taped to a door that was decorated with a rainbow of colored pencils and only three big, bubbled letters: GSA. Meeting times for the group were listed below it.

Lara stopped and pointed it out to Paige. "There's a gay-straight alliance now. We didn't have one when I went here."

Paige assessed the sign as carefully as Lara and pulled out her notebook. "Was it hard being gay here?" she asked. She wasn't using her professional interview voice. She was all genuine curiosity.

"If I'm being honest, not particularly. It was kind of weird being basically the only gay person I knew—and I still don't know a lot of other queer people from Perry—but no one was really hostile towards me. Not for being gay, anyway. It was worse to be a Spellmeyer than a lesbian."

"No one else ever came out when you were in high school? Not even after you did? I knew so many gay people when I came out in OKC."

More reason to love OKC as far as Lara was concerned.

"Not really. Like I said, Perry's so small that I don't think there were many gay people *to* come out."

"Must've been rough. I've got to give you credit for going it alone."

"Credit for what?" Lara asked. "Being myself? Living my life?"

"Yes. Some people never get that chance. It's admirable you have the courage to."

Lara had heard that before from her grandmother. "That's a pretty low bar."

"Unfortunately, you're correct."

Maybe Lara *was* brave in some way. She was forgetting someone.

"Actually, there was someone else, though I don't think I realized it at the time. Kerry never came out during high school, but she said that she always admired me for having the courage to be out. I don't think courage was the real issue, though. It's more like I had accepting parents that allowed me to be myself without fear. She didn't. But she got to live vicariously through me for a little while until she was able to safely come out herself." She paused, thoughtful. "I guess that's pretty cool."

"That is pretty cool." Paige gave a weak smile, but it didn't last long. She went quiet and spaced out, lost in her thoughts. It was a familiar kind of moment. Once upon a time, Lara took it as her responsibility to snap Paige out of her hyperfocused episodes. Now, she noted, Paige was composed enough after a moment to dig herself out of her hole.

"Kerry's the girl you're seeing, right?" Paige asked.

"I guess you could say that."

"You guys have known each other since high school. You can't be that nonchalant about her. Plus, you looked pretty close at the parade."

Lara tensed up. "We've only been on a couple dates." She didn't know why she was downplaying it to Paige. The dates weren't a big deal, but if Paige was as jealous as she'd seemed at the parade, then Lara was feeding her what she wanted to hear, and Lara didn't know how she felt about playing into Paige's hand.

"When's the next one?" Paige asked. She tried to chuckle through the question, but Lara could sense more anxiety in the words than humor.

"I don't know if there will be one," Lara said. "It really isn't a big thing. We're not that serious." Lara chewed a loose piece of skin off her thumb and worked up the courage to ask her own question. "Why do you want to know?"

Paige's throat bobbed as she swallowed. She opened her mouth to speak, but the only noise that followed was the bell. As students poured out of their classrooms, Lara hugged the lockers to step out of their way. When they were gone, so was the moment. Paige checked her watch, and Lara couldn't help but think it was to avoid looking at her. "It's been twenty minutes," she said. "We should probably get back."

Lara nodded and led Paige back to the office.

It was a long half hour of chatting with the receptionist while she waited for Paige to finish up her interview. When Paige stepped out of the principal's office, a jolt of glee ran through her, but Lara chalked it up to being happy that they could finally leave.

There was another long minute of silence as they signed out and headed back towards the parking lot.

Paige cleared her throat before she spoke, but the words still came out shaky. "Do you want to come back to my place for a bit?"

Lara's body immediately tensed. "I don't know if that's such a good idea, Paige."

"Why?" Paige's head jerked towards her.

"You know why."

"I want to hear you say it." Paige's voice was low and serious.

Lara sighed. The car was within reach, and Lara waited until she could lean against it and ground herself before starting this conversation. They were practically alone in the parking lot, but her voice was still a whisper. "We can't do this, Paige."

"Can't do what?"

Did she want Lara to say it? Did she want Lara to define whatever it was that was happening between them? Did she expect Lara to have answers for that?

"You know what I mean," she said.

"No, I don't." Paige tried to grab Lara's hand, but she recoiled from the contact immediately. Paige got the message and backed off. "I know what *I* mean, but I'm not at all sure what you're thinking." She folded her arms across her chest. "Look, we don't have to define this. We don't have to make it a *thing*. We can feel it out. We can do whatever feels right. But kissing you, it felt right. Don't tell me you regret it. Don't tell me you didn't feel it too, because I know you did. You kissed me back."

"Paige…"

"I didn't plan for this to happen," Paige said. "I didn't plan to kiss you. I didn't think before I acted. But seeing you with another woman… I couldn't take it. Something snapped, and I had to go for it. It felt right, and in that moment, everything fell into place. I haven't felt like that in so long, Lara."

Lara didn't know how she felt. The weird thing about it, the thing she'd kept thinking about all night last night in bed, was that it was almost like the kiss had never happened. The few times Kerry had kissed her, it had been an event. Lara had been hyperaware of every detail in the moment. They were first kisses, with all the usual emotional fanfare that went with them. They were the start of a thousand what-ifs.

But when Paige kissed her, it was another kiss added to hundreds of kisses. Familiar. Comfortable. It was something Lara had taken for granted on a daily basis for years. It was a routine that she could easily slip back into. It was home.

"Please tell me you didn't hate it," Paige said. She stepped forward so Lara's body was trapped between her and the car. It would be so easy for Paige to lean down and kiss her again. "I know you didn't hate it. Please don't say you did. Please be honest."

Paige's tone hurt too much to look her in the eye, so Lara looked at their feet instead, only an inch or so apart on the asphalt. Paige's feet had closed themselves back together.

Lara spoke quietly. "I didn't hate it, Paige."

Paige sighed in relief, and Lara could hear the way her smile shaped her exhale. "Then what's the problem?" She reached out to Lara's arms, which were crossed now, and gently tried to coax them apart. This time, Lara let Paige touch her. "If we both liked it, then what's wrong?"

Lara tried to keep her arms rigid, but Paige's warmth melted into her skin. "We just can't, Paige."

Paige's voice quivered with her lip. "Because of Kerry?"

"No, not because of Kerry." Lara sighed. "I don't think I can be that serious with her either."

Paige looked even more confused. "Why not? There's not someone else, is there?"

"No, nothing like that. I'm just… I'm not looking for anyone right now. I don't think it's a good idea to get attached to someone."

"Why aren't you looking for anyone? Don't you miss being in a relationship? Don't you miss having someone to come home to?"

"What do you even know about missing…" No, she wasn't going there. It didn't matter anymore. Paige wasn't that person anymore. She had taken their relationship for granted once upon a time, but she'd already admitted that she regretted it, and Lara had already admitted that she regretted the way things had ended between them too. It *would* be nice to have someone to come home to, and Lara did want it someday, but right now she had bigger things to worry about.

"I'm going back to Oklahoma City, Paige. I'm not staying in Perry."

Paige searched the ground for answers.

"Did you forget?" Lara asked. Her tone was more accusing than she'd meant it to be. But maybe that was for the best. If she hadn't let her guard down around Paige in the first place, none of this would have happened.

"I didn't forget," Paige snapped. "I just didn't think you would actually go back."

Now it was Lara's turn to feel defensive. "Why wouldn't I?"

"I don't know." Paige sighed. "I guess I'm an idiot. I thought that maybe you'd want to stay this time. Things are good here for you now, aren't they? You have Tight Knit. You have your friends. You have your grandma and your parents and the rest of your family. You have Kerry, I guess." Paige's voice was so quiet that Lara almost didn't hear her add, "You have me."

Things *were* better. That was hard to deny at this point.

"Look, I don't know, okay?" Lara explained. "I'm not leaving right now, but I still want to leave. Even if I hate it here a little less than I used to, and even if I decide to come back someday, this is still far from my perfect life. I don't want to feel like I'm stuck in Perry forever. Life was good in Oklahoma City. Not perfect, but good, and I want that again."

Paige said nothing. Did she have nothing to say, or did she have too much to say?

"Can't we try?" she finally asked. She took Lara's hands in her own and stroked them with her thumbs. "At least until you leave. Whatever this is, I want to give it a shot, even if it ends up being temporary."

Paige was stubborn, but Lara didn't think she'd be this stubborn. A rejection was a rejection. Even Paige should understand that. "Why are you doing this?" Her voice rose an octave. "What do you want out of this? Friends with benefits? A fling to remind yourself that you aren't entirely out of the dating game? Seriously, are you going to fall in love with me again and move to Oklahoma City with me when I leave this time?"

"I don't know," Paige said. She sounded miserable, but Lara could appreciate the honesty. "All I know is that kissing you made me the happiest I've been in a long while."

Paige's eyes were gleaming. The dark brown of her irises brimmed with tears. It was hard for Lara to keep her resolve while looking at her. She looked to the asphalt again.

"Paige, I can't give you an answer right now. I don't know what I want. Long-term or temporary."

One of her hands let go of Lara's momentarily to brush back a tear. She huffed out a breath. "That's okay," she said, giving Lara's knuckles a gentle squeeze. "I'll give you time."

Chapter 18

They may have been at April's house, but Glenda was the main attraction. The matriarch of the group had taken a liking to April's rocking chair, and she loomed over a hoard of followers. The group was made up of the same elderly ladies that always followed Glenda around, but a few of the younger gals had joined their crew. They sat around her in a circle, looking at Glenda like she was their chief, the leader of the most benign cult in the world.

Glenda was clearly teaching something. She held out her work in example as the other women replicated what they were being shown.

"Hey, Glenda!" Glenda looked up from her work. The rest of the group did, too. "How's Betty's welcome home party coming?"

Excited chatter erupted around the group.

"It's almost finished," Glenda said. With a smile, she set her work down on the armrest and stood from the chair. "We should do a bit of pre celebration. April, get the wine."

April clapped her hands together and stood up from where she was seated on the floor. "Should I get the white or the rosé?"

"Why not both?

"I like the way you think."

A few more cheers escaped from the circle, and that was Lara's cue to leave. With a smile on her face, she set off for the back porch.

April's yard was beautiful. It was the kind of groomed that shouldn't be possible when April was a working mother with young children. The float stood as a temporary centerpiece, outshining the size and grandeur of the swings and slide.

"Were the old ladies too much for you?"

This time Lara recognized the voice immediately. Kerry was starting to make a habit of sneaking up on her. Lara had to admit she was starting to mind it less and less.

"Not too much. I'm just…" Lara took a deep breath. She stretched out her arms and let the wind grace past her fingertips in a gentle handshake, "enjoying the weather. Taking in the air. I heard on the radio it's supposed to get colder soon."

Kerry leaned against the railing, nestling in beside Lara close enough for their sides to touch if Lara shifted the weight in her hips. Having Kerry so close made the space that much warmer. It was comforting.

"My grandmother is getting out of the nursing home soon," Lara said. "She gets to come back home."

"That's good news. Was she in there for a while?"

"Too long. A couple months."

"Wow. I'm sorry to hear that."

"It's alright. Her being in care was better than her being in the hospital. We're throwing a welcome home party for her this Friday. A lot of the people here know her, and I was just talking to some of them about it."

"That's awesome. I'd offer to be your date, but I don't want to intrude." Kerry scooted closer. Their sides bumped.

"I have to be honest with you," Lara said.

"Oh no."

Kerry chuckled lightly, but Lara watched the way she pushed her bangs away from her forehead and covered her eyes.

"It's not awful, don't worry."

"But not good either?"

Lara cringed. "I just don't know what I'm looking for right now. There's a lot going on in my life, and I don't know how much room there is for a relationship. Or if I even want a relationship. Or who I want a relationship with." Lara took a deep breath.

"Is there someone else?" Kerry asked.

"There is someone." Lara was admitting it to herself as much as she was admitting it to Kerry.

"Your ex? Paige?"

Lara nodded.

"Is it serious?"

"I don't know. I've been telling her the same thing I told you. I don't know what I want yet."

Kerry stepped away from the railing and settled into April's porch swing She sat on one side, leaving room enough for Lara to sit on the other, but Lara stayed rooted at the porch railing. Gently, the tips of Kerry's toes rocked her back and forth.

"If you have unresolved feelings for her, you should explore that."

Lara looked up, surprised. "Really? You'd be okay with that?"

Kerry shrugged. "It's not really about me. You have to do what you want to do."

Wise words. Still, Kerry had to be censoring herself. "How do you feel, though?" Lara asked. "I want to know. I don't know if you're looking for a commitment, but if you are, I don't think I'm the person that can give it to you."

Kerry swung a little higher. Her toes launched off the porch a little harder. "I guess I am looking for more. I've had flings, off and on relationships, but nothing serious. It would be nice to have that, to settle down someday."

"I can't even picture that right now. Settling down." Lara stared out into the expanse of April's yard. Her spring flowers had been replaced by fall cucumbers and tomatoes. All of it looked good enough to eat. April would pick it soon, then let the ground frost over for winter. "I could once upon a time, and I hope I can again someday, but not right now. This feels like a fling to me, if I'm honest." Lara gestured between the two of them. "A good fling. Maybe one I needed. But I don't know if it will ever feel like more than that."

"I guess we're in different places, huh?"

"I guess so."

Lara hadn't expected this to be so easy. The conversation had seemed so intimidating when she'd imagined it in her mind. Part of her had been tempted to ghost Kerry, but she had already tried that with Paige. It hadn't worked. It had just made both of them resentful and angry and searching for closure. Lara was glad she hadn't given history a chance to repeat itself.

"If I'm honest," Kerry said, "I kind of found someone else too."

Lara was surprised by the revelation, but even more so by how jealous she didn't feel. "Really?"

"Nothing serious," Kerry promised. "I just met her. I could see myself going out with her."

"Then you should do it," Lara said. It felt like giving advice to a friend.

"Yeah?" Kerry smiled. Her legs stopped swinging. Her feet fell to the ground, and slowly the swing came to a halt too, each rotation back and forth a little shorter than the last, a little lower to the ground. She stood.

"Are you ready to go back inside?"

Lara looked out into the yard again at the trees and the playset and the birdbath. She smiled a little as the wind kissed her cheek. "Yeah."

Kerry held the door open for her.

Lara had the only job in the world that could make her enjoy checking her email. The past couple of months had been a little rough, but now her inbox was mostly full of the usual cat pics and positive reviews again.

Lorraine had been right about sharing the *Daily Page* video to her audience. Apparently people actually liked learning more about her. Most of the comments were good now, even most of the articles were nice. There were fewer of them than there had been when Lara first became popular, but it seemed like the people who had stuck around genuinely cared about her and her work. Lara was fine with that. She would rather have a few loyal fans than a lot of random followers uninvested in her well-being.

Lara was just about ready to call it a night. She was curled up in bed with Rocket by her side and a small smile on her face from a particularly funny photo of an orange cat in an orange sweater camouflaged in a pumpkin patch. She scrolled through the last few emails and paused. The message was titled no differently than any of the others. *Cat Pic :)* was an email Lara received on a daily basis. But the email address was new.

Lara did not get cat pictures from Paige Daley.

Out of curiosity, she opened the email.

One for your Instagram :) was all the email said, and Lara opened the attachment, half expecting some chain email cat meme. What loaded was a picture of Paige and Cosmo wearing the matching sweaters Lara had made them. Paige's smile was sweet as she eyed Cosmo lovingly and scratched beneath the calico's chin. Lara could practically hear the purring as Cosmo stared back at Paige through hooded eyes so golden they put Paige's blue ones to shame. Paige looked beautiful in the photograph.

It was the cutest thing Lara had ever seen, and she tried desperately to ignore the migration of butterflies fluttering in her belly.

She saved the picture to her phone before she decided whether or not she was going to post it. There was no reason she shouldn't. It was a cute photo. Paige had given her permission. It was exactly the kind of thing she posted every day and exactly the kind of thing her audience would love. But it felt too intimate. Lara knew Paige, and it was so rare to see such a beautiful, vulnerable moment from her. She ran her finger slowly over the screen, along Paige's cheek. No, she couldn't bring herself to share this with the world, not quite yet.

If she posted a picture of Paige, everyone in Perry would see it. April would think they'd gotten back together. Her mother would see it and ask her why in the world she was giving Paige Daley the time of day after what they had been through.

They were all good enough reasons not to share the photo, but none of them were why Lara was so hesitant.

She imagined putting the photo out into the void of the Internet: strangers would critique the lighting or comment on how much cuter their own cat was or how the gap between Paige's teeth made her ugly. No, she wanted to keep this moment to herself. This was a photo that belonged in a family scrapbook. It was a memory. It was something to cherish.

She made it Paige's contact photo and shut her phone off to charge for the night.

Chapter 19

"Did you get my email?"

Paige was supposed to be working, not talking. Lara was here to keep her company, not distract her.

"Yes, I got your email."

Paige's grin was all cheese. The light from her laptop made her smile shine even brighter. "Cute picture, huh? When are you going to post it?"

Lara sifted through a couple more pages of the photo album in her lap. There was a grainy shot of Betty and her first car that Lara had never seen before. Cute, but not exactly the type of photo that was worthy of being hung up at Betty's welcome home party. She thought for sure these old albums she'd found while cleaning out Betty's house for the party would be more helpful, but in hindsight, there was probably a reason they were tucked away instead of on display.

"I don't know. Are you sure you're ready to be an Internet celebrity? Someone's going to make fun of your drug store mascara, and I don't want to have to console you when you cry it all away."

Paige chuckled. "I'm a big girl. Besides," Cosmo slinked into the living room and Paige scooped her up before she could scurry away, "Cosmo wants to start her modeling career. She needs her mommy's connections."

Paige made kissy faces at the cat, and Lara looked away so that she didn't have to think about how sickeningly sweet it was. Paige pushed closer to Lara on the couch and shoved the cat between them, still cradling her in her arms and showing her off like Cosmo was a newborn infant.

Paige adopted a baby voice and spoke on Cosmo's behalf: "Post the photo, Mom, so Grandma Daley can see it. I want her to see how popular I am."

"Does your mom have Instagram?" Lara asked Paige.

"Oh, yeah," Paige said, her voice returning to normal. "She sends me things all the time. I keep hoping her phone logs her out one day and she forgets her password."

"Do you have Instagram?"

"God, no. Instagram, Facebook, it's all the same to me. I don't bother with social media. Waste of time."

Paige was right about one thing: Barbara Daley would absolutely love to see that picture of Cosmo and Paige.

"Couldn't you text your mom the picture? You do believe in texts, right?"

Paige pouted. "You're no fun." She rocked Cosmo back and forth, consoling her as if the cat was the one upset. "Is something wrong?" she asked more seriously. "You're acting weird about this. Is the picture not good enough to post or something? Is it the wrong dimensions? Wrong lighting? I used my camera and everything. I didn't even take it on my cellphone."

"It's not that," Lara said. "It is a good picture. It's a great picture. I just don't..." Lara didn't know where she was going with this. She didn't know what to tell Paige. She didn't know what to tell herself.

"What?"

Lara sighed. Paige tensed up, and Cosmo stopped purring in her arms. "It's not that. It's a privacy thing. It's so personal. Why ruin such an intimate moment by sharing it with the world?"

"Newsflash: you and the world can both enjoy the photo at the same time."

"It's not the world, it's this town. People talk, Paige. It'll make everyone feel like they're entitled to our personal lives. I don't want to hear a bunch of rumors about whether or not we're back together. I like to have some things that I can keep to myself."

Paige scoffed. "Let them say whatever they want. It doesn't matter what they think. You don't know those people."

"No, you don't know those people," Lara said. "I know everyone. Even if I don't know them, I know them. That's what it's like growing up here, Paige. You don't have to deal with it because you aren't from here. You've only been living here for a few years."

"This again?" Cosmo jumped from Paige's arms. Paige took a moment to center herself. She wiped a few stray cat hairs from the front of her shirt. "Look, I don't pretend to know what your childhood was like here. I know we grew up in different environments. I know we turned out to be different people. I know it's hard to ignore whatever criticism you think you'll receive, but the more you can learn to block it out, the better off you'll be. You can't spend your entire life worrying about what people think about you or what they're saying about you behind your back. You need to distance yourself from that mindset."

"I know. That's why I moved to Oklahoma City and put literal distance between myself and that mindset."

"Running away won't solve your problems either," Paige said. "You might be far enough away that people will start to forget about you, but it doesn't solve the root of the problem, which is that you care too much about something that you don't have any control over. You focus on pleasing other people more than you do on getting what you want out of life. It holds you back. It's not that Perry is an awful place; it's that you don't take advantage of what it has to offer because you're afraid of what others will say."

Lara scoffed and sunk further into Paige's lumpy couch. It was more uncomfortable than it had been two minutes ago. "You don't know what you're talking about."

"I know you, Lara. You have things you love here." Paige gestured to the photos of Betty in Lara's lap. "You have your family, and yet you're willing to leave them behind to escape the things people say about your grandfather. You have a club for your favorite hobby with your best friend, and you'd rather move away and knit in some dinky apartment by yourself to avoid the possibility that you might hear gossip about yourself. You had a job you loved that you got yourself fired from because you were more willing to start a fight than to professionally report your boss for having an unfair bias against you for something you were never even responsible for. The longer you keep caring so much what other people think, the more things you're going to lose. What happens when you stay in Oklahoma City long enough for people to get to know you? What if you play your music too loud and your neighbor starts hating you? What if your regular Starbucks barista starts resenting you because your morning order is too complicated? You can't keep moving your entire life to prevent people from holding you back. The only person holding you back is yourself."

Lara hated how Paige always sounded so sure that she was right. Lara hated more that Paige probably was right in this case. "You don't want me to move back because you aren't over me. You still have feelings, and you want to keep me to yourself."

Paige startled. She was a lion who didn't expect the mongoose she was toying with to fight back. "You know it's not just that, Lara. I really do want what's best for you."

Paige didn't even know what was best for herself. Her living room was nicer than Lara remembered it, but the couch had more cat toys on it than it did pillows.

Lara wouldn't be sitting on it if she weren't so tired. She'd stayed up half the night finishing the week's orders so that she could devote the entirety of today to setting up for Betty's party.

"I don't really want to talk about this right now, Paige. I'm gonna be late."

"Wait. I wanted to show you something."

Lara huffed. "Make it quick, please."

Paige disappeared into her bedroom and returned in moments with her hands full. The hanger she presented carried an article of clothing that Lara hadn't seen in four years.

"You kept the sweater?"

Paige's smile was beaming. "Of course I kept the sweater," she said quietly. "I was never going to throw it away or anything like that. I know it seemed like I didn't love it when you gave it to me, but I did like it back then, and I still like it now. I wear it every once in a while. It does spend most of the year in the back of the closet, but every time the weather starts getting chilly, I bring it out. It's a good sweater. It's warm and nicer than most of the other ones I have. I've always liked it." Paige cradled the sweater in her arms as she spoke, talking to the fabric like a long-lost friend.

Lara wasn't sure what to say. She had spent years thinking her work was unappreciated, but here it was, dangling in front of her in Paige's arms. "You're just saying that because I called you out on it," she grumbled without much heat.

"No, I mean it."

Lara thumbed the material. It wasn't her best work. She was a lot better now than she had been four years ago, but she had poured so much love into Paige's sweater that it had been one of her best pieces at the time. That was back before Lara took herself seriously as a knitter. It was before Festive Feline Fashion, and it was before Lara decided to find a group of people that would appreciate her knitting more than she thought Paige had.

Still, it was a good piece. At least Paige was getting some use out of it, even if the thought of her wearing the sweater brought out a painful clench in her chest.

Lara's instinct was doubt Paige, but somehow Paige kept finding ways to convince her that she was genuine now. This was new. Lara wasn't used to it. The old Paige would never have been this sweet or this vulnerable. Something had happened over the last four years. Either Paige had grown up or she'd become a better liar. Lara didn't know which one was the truth or which one she wanted to believe.

When Paige cupped Lara's face in her hands and kissed her for a second time, God help her, it was all too easy to let it happen.

Lara could feel herself sinking. It was a familiar feeling, one she was afraid she'd never escape. For the past four years, it had always felt like she was drowning—into pits of despair, into her own thoughts—but this time, she was falling into Paige's arms, and Paige was there to help pull her back up to the surface. Finally, Lara had access to fresh air, and she took a deep gulp of it when Paige pulled her lips away from the kiss.

Paige's forehead was warm pressed against her own. Her breath was hot on Lara's lips as she spoke in a gentle whisper. "I've wanted to do that for days. I'm so happy you let me." Another kiss came, this time feather-light across her cheek.

Lara wasn't sure it was a good idea, but right now, whatever this was, she needed it. At least until she got out of Perry. She let herself be held for a moment until Paige pulled away.

"I'll see you tomorrow at the party?" Lara asked.

"Wouldn't miss it." Paige grinned.

Time travel was entirely possible.

Lara was transported back twenty-five years. The *Welcome Home* sign above the door was a *Happy Birthday* banner for a five-year-old who wanted a dinosaur-themed party and a zoo of stuffed animals. The row of presents on the kitchen table was that army of stuffed bears and giraffes. The scent of freshly Febreezed furniture and lit candles was the aroma of homemade birthday cake fresh out of the oven. Betty had given Lara so many good parties here, and Lara was overjoyed to finally be able to return the favor.

"Lara, dear, can you help me with the cake?"

It was carrot cake. Betty's favorite. Lara's favorite too. The baker was Evelyn, one of the Tight Knit ladies who was supposedly even better in the kitchen than she was in the sewing room. She was a double threat, and she only needed Lara's help piping the icing. The arthritis had gotten to her hands, she said, and she didn't have the fine motor skills. It was Lara's hands that wrote out *Welcome Home, Betty!* in cream cheese. She had never used a piping bag before, but it was really no different than drawing. The ink just came out slower.

Taking a second to admire her work, Lara licked the remnants of icing from her fingertips. The dyed pink paste was way too sweet, but so was life right now. Lara wouldn't have it any other way. Evelyn rewarded her job well done with a smile and left to join some of the other ladies in the living room.

The clatter of metal folding chairs collided with the sound of soap operas playing too loudly on the television. Lara felt rather than heard her phone vibrate in her pocket. She retrieved it and swiped a sticky line of sugar across the cracks in the screen as she answered her father's call.

"Hey, honey, I've got—" A chair scraped against the wall, and a screaming ambulance caused panic on *General Hospital*. Lara pressed her index finger into her ear, but the underwater effect it created did little to block out the noise of the living room. It only distorted the sound.

"What? Hold on, Dad. I can't hear you."

Lara stepped over the threshold between the rooms and found her shoes among the growing pile that was forming in the living room. She pushed the screen door aside, then did the same to the front door and stepped out into the driveway. A quick search of the fleet of cars showed her that Hank would have no room to park when he did get here.

"What's up?" Lara asked. "Are you guys almost here?"

"Honey, are you sitting?"

"No, I'm standing. Can you see me in the driveway?"

Lara started toward the head of the drive. She looked both ways, but Hank's car wasn't up either end of the street.

"We're not going to make it, sweetie."

The air turned colder. Lara had rushed outside without thinking to grab her cardigan. She had no protection. The wind bit into her skin like lashes from a whip. "Why not?"

"We're at the hospital right now."

Lara stared ahead, eyes fixed on the end of the road. Any second her father would pull up and tell her this was all a prank.

"What happened?"

Hank's voice crackled on the other end of the line. For a second, Lara thought he'd hung up, and for a second she wished he had. If he didn't tell her the story, then it wasn't real.

"She stopped breathing."

Lara stopped breathing too.

"Is she okay?"

Silence.

"I don't know," Hank said. "I don't know. Your mom and I are still waiting."

There was a rustle of fabric on the other end of the line, followed by a jostling of the phone.

"I'll be there," Lara said, and the promise was the only thing that convinced her body to move against the wind.

Was there ever a point where it was appropriate to stop calling a waiting room a waiting room? What if the bad news being waited on had already been delivered? What if no one knew what they were waiting for? What if someone was waiting for something that would never happen?

The hospital lights were too bright, and the grief of everyone around her was too much to handle. Legs tucked against her chest, Lara pressed her knees into her forehead like a bad headache. The pain was the only thing she allowed herself to feel, and she closed her eyes to savor the sensation.

A flash of light disrupted the dark cocoon she'd created for herself. She opened her eyes to see her phone blink up at her from her lap. 6:06 p.m. Betty had passed over an hour ago. Lara was so distracted thinking about the time that she barely caught sight of the text notification before her phone screen faded to black.

I'm back. Be in with you in a second.

The smiling picture of Paige and Cosmo on the screen almost made Lara feel something for a split second, and there was a definite murmur in her heart when she felt a body sink into the seat beside her. A strong arm wrapped around her back, and Lara abandoned the comfort of her own lap to curl into Paige's side and fall into the embrace.

"How are you doing?" Paige asked. Her voice was nearly a whisper in Lara's ear. They weren't alone in the waiting room, but they were off in their own little world together regardless.

How did Lara respond to a question like that?

"Right," Paige said. "Stupid question." There was a bite in her voice. Lara could feel her wince. "Did everyone else leave? Are your parents still here?"

"They all went home. I told my parents I was going to stay with you tonight." Lara's voice was hoarse, but her words came out more level than they should have. She should be crying. She should be choking and sniffling and forcing her lips to stop quivering, but she couldn't bring herself to feel anything. Her voice was steady and monotone. If she didn't feel her mouth forming the words, she wouldn't have recognized them as her own. "I can't believe she's gone. Just like that. She was supposed to come home today. She was supposed to be better. She was supposed to die peacefully in her own bed, not in a hospital."

Paige hugged her a little tighter. She smelled like jasmine, and the scent was so soothing compared to the clinical smell that hung over the hospital. Lara never wanted to leave her side; Paige's arm around her felt like the only slice of happiness she had left.

"I didn't even get to say goodbye," Lara said. "She was out of it before I got here, and I never got a chance to talk to her before she…" Lara couldn't force the words out of her mouth even if she wanted to. It was out of her hands. Everything was.

"She knows how much you love her," Paige said. "You didn't need to say it for her to know. Everything you've ever done for her said it for you."

Lara hoped so. "It's not fair."

"You're right," Paige said. "It's not. Nothing is. We all lose people eventually, and it sucks every time. All you can do is look back on the good times and appreciate the time that you did have with those people. You two had thirty great years with each other, and I promise that she loved each and every one of them as much as you did."

"More," Lara said. "I was a kid for most of it. I never appreciated her as much as I should have. She loved me more."

Paige fell silent. The noises of the hospital returned to Lara's consciousness. Sneakers scuffed on polished tiles. Gentle whimpers reached her from the other side of the waiting room. An ambulance activated its sirens outside.

"Why don't we get out of here?" Paige asked. "I packed some clothes for you. I fed Rocket. You don't have to worry about anything. Let's get you back to my place where you can have a nice bath and settle down. I'll make you food and make sure you fall asleep, okay?"

Lara nodded. She hadn't been able to bear the thought of going home like this was any other normal day. She couldn't tuck herself into her cushy bed in her nice house and wake up in the morning and follow her normal routine. Staying with Paige was the only way she'd get through this night.

Lara's legs were weak as Paige guided her back out into the real world. It was darker than she'd thought it would be, calmer, too quiet. She felt guilty for enjoying the fresh air and the smell of recent rainfall. All things Betty would never experience again. Trapping herself in the front seat of Paige's car was refreshingly claustrophobic. She strapped the seatbelt tight against her chest and squeezed Paige's hand in her lap even tighter. Neither of them let go during the ride.

At Paige's place, she felt just as out of control as she had at the hospital, but here Paige was around to be in control for her. It was nice to hand over the reins to someone she could trust.

"I could run you a bath. I have those salts that smell like lavender." Paige posed it like a question. It was Lara's choice.

A bath sounded as good as anything else. "Sure. Thank you."

Paige slipped into the master bath, and the roar of the faucet filled the house. Lara waited in the bedroom, tucking the sheets across the corner of the bed to give herself something to do. An image of her own smile caught her eye: Paige hadn't removed the picture of them. In fact, she'd added another. The twin smiles stared up at her, and for the first time, the photos didn't feel like ancient relics of another time.

She looked the same. Paige looked the same. The photos could have been taken days ago. She hadn't realized how happy she had been over the last few days until she had this moment to compare it to.

The spout creaked as Paige turned the water off. Lara let herself be caught admiring the photos as Paige exited the bathroom.

"Bath's ready," Paige said. "I'll make you dinner. Give you a little time alone."

But Lara didn't feel alone. Paige was still near. Her footsteps were in the kitchen, as was the banging of pots as she rummaged through her cabinets. And that was good. Lara wasn't sure she really wanted privacy right now. She stripped, slipped into the water, and let the steam engulf her. The bath was too hot, and it turned her thighs red where the water swallowed her, but the scald felt nice, and the scent of lavender soothed away the pain.

When was the last time Lara had taken a bath? It was probably four years ago, with Paige taking up half of the tub and a bottle of wine precariously balanced on the ledge between the shampoo and conditioner. Lara worked the former into her scalp and tried to stimulate memories of better times.

A series of knocks sounded on the door, and Lara brought her head above water. A ring of suds cascaded around her. "You can come in."

Paige did. She kept her eyes on the tile, purposefully avoiding looking at Lara's body. Gently, she placed a folded towel and Lara's nightgown on top of the sink.

"You've seen me naked, Paige. You can look."

Paige's face turned red. The sauna-like heat of the room didn't help to hide her blush. "Sorry." Paige chanced a glance, meeting Lara's eye, but only after a moment of taking in the rest of her, too. "The food's ready whenever you're done."

"Thanks."

Paige dropped her gaze back to the floor and slinked out of the room, leaving the door cracked behind her. The chill of the air nipped at Lara when she stepped out of the tub, but the warmth returned as she stepped into her clothes.

Lara wasn't sure what dinner would look like, but breakfast in bed wasn't what she'd expected. Paige had set up a TV tray with a stack of pancakes and a glass of orange juice on the left side of the bed. Lara's side.

"This is surreal."

"You'll probably feel like that for a while," Paige said, settling into her side of the mattress. While Lara was changing into pajamas, Paige had done the same. "Give it time."

"I meant this." Lara gestured to the tray. "You used to make me breakfast in bed all the time. Birthdays. Anniversaries."

"I know. You love breakfast in bed."

Lara rounded the bed. She saw the picture of herself again and the clock beside it. It was late. Lara felt tired, but not in a sleepy way. "Usually breakfast in bed happens in the morning."

Paige leaned back against the headboard and shrugged. "There's no bad time for pancakes."

Lara shook her head as she sat down and moved the tray into her lap. "That's because pancakes are the only food you know how to make."

"Why be a jack-of-all-trades when you can master the only food that matters?

Lara chuckled, but the rumble of her body only made her stomach more uneasy. "I'm not feeling too hungry."

"You should eat something. At least take a couple bites for me?"

Lara obliged, cutting the cakes into neat triangles. The dough dissolved into a sickly sweet cloud of butter and syrup on her tongue.

"I should have made silver dollar pancakes," Paige said. "It's a new recipe I'm trying out. Well, the exact same recipe, but smaller portions. Doc says I should cut back on sugar." It was a joke, but Lara wasn't laughing. "Shit, I shouldn't have mentioned doctors, should I?"

Her words made Lara's blood run cold. She took a sip of orange juice to kick start her system. "It's fine."

"Sorry. I use the whole humor-as-a-coping-mechanism thing. It seemed like you could use a laugh."

The next bite went down a little easier, but she was already full. She moved the tray to the nightstand. Her head found the nook of Paige's shoulder. "You don't have to make me laugh. Just be here with me."

"I'm not going anywhere."

"Promise?"

"Promise."

Lara welcomed Paige's kiss, then welcomed sleep.

Chapter 20

"Today is all about you," Paige said. "Whatever you want to do, it's on me. I'll take you anywhere you want to go."

Could Paige take her back in time?

So far Paige had taken her home to drop off her dirty clothes and feed Rocket, and if Lara had her way, that would've been the only place they went today. All she wanted to do was mourn in bed, but Paige wouldn't let her, citing some bullshit theory about staying active and carrying on with life instead of letting the grief take over. Lara wasn't sure there was anything to do or anywhere to go that could stop her from feeling empty.

"I told you. All I had scheduled for today was to get my phone fixed."

"And that's why we're here." Paige gestured to the bustling maze of shops around them. "But I mean after this. There's got to be something else you want to do."

No. Lara didn't want to do anything, but she also didn't want to think about what had happened. Her skin felt rice-paper thin, and her muscles were jumpy and anxious. One wrong move could push her over the edge, and she didn't know what would be at the bottom of the ravine. She had to stay as far away from the cliff as possible. "Not really."

"Well, we're already at the mall, and we have to wait for the tech guys to fix your phone anyway," Paige said. "We may as well do something while we're here. It'll be like our mall dates back in OKC."

It was not like their mall dates back in OKC. Back in OKC, she and Paige were innocent kids with their whole lives ahead of them, and the malls in Oklahoma City had more than fifteen stores, and actual food courts instead of a single cafeteria that only old people ate at. Looking at the diner's sign at the end of the hallway reminded Lara of Betty having luncheons with her friends. The smell of the roast wafting from inside made her nauseous. "This isn't a date, Paige."

"Whatever helps you sleep at night—which was me last night, in case you'd forgotten."

Lara rolled her eyes, but she couldn't stop the small smile forming on her face when she saw Paige's. It was nice to feel her frown ease. At least one of them could still feel humorous. "Slow down, Casanova." Lara wasn't ready to think about what they were—analyzing what it all meant required thinking, and that was not on the day's agenda. "We're just here to get my phone fixed."

Paige sighed as they walked further away from the Apple Store. They were lingering in the middle of the aisle, taking short steps and making little progress on their journey to an undetermined destination. "What's up with you getting your phone fixed anyway? I thought you were getting a new one."

Lara shrugged. "I changed my mind. It's not totally broken, and it's worth saving."

Lara had forgotten how much she liked malls. This mall wasn't great, but if there was one place in Perry that could be described as busy, it was here, and Lara liked busy places. The building was so full of life that it distracted Lara from the life she'd lost. Her grandmother was gone, and Lara couldn't follow her normal routine anymore, but the rest of the world could. Lara couldn't decide if the general indifference to her radically altered life was morbid or comforting.

"Okay," Paige said. Her hand found Lara's and laced their fingers together. Lara didn't have the energy to stop her. She wasn't sure if she wanted to. "We have to do something while we wait. You can pick. Either we eat lunch, or you let me take you on an adventure."

"Ugh." Those sounded like Lara's least two favorite things. She squeezed Paige's fingers a little harder than necessary as a subtle threat. "I pick option C: none of the above."

"Adventure it is, then." Paige tugged on her arm so hard that Lara thought her shoulder might pop out of its socket. Paige picked up her pace, and Lara had no option but to rush to keep up with her.

"I know this won't help," Paige said, "but every time I'm sad, I go to Bath and Body Works and smell things. It never solves any of my problems, but sometimes it's nice to waste money on a mango-scented bath bomb, then go home and pretend you're at the beach in the tropics reading a book and drinking a glass of wine." Paige paused for a moment as she let Lara cross the threshold of the store first. "Or, in your case, grape juice? I think I have grape juice at home."

Lara wanted to be mad, but that was difficult when her nose was clogged with the scent of coconut and passion fruit so potent that it transported Lara to an imaginary tropical island where only she and Paige existed. Like Paige said, this definitely wasn't going to solve any of her problems, but if Lara had to spend her waiting time adventuring, then candle-smelling was a level of escapade that she could handle.

"Pick anything you want," Paige said. "My treat."

But Lara didn't want anything. She'd never felt so numb in her life. Any other day she might have been excited over the prospect of trying a new mixed-berry-scented lotion or an avocado face mask, but that type of luxury was the last thing on her mind right now.

Paige busied herself with a selection of body wash sprinkled with seaweed glitter, and Lara pretended to pay more attention to the products than the people around them. This was not the kind of place Lara frequented, and, yet, in true Perry fashion, she felt like she knew everyone here. The woman in her mid-forties with the "can I speak to your manager" haircut was the soccer mom who bragged that her lemon bars outsold April's peanut butter fudge every year at the annual bake sale. The woman trying and failing to hide the miniature Yorkie in her giant purse was the same woman Genie used to catch doing the same thing in the library.

This judging people based on nothing but secondhand stories thing was kind of fun when it was harmless like this. Lara could see why the Perry gossip vine had grown so strong. Then she spotted someone that she truly did know.

Kerry was in line at the register, and she wasn't alone. At first, Lara assumed the woman beside Kerry invading her personal space was passive-aggressively trying to cut her in line. But then the two made pointed eye contact, and a smile and a laugh followed. The woman was acting too familiar to be a rude stranger, and her suddenly obviously gay flannel shirt should have given away what she was to Kerry. Kerry was holding her items in one hand and the other woman's in the other.

"Holy shit, that's my ex."

Lara was thinking the words but wasn't the one who said them. It was Paige.

Paige ducked behind a display stand like a poorly hidden protagonist in a children's cartoon. "Okay, don't panic," she said, as if Lara was the one panicking, not her. "Remember when I told you I'd only been on one date since you left? It was a one-night stand a couple years ago, and I don't know if she remembers me, but we should still get out of here. I'll buy you lotion some other time, I promise."

Paige grabbed Lara's hand and tugged her out of the store; Lara was forced to stash the shampoo she was holding on a shelf of conditioner. They were halfway across the mall by the time Paige stopped power walking.

"See, this is what happens when you live in Perry," Lara said, mildly annoyed. "All of the lesbians have slept with each other, and you can't go anywhere without running into an ex or an ex of an ex and making things awkward."

"I'm pretty sure that's every lesbian community in every city ever," Paige said.

"If that's the case, then you should get used to it. Stop caring so much about other people and live your life. Sound familiar?"

Paige conceded with a small nod. "Yeah, yeah," she grumbled. "You're right."

"I don't know if you saw, since you rushed us out of there like we were running from the mob, but that woman that your ex was with was Kerry."

Paige winced. Lara couldn't tell if Paige was empathizing with her or feeling a pang of jealousy over hearing Kerry's name. "Uh, sorry, then," Paige said. "Are you okay?"

In general? No. About this fiasco? Surprisingly, yes. Aside from a bit of awkwardness, Lara felt no emotions about seeing Kerry with someone else. She looked happy with that woman. Good for her.

"I'm fine. Are you okay? You seem more caught up in this than I am."

"I'm good," Paige said, only a little out of breath from her jog and her borderline anxiety attack. "Thanks for caring enough to ask. You were right, adventure was a bad idea. Let's go see if your phone is ready."

It was. Lara was happy to have it back. It was like a phantom limb that her body subconsciously knew she was missing, and the dull ache wasn't relieved until the phone was reattached to her hip. If only Betty could come back; that same empty feeling in Lara's chest would dissipate.

"One more pit stop." Paige cut off Lara's groan with a single word. "Pretzels. You can't take a trip to the mall and not get a soft pretzel."

Lara could, in fact, do that, but it didn't look like that feat would be achieved today. "You're paying. I'll find a table."

When Lara took the first bite, she realized how hungry she was. Her stomach was still a bit queasy, but she needed to put something in her body, even if the salt of the pretzel made her already dry throat feel even drier. She took a sip of lemonade and winced from the burst of sour on her tongue as she watched Paige play with her phone.

"What are you doing?" Lara asked.

"I'm writing something."

"Like a book?"

Paige glared at Lara like she'd told a terrible joke. "The obituary."

Right. That. Paige had asked if Lara wanted to do the honors, but she couldn't bring herself to. She didn't know how to talk about Betty in the past tense. If anyone had the writing skills to do the obituary justice, it was Paige.

Lara pulled her own phone out of her pocket and set it on the table next to her pretzel. No new messages from her parents. That was a blessing, honestly. What would she say to them? She wasn't ready to talk to anyone right now, and especially not about Betty.

The only thing on her phone worth looking at was the photo of Paige and Cosmo. It had been upgraded from contact photo to home screen photo, and Lara stared at it wistfully until her phone timed out and faded to black of its own accord. Lara hit the home button again and watched the image come to life once more.

Fuck it. It was a wonderful photo. Memories as good as that deserved to be immortalized.

With the press of a few buttons, the photo was soon front and center on Lara's Instagram page. With a quick refresh, the photo already had ten likes and one comment: *Meow-gnificent!*

Lara took another bite of her pretzel. It went down a little easier.

"My phone feels a lot better." It was nice to be able to swipe across the screen without worrying about cutting her fingers. It was also a bonus that Paige and Cosmo's picture looked even cuter without the jagged lines obscuring their faces.

"I'm glad," Paige said. She popped the last bite of bread into her mouth and wiped the salt off her fingers. "Let's get out of here."

Outside the car window, Perry flew by. None of it looked like it had before: Perry's Pins wasn't a bowling alley; it was the place where Gam Gam had helped organize Lara's eighth birthday party. The grocery store was the place where Lara helped her grandmother carry home heavy bags. The pet store made her think of her cat, which made her think of her knitting, which made her think of her grandmother. Everything was tainted now by the memory of Betty.

Paige was driving, and Lara didn't know where they were going. Home? Did that mean Paige's home or Lara's home?

"Do you mind if we stop by the office for a minute?" Paige asked. "I have something I need to pick up."

"Sure." The *Daily Page* headquarters was maybe the only place in town that wouldn't remind her of Betty. She could only associate the building with Paige, and Lara already missed that time in her life when Paige was her most painful memory.

Paige drove on, and Lara tried to let the speed of the car blur the buildings enough that she didn't have to look at them.

"Do you want to come in or stay in the car?" Paige asked when they'd parked. "I won't be long."

Across the street was Mozart Cafe, an Italian restaurant the Spellmeyer family had eaten at together a thousand times, and a bar that no doubt the Spellmeyers were banned from. It wasn't a view Lara could stomach for more than a few seconds. "Uh, I'll go in."

Even for a Saturday, the office looked remarkably empty. Only a handful of workers had stayed until the late afternoon, apparently to print the next day's paper, and Lorraine, one of the few still lingering, lit up when she saw Lara. For once, Lara found her enthusiasm admirable instead of annoying. Lorraine's happiness was far from the worst thing in the world.

"I'll wait for you out here," Lara said.

Paige headed for her office, and Lara headed for Lorraine's desk. Lorraine pushed her chair away from her workstation and turned to face Lara. "Hey, I heard the news. How are you doing?"

"Honestly? I've been better."

"I'm so sorry to hear that." Lorraine's smile was replaced by a sympathetic frown. "Do you want to talk about it?"

"Not right now. I wanted to thank you."

Lorraine's brow twitched quizzically. "For what?"

"For suggesting that I share that video on my Instagram. You were right. People loved it."

"I saw that!" Lorraine's face lit up again. Her emerald green eyes sparkled. "I saw that picture you posted of Paige, too." As soon as Lorraine said it, Lara realized that she didn't care what people thought of her posting pictures of Paige anymore. After last night, it was hard to deny that something was going on between them. Let the world know. Who cared? "Super cute."

Lara glanced towards Paige's office. The door was cracked open, and Paige was visibly digging through her things like a hamster tunneling into its bedding. "She is, isn't she?"

"Only when she's with you. Everything is so much better here lately, Lara. You really saved us."

Lara scoffed. "Please. I know you think of me as a Hometown Hero and all, but I don't think I've saved anyone. Nothing I've done warrants a claim like that."

"I don't mean all the stuff we covered in the project, I mean the project itself. It's exactly what we need. I don't know what we would've done if we hadn't found you and Betty. Between the two of you, we have a real chance of winning now, and boy do we need it."

Lorraine was passionate about her work, but Lara had never seen her particularly excited about the contest itself. Now she was all about it. "What do you mean? It can't be that big of a deal. No offense, but I've never heard of the Oklahoma News Organization, and I doubt any organization named after the state of Oklahoma is that prestigious."

Lorraine shook her head. "It's not just the prestige. We aren't entering for the accolades. It's the prize money. You wouldn't believe how much an 'organization named after the state of Oklahoma' is willing to pay to support its journalists. And if we can get pull with them, we can get funding from other places too. The prize money will tide us over until that happens. It's a whole new start for the business. We're this close to going under."

There was money involved in this? Lara couldn't believe it. She had actually bought Paige's bullshit lie about wanting to improve the image of the community and help Perry stand out as one of the greatest cities in Oklahoma. What a load of crap. What else was Paige not disclosing?

Lara's most firmly held belief was that she knew two things in this world. One: Perry, Oklahoma, was not as great as everyone made it out to be. And two: Paige Daley had always been and always would be a selfish liar willing to do whatever it took to climb to the top. Lara had been so distracted by the first truth lately that somewhere along the way she had forgotten the second.

Lara's fists balled at her sides, but she had nowhere to unleash the anger. Lorraine didn't deserve it. The energy bubbled in her palms with nowhere to go. She was static ready to shock the first object that dared to touch her.

"Is that really why Paige wanted to enter the contest?" Lara asked. "Just for the money?"

"Well, I doubt that's the only reason. It's a cool project. I've had fun working on it, and I'm sure she has too. She's put a lot of effort into this."

Lara scoffed at Lorraine's naiveté. "Yeah, because if she doesn't, she's apparently going to lose her business."

Lorraine was noticeably taken aback by Lara's change in mood. She leaned back in her chair a little more, trying to calm Lara by showing her how at ease she was. "Come on, Paige likes what she does."

"Yeah. Too much. This paper has always been the only thing she cares about. How long has she known it was in trouble?"

"I-I'm not sure," Lorraine stuttered. "For a while, I'd imagine."

"Did she ever mention when she was going to tell me this?"

Lorraine rolled backward in her chair, putting distance between herself and Lara. "I don't know. I didn't know you didn't know. She probably didn't want to bother you with her work problems."

Lorraine didn't know Paige like Lara did.

"No. She was fine with bothering me when this project started. She didn't tell me because she knew I never would have agreed to help her if she had." Lara shook her head, trying to make sense of it all. "She was a complete asshole to me for years, and I should have known better than to trust her. She was using me right from the get-go." Lara's chest tightened. She wanted to be angry, but she couldn't. She was too hurt.

It wasn't the using that bothered Lara; she had always known Paige was using her to win the contest. They had been using each other. What bothered Lara was that after all they had been through, Paige hadn't come clean about it. After all the time they'd spent together, after all the reconnecting they'd done, Paige still wasn't comfortable sharing her life with Lara in the way Lara had shared hers with Paige.

Lorraine took Lara's words at face value, but Lara could see her brain working to connect all the pieces of the story. She'd never be able to. "Are you alright, Lara?"

"No." Lara shrugged her jacket back on. The thought of staying in the building for one more moment made her skin crawl. "When Paige finishes, tell her I didn't wait for her."

Chapter 21

The roar of a hundred voices surrounded her. Lara watched as new face after new face passed by her table outside the café. Businesswomen powerwalked their way to work. Cars honked through the traffic of the crowded street. A group of teenage boys skated off to class. There was an urgency. An excitement. An anxiety. No other place in the world was more suited for Lara Spellmeyer at this moment than the heart of downtown Oklahoma City.

The busy din drowned out her thoughts, but that was the best thing about it.

Lara took a bite of the muffin she had ordered. The cake was dry, or maybe that was her throat. Either way, it scratched on the way down, and the artificial blueberry flavor that was left on her tongue was nearly as unpleasant.

The phone in her hand rang three more times then went to voicemail. "You've reached Janet Westler, landlord for Paradise Springs Apartments. I'm unable to answer the phone right now, but if you leave your name, number, and apartment number I'll get back to you as soon as I can."

"Damn it, Janet."

Lara ended the call. Maybe this wasn't the best time to start apartment hunting, but Lara didn't care. She needed out of Perry. She needed away from everyone. She'd call Janet back later, or she'd try another place. Oklahoma City had plenty of apartments, and Lara had enough saved up to book a hotel room until she figured something out. Once she had a plan, she could go back to Perry, get the rest of her stuff, and move back for good.

Lara pocketed the phone to save her battery.

She had nowhere to go, but that was the point. OKC was her oyster now. She could go anywhere she wanted.

She finished her muffin, downed her coffee, and set off down the busy street of shops. Aside from the restaurants, there were a few street vendors. Most were tourist traps selling nothing but trinkets, but a small stand caught Lara's eye.

The newspaper stand was small but well-stocked; a single worker sat on a stool next to a cash register. She expected to pick up a copy of some national tabloid, and, if she was lucky, something international as well, but more of the newspapers than Lara expected were local. *The Guthrie Gazette. The Checotah Chronicle.* And right there amongst them all was the very thing Lara was running away from. That day's copy of *The Daily Page.*

Lara grabbed the top paper from the stack. The pile was significantly higher than all the others. No one was buying them, and Lara wasn't surprised, not after what Lorraine had told her. She couldn't help but feel bad, as if her own hatred for *The Daily Page* had somehow helped caused this. She thought of Lorraine and the rest of the workers who would suffer if the paper went under. She thought of Paige, who was on the brink of losing her dream. Paige had sacrificed so much for this paper, including Lara, and it was all on the verge of being for naught. Once upon a time, Lara would have felt validated watching Paige crash and burn, and some of that resentment was still there, but now for the most part she just felt sad. For Ferry. For Paige. For what could have been if things had been different between them. If they had been different people, now or back then.

But it wasn't Lara's problem anymore. She couldn't help if Paige didn't let her. She couldn't let herself get trapped in another relationship if Paige was just going to push her away again. She needed honesty. She needed communication. She needed someone willing to sit beside her on the train ride of life.

So why couldn't she put the paper down?

"You gonna pay for that?"

Lara fished the money out of her pocket and regretted it as soon as the coins fell into the vendor's hand. Was she really spending money on this? Apparently. She grabbed a copy of a different paper and gave the vendor money for that too

Lara resumed her trek down the street, partially out of shame for what she was doing and partially to find a spot quiet enough where she could sit down and read.

There was one place in OKC that could always bring her clarity. The Bricktown Canal was to Lara what Clandestine Orchards was to Kerry. Sitting along the water and watching tourists pass by the storefronts and enjoy the bit of nature in the heart of the city was Lara's way of connecting to the natural elements of the world around her.

She took the stairs down to the water and sat on the final step. With the papers splayed out on the concrete beside her, Lara began sifting through the pages to find the only article she really cared about.

"Beatrice Spellmeyer passed Friday evening after a long bout of respiratory problems. Born on May 8, 1943 in McClean, Virginia, Betty moved to Perry with her late husband Daniel in the 1960s. A retired attorney with a heart of gold, Betty became a pillar of the Perry community in her final years and has single-handedly made the Spellmeyer name one of the most beloved in Perry. Her loves included knitting, fudge-making, and her ultimate pride and joy, her beautiful granddaughter Lara. She is survived by Lara, her son Hank, and a bounty of close friends who will miss her dearly."

Lara put the OKC newspaper on the ground. She didn't need it. Nothing in it would top the obituary. She wasn't in the mood for political going-ons or crime reports any longer.

How could someone so imperfect have written such a wonderful obituary? How could she know exactly what Lara needed to hear? How could Lara never stay mad at Paige for more than a day?

Lara had her own corner of solitude down by the waterfront, but she was far from alone. Above her, a busy footbridge crossed the canal, and below her the ferries passed by on the water. Lara paid the passersby no mind until she heard footsteps on the stairs behind her.

She scrambled to move her newspapers and give the stranger space to pass her, but when Lara looked behind her, it wasn't a stranger. Lara let the papers be and turned back around to face the water.

"How'd you know I'd be here?" she asked.

Paige crept her way down another step. She approached Lara slowly, as if she were a wild animal. "You weren't at home. Where else would you be?"

"What'd you do, break in and check?"

"Is it considered breaking in if I used a key?" Paige sat down on the steps next to Lara. The newspapers divided them like a barrier.

"How'd you get my house key?"

"Betty gave me her copy." Paige exhumed the key from her back pocket as proof. "She said I'd need it more than she would."

"She really thought I'd let you back into my life that easy?"

"It didn't seem that farfetched to her."

Lara scoffed. "Only because you tricked her. You tried so hard to worm your way back into my life over the past two months. Then I finally let you in, only to find out that you weren't being honest with me. Again. Did you really expect me to stay?"

"What are you talking about?"

"The contest?" Lara waited for Paige to realize that Lara knew what she was up to, but there was no flash of panic on Paige's face. There was nothing but hurt and sunken cheeks and pouty lips. "Lorraine told me what you were up to. This stupid contest isn't about Perry at all. It's about you saving your ass and winning the prize money. Using my life story for monetary gain without telling me is one thing, but using my dead grandmother's? That's a new low, even for you, Paige. She spent some of her very last moments with you. You realize that, right? You should feel honored that you got to bear witness to those stories. You should have had to pay to hear them, not get paid to regurgitate them and butcher them with your shitty writing."

"That's why you're mad at me?" Paige asked. Her tone wasn't accusatory. It was contemplative. "You told my intern to tell me to leave you alone because you think I'm doing this for money?"

"Why'd you think I said it?"

Paige chuckled. "Could have been anything, honestly. I thought maybe I was taking too long in my office and you thought I was choosing work over you again." Paige leaned over and gave Lara a light shoulder bump, but Lara refused to be moved by the momentum. "That was kind of a joke," Paige said. She swallowed hard and replicated Lara's stony composure. "I didn't know why. I thought maybe you were just upset over Betty and broke down. I didn't take it personally. Are you really mad at me?"

She was mad at Paige. She was mad at herself. She was mad at the world.

She felt nothing.

"Is it true?"

A noisy group of college kids passed by on the walkway behind them. Their laughter stung. Paige waited for them to pass before taking a deep breath and scooting an inch closer to Lara. The newspaper wrinkled between them. "It's true. If we don't win this, the paper will be in trouble. Bransom blames the industry, but I blame myself. If I lose this, I failed, and that hurts."

"Don't you think I deserved to know about this?" Lara asked. "I get why you didn't tell me at first. I really do. If you had, I probably wouldn't have agreed to do the contest just out of spite. But things aren't like that anymore, Paige. I've told you everything these last few weeks. I've opened up to you like I haven't done with anyone in years. You made me feel safe. You made me feel *loved*. I told you personal stuff, and you didn't even feel comfortable telling me about your problems at work? If you had told me, I would have tried to help you, you know. Why keep it a secret? Why couldn't you trust me?"

"I'm sorry," Paige said, and the guilt in her voice made Lara believe the apology. "I do trust you, Lara. I wasn't trying to keep secrets from you. I didn't tell you because it doesn't matter. It's on me to write the article and win, not you, not anybody else. The contest is about highlighting Perry, and that's what I wanted you and Betty and everybody else to focus on. That's what I wanted to write about. I thought if you guys didn't know, I could get better material out of you and it wouldn't feel so staged.

"But then I didn't mention it because I've barely been thinking about this damn contest." Paige took a deep breath. She picked up a loose leaf and tossed it into the water. "I don't care anymore. If we lose, then so be it. I didn't want to admit it, but I'm not cut out for this job. I hate it. I'm overworked. I thought this was what I wanted, but I was wrong. You were right when you left me. My priorities are all fucked up. I should have asked for help. I should have talked to you more. I should have realized that you were more important than some job or some city. That's why I followed you this time."

Lara didn't know how to process this. She'd expected Paige to argue and cover her ass and defend what she'd done. Lara knew how to fight, but she didn't know how to accept victory over someone willing to throw in the towel.

Paige picked up another leaf. She shucked the dead foliage and rolled the stem between her fingers. "While I'm at it, I may as well come clean. That wasn't the only lie I told you about the contest." Paige let the leaf drop to her feet and reached into her bag. The binder she pulled out was brand new, black, sleek. It was nothing like her usual messy notebooks. She weighed it carefully in her hands, keeping it steady in her palms as if the slightest movement might damage it the way she damaged everything. She handed it to Lara reverently. "The votes have been in for a few days now."

Lara peeled the cover back slowly. The headline was nothing fancy. The format wasn't breathtaking. It was normal, professional. The center photo was black and white, ancient.

The Heart of Perry: Beatrice and Lara Spellmeyer.

Betty's face stared up at her, and for a moment it was like she was alive again. Lara remembered that smile so fondly. Her grandmother was so young in the photograph. So full of life. And cradled in her arms was a baby Lara, swathed, smiling, innocent and protected from the world.

"What is this?" Lara asked. Her fingers shook as she caressed the photo. It was smooth and glossy against her fingertips.

"When we tallied the votes, your grandmother was way ahead of everyone, and I told her she won. She would only accept if the article was also about you. She never stopped talking about you. Even when I asked her questions about herself, she always circled back to her granddaughter. It was pretty obvious that Perry had more than one Hometown Hero, and there's nothing in the contest rules that say I can't write about a hero and her sidekick. You came in a close second."

Lara skimmed through the article. It was the perfect way to highlight everything her grandmother had done for herself and everyone around her. It was the perfect memoriam, even better than the obituary.

Now she understood why Paige had handled the folder so carefully. Lara couldn't be gentle enough with it herself. She wanted to protect it with everything she had.

"You really think I deserve this?" Lara asked. She felt selfish. It didn't feel right to take any of the spotlight away from Betty now that she was gone.

"You've seen the videos and the comments and the support. You and your grandmother both mean something special to Perry. Of course you deserve it."

"You deserve this too," Lara said. "You can't give up. You love that paper. It's the only one in town, and it's the only one doing what you're doing. You were right. This small-town journalism is important, and you need to keep doing it. Someone has to." Betty smiled up at Lara from the page, and Lara clutched the binder to her chest again.

"I don't know. You really think I can pull this off?"

"Of course you can. If you got me to agree to all of this after how much I hated you…" Lara paused, staring out over the water as her thoughts cleared. "If you got me to love you again after how much I hated you, then you can do anything. Just stop trying to do it alone."

A ferry passed by. The young lovers on board tucked themselves into each other's sides, the boy's hands mindlessly reaching out to grasp his lover's fingers in her lap. They smiled. The ferryman rowed on.

"You were right the other night," Paige said. "I am selfish, and I do want to keep you to myself. I wanted an excuse to spend time with you. A way to be your friend again. A way to be more than that. I want you back, Lara. I have since the day you left. But what is it that you want?" Paige asked. "And don't say to run away, because that's not what you want. What are you looking for that you think you can only find outside of Perry?"

Lara looked at the couple again. The boy wrapped his arm around the girl's back, and the small gesture of affection made Lara feel even emptier inside.

"I want to be happy," she said.

"Well, what makes you happy?"

"My grandmother. She always has." And now that happiness was gone. Nothing would bring it back, not running away or staying in Perry.

"What else?" Paige asked.

Lara had to think, but not as hard as she'd expected to. "My knitting. At first. Back when it was just something I did for fun and no one judged me on it."

Paige hummed along.

"Tight Knit," Lara continued. "I know I told you it wasn't my idea, but it was, and I love everything about it. I'll miss it if I leave."

"What else would you miss?"

"My parents. April." Lara paused. "You."

Paige's eyes mirrored the river, a wave of blue with gentle ripples. She hesitated. She thought before she spoke. It was so un-Paige-like. "Me?"

Lara nodded, finally sure of adding Paige to the list. "Yes. You make me happy too. Sometimes," Lara was quick to add. "The obituary. This contest entry." Lara placed a palm over the pages in her lap like she was putting her hands over a Bible in court. "The other night when you took care of me and let me cry on your shoulder. That was nice. That made me happy. But when we broke up, that did not make me happy."

"Do you know why I cared so much about *The Daily Page*?" Paige asked. "Why I spent so much time working nights and sucking up to Bransom and trying to get you to stay in Perry with me?"

"Because you're neurotically ambitious and desperate to prove you're successful and better than everyone else?"

Paige acquiesced with a half shrug, half nod. "Okay, that, yes, partially." Her tone softened and shifted to something more serious. "But every time I get overly ambitious like that, I always have a goal. It's never only about success or showing someone up. I wanted to do this contest and save the paper so Perry still has something local to cling to. I wanted to take over the paper because I believed in

Bransom's vision, and I wanted to make sure his legacy lived on. I was so anal in school because I wanted to make sure I graduated and got a good job to support us. And I picked up all those extra hours and took those promotions at the paper because I was saving up for something important."

"Saving up for what?" Lara asked. They'd been far from rich back then, but they weren't struggling. The newspaper was a good job. The library was a good job. It was more than enough to support the both of them. They were supposed to use that savings to move to OKC. That had always been the plan, and Lara had followed through with it, even if Paige hadn't.

"A ring."

The words hit Lara like a punch in the gut. "Oh."

"Yeah."

Paige's hand crept across her lap and settled into Lara's palm. It was a perfect fit, the same as Lara remembered it being. Paige's thumb brushed across her ring finger, and Lara could all too easily imagine the weight of a diamond there in place of the pressure of Paige's skin.

When Lara moved to lace their fingers, the warmth disappeared. Paige stood up.

"Where are you going?" Lara asked.

"Home."

"You're not going to try to convince me to come back with you?" Lara asked. "You're not going to give me another speech about how I'm running away from my problems instead of facing them head-on?"

Paige shook her head. "I already gave you that speech. You heard me the first time, and you know where I stand. I want you to come back to Perry, but this is your life and your decision. If this is what you want, I'm not going to stop you."

For the first time, Lara felt free. Finally, this felt like her decision, and no one was dragging her down and telling her what she should or shouldn't do. Paige was the first person who was trusting Lara to make the choice for herself. She was the first person offering support. It was the first time Lara didn't feel quite so alone.

"I'm gonna go, Lara." Paige gathered herself. She stood from the steps and brushed the dirt off her pants. Her palms were speckled with indents from the concrete. "I'm gonna go, and if you ever decide to come back, I'll be there waiting for you. We all will."

Epilogue

The entire point of owning an alarm was to utilize the snooze function. Paige did not get the memo.

"Babe, come back to bed." Lara's voice was groggy. She could barely hear herself as her mind sorted through the fog of what was real and what was left over from her dreams. Her eyes were closed, but the empty bed beside her radiated a loneliness too overbearing to be ignored. She was so used to sleeping with Paige by now that the absence was impossible to miss.

"It's Tuesday!" Those two words had never been uttered with such enthusiasm.

Lara groaned. "It's your day off. Why are you up earlier than me?"

"I'm too excited. I want to unpack." Another string of words that did not make sense to Lara at seven in the morning.

When Lara begrudgingly lifted her heavy eyelids, only the bedside lamp was turned on, and she silently thanked Paige for sparing her vision. In the half darkness, Lara could make out Paige's figure crouched over a box in front of the dresser. Lara admired the curve of her spine and the wings of her shoulder blades across the bare expanse of her back. Not a horrible first sight of the day.

"Which one of these sweaters should I wear?"

More absolute nonsense. "Why do you have to put on clothes?"

Paige turned around to give Lara a chastising glare before standing and flipping on the lights. Lara winced as bright spots swarmed her vision. A few blinks showed Paige back at the dresser stuffing some of her clothes into the empty drawers and reserving a few sweaters by laying them out on the bed.

"I love these new patterns," Paige said, as if Lara hadn't heard the compliment a million times in the last few weeks.

"Tell that to my grandma, not me. I didn't design them, just knitted them."

"I'm just glad you're making sweaters for people now. I'll never spend money on shopping again."

She'd better. Lara was not about to start knitting an underwear line just to make her girlfriend happy. She wasn't about to start knitting anything to make anybody happy anymore. Except for herself. She only took orders on projects she really liked when she really wanted to. She just happened to really like knitting sweaters for Paige. "Thank the market. Turns out you're not the only crazy cat lady that wants to buy a set of matching sweaters for them and their pet."

Paige put a few more tops away until she was down to two. Lara was just happy Paige finally turned around to give her the full frontal view. She held up both sweaters for Lara to see. "Okay, which one should I wear? I like this one more, but I feel like the pattern looks better on Cosmo than it does on me."

"Actually it looks better on Rocket than both of you."

Paige pouted. "You can't play favorites with our children while they're in the room."

Lara glanced over the edge of the bed. Both cats were still asleep where they had lain down the night before. Cosmo was getting reacquainted with her old cat bed, and Rocket was happy to share it, letting his sister take the middle while he draped himself over the edge at an impossibly awkward angle.

"I still vote no sweater," Lara said. "I also vote you come back to bed. You don't have to unpack now. You have all the time in the world. You live here now."

"It'll feel more like I live here when all my stuff is put away."

"It'll feel more like you live here when you come back to this bed and never leave it."

Paige chuckled. She laid the sweaters back down on the bed, and Lara hoped her body would soon follow. "You make a compelling argument, Ms. Spellmeyer, but..." Paige leaned over Lara, inching closer but staying much too far away. "We can't stay in bed all day or you're going to be late for work."

"Who cares?" Lara asked. "Genie's late every day. She'll never know."

Paige climbed on top of the mattress, then on top of Lara. Lara wished there wasn't a blanket between them. "You're bad," Paige whispered. Her breath was warm against Lara's lips, and Lara struggled not to lean forward and claim Paige's mouth right there and then. "Somewhere outside the library, there's a little kid waiting for someone to open the building so he can borrow a book about trains."

"I can assure you that that doesn't happen on a Tuesday morning in the middle of the school year in the middle of winter."

Appeased, Paige pressed into the kiss, and Lara melted into the sheets, victorious. Keeping their lips melded together, Paige swung a leg around to straddle Lara. Lara welcomed the pressure of Paige's body atop hers until a knee jammed into her side.

"Ow, careful. I'm still sore from last night."

Paige raised an eyebrow and lowered her voice. "Me too."

Lara rolled her eyes and pushed Paige's leg away from her hip. "Not from that. Although I'm sure that didn't help." Paige's smirk intensified. "I meant from moving all your boxes."

"Please." Paige scoffed. "You're weak. Yesterday was nothing. I dropped off twice as many boxes at Goodwill the other day."

Lara ran her hands up Paige's biceps, letting the heat melt into her palms. The muscles were far more toned than they had been four years ago. Quitting smoking and cutting back on pancakes had done wonders for Paige's body. Lara wasn't complaining. "How about you show me how strong you are, then?"

Lara knew Paige couldn't resist the challenge. She moved the blanket, lifted Lara by the back of her thighs, and dragged her closer, putting less pressure on her side this time. Her kiss was less careful, more forceful, and Lara parted her lips to accept Paige's tongue.

A phone chirped from the nightstand, and Lara hoped she was imagining the ring. When the phone chimed again, Paige was much too quick to reach for it. "I have to get that. It's Lorraine."

Lara threw her head back onto the sheets, out of breath. "I thought the whole point of promoting Lorraine was that you wouldn't have to worry so much about work."

"Who says this is about work? I have her on a special project." Paige's eyes scanned the screen. The small smile on her face grew larger.

"Special project? Isn't that the same thing as work?"

"I told her to text me as soon as it came out. Guess whose new *Trend Bender* article is live?"

Paige shoved the phone in Lara's face, and Lara swatted it away like a fly. "No! I am not about to get cock-blocked by Roger Feldman."

"I'm going to read it."

"No!" Lara reached for the phone, but instead of playing keep-away, Paige kissed her. The surprise was enough to stop Lara from protesting, and the confidence in Paige's voice when she spoke was enough to put Lara's stomach at ease.

"Hey. You don't have to worry this time. You killed that interview." Paige kissed her again, soft and sweet, and Lara let her hands settle back into her lap. "Can I read it to you?" The way Paige asked made Lara believe that if she said no, then Paige would put the phone down and act like Roger Feldman never existed.

It was all the comfort Lara needed to say yes. She had been waiting for this too, if not as diligently as Paige.

"Yeah. I'm ready."

About Shaya Crabtree

Shaya Crabtree was born and raised in the Midwestern United States, where she studied English and Creative Writing at university. At age twelve, she began writing and never looked back long enough to put down the pencil. She prefers writing to reading and has an affinity for cryptozoology, conspiracy theories, and cooking competitions.

Other Books from Ylva Publishing

www.ylva-publishing.com

You're Fired

Shaya Crabtree

ISBN: 978-3-95533-754-4
Length: 193 pages (61,000 words)

When poor college student Rose Walsh gives out an inappropriate gag gift at her office Christmas party, it backfires horribly. The gift's recipient is her boss, the esteemed president of Gio Corp., Vivian Tracey, and the only thing that can save Rose now is her smarts.

Instead of firing her, Vivian blackmails math major Rose into joining her on a business trip to New York to investigate an embezzlement. A week out of state with a woman she can barely stand seems like the last thing Rose wants to do with her winter vacation. Only, maybe Vivian is not as bad as she seems. Maybe they can even become friends…or more.

Rewriting the Ending

hp tune

ISBN: 978-3-95533-503-8
Length: 286 pages (107,000 words)

Juliet is an author with a deadline. A big deadline…and a ratty old backpack, and she's on her way to Belgium.

Mia has a one-way, first class ticket to anywhere. Today anywhere happens to be Scotland. The one thing she knows is that money can't buy happiness, and she has no idea what does.

A chance meeting in an airport lounge and a shared flight itinerary leaves Juliet and Mia connected. They've known each other for only twenty-four hours and they are destined for separate countries. How do you forge a future when the past keeps pulling you back?

A Story of Now

(A Story of Now Series – Book 1)

Emily O'Beirne

ISBN: 978-3-95533-345-4
Length: 367 pages (128,000 words)

Nineteen-year-old Claire knows she needs a life. And new friends. Too sassy for her own good, she doesn't make friends easily anymore. And she has no clue where to start on the whole life front. At first, Robbie and Mia seem the least likely people to help her find it. But in a turbulent time, Claire finds new friends, a new self, and, with the warm, brilliant Mia, a whole new set of feelings.

Food for Love

C. Fonseca

ISBN: 978-3-96324-082-9
Length: 276 pages (96,000 words)

When injured elite cyclist Jess flies to Australia to sort her late brother's estate, the last thing she wants is his stake in a rural eatery. She'd rather settle up, move on, and sidestep the restaurant's beautiful owner, Lili, and her child. Given her traumatic life, Jess isn't sure she'd survive letting her guard down.

A lesbian romance about how nourishment is much more than the food we eat.

Tight Knit
© 2019 by Shaya Crabtree

ISBN: 978-3-96324-239-7

Also available as e-book.

Published by Ylva Publishing, legal entity of Ylva Verlag, e.Kfr.

Ylva Verlag, e.Kfr.
Owner: Astrid Ohletz
Am Kirschgarten 2
65830 Kriftel
Germany

www.ylva-publishing.com

First edition: 2019

Credits
Edited by Michelle Aguilar and Alissa McGowan
Cover Design by Streetlight Graphics

www.ingramcontent.com/pod-product-compliance
Lightning Source LLC
Chambersburg PA
CBHW030546030726
47495CB00004B/1150